RISING RIDGE

Alexa Jacobs

CreateSpace Independent Publishing Platform
North Charleston, SC

For further information & permissions:
www.alexajacobs.com

Library of Congress Catalog-in-Publication Data
Jacobs, Alexa
Rising Ridge / Alexa Jacobs
ISBN-13: 978-1517773366
ISB-10: 1517773369
2015917921

Publishing History
CreateSpace paperback edition / November 2015

PRINTED IN THE UNITED STATES OF AMERICA

10 9 8 7 6 5 4 3 2 1

Cover Design by RL Sather
Cover image: "RLSather_19729" by RL Sather

For the real life Elle

The teeter to my totter you will ever be.

May this bring the
Sweetest memories of
your first love back

to you.

— Alexa Jacobs.

With Gratitude

This book was a true labor of love. I would like to thank those people who took part in getting the details of my mind onto paper. For every friend who has suggested along the way that I should be a writer, thank you for believing that I could be. For my children, thank you for adjusting to Mom having a job, and eating silly dinners far more often than you should have to. For my husband, who gives the best of himself so that I may live this life…I am so grateful, and love you. Every good heroine needs her best girlfriends to keep her sane. To my best girl, thank you for coming along on the ride. To my friends who find their names here, I love you, and I keep you close to my heart. For the man with all the words, thank you for being better than Google, and for the amazing soundtrack. Thank you to Mark for the encouragement and a push off the diving board. For Eliza, thank you so much for inviting me into your world, I hope I get to stay a while. To Virginia at First Editing, thank you for your time, help, and thoughts. I would like to thank RL Sather for the beautiful cover artwork. It could not be more fitting for my small town girl with a case of wandering feet.

One

Hot tea.

Her eyes were closed. She willed herself to sit up. Just sit up, and the day will begin, she thought. Imagining her favorite spiced chai, filled to the brim with intoxicating aromas all but moved her from beneath her blanket. Yet, the sunlight that poured through her bedroom window was warm and wrapped around her, enticing her to stay put. Maybe just a few more minutes of this.

"Get up," she moaned. For the first time, she opened her eyes and saw daylight fill her room.

Olivia preferred natural light, and as annoying as it was to be awake at 7 a.m., she loved being woken by the peeking rays of sunlight through her blinds rather than the blaring noise of an alarm clock. Just to be responsible, she would set her clock for 7:30, but found that she rarely needed it. No, dreams of that hot cup of chai were enough to move her from the bed.

Finally giving in to get her day started, she slid out of bed and stretched. As with every morning, before moving one inch, she gazed outside the window looking for nothing in particular. She just wanted to see "it"—FREEDOM. She smiled. Now the day could begin.

Making that chai was now her only goal. As she walked into the living room, she noticed that Debi, her roommate, had already left for the day. Debi was in nursing school and was the perfect roommate. They met a party, and hit it off. Although Debi was her exact opposite, Olivia loved her for it. She was tall, loud, fun, and free. Everything they did together was an adventure. It was just what she needed at this time of her life.

They found a small one-bedroom apartment that was way too expensive for either of them to afford alone, but together they could swing it. Best of all, it meant they didn't have to live in New Jersey. Together, they painted the walls a warm yellow and filled the small rooms with sensible furniture of multi-purpose from Ikea. Debi chose to sleep on the pullout sofa in the living room because of her long, hard hours in nursing school. In exchange for the bedroom, Olivia would do all of the cooking. It was a partnership that worked well for each of them.

After whipping together a quick breakfast of eggs and toast to go with her chai, she ate while scrolling through the morning news and social media feed on her laptop. Nothing caught her attention this morning, so she closed it and started to wash her dishes. Then the phone rang.

"Hello?"

"Are you ready for this? Are you sitting down? Jesus Christ, Livy."

Olivia smiled. Wiping the eggy soap off her hand, she sat down as Elle recommended. Elle was one of Olivia's oldest friends, and of all of them, her favorite.

"I'm sitting," she said as she wrapped her hands around her second cup of tea that had been waiting for her on the table.

"Everyone on earth is an asshole today," Elle informed her.

"Oh? Why is that?"

"Because they are. I started my day getting pulled over, and it's been downhill since then."

"It's only…" Olivia looked at the clock on the stove "…7:30, Elle. This is a record for even you. You got pulled over?" she chuckled.

"This morning at six. Running a red light."

"Why did you run a red light?"

"There was a bee in my car! A big, fat, monster bee!" she shouted. "I was sitting at the light, feeling all good about myself. I've got this new shirt, and it makes my boobs look fantastic. I've got the music turned up, singing along. And then this thing zips by my face. It was a freaking killer bee! I panicked and hit the gas, and it made me go through the light."

"Elle!" Olivia smacked her free hand on the table. "You have got to get over your fear of bugs! They're not going to kill you!"

"Whatever, be quiet. OK, so I get through the light, and I pull over as quickly as I can so I can get that bee off me. I'm waving my hands like a maniac trying to keep from getting stung. And wouldn't you believe it? There's a freaking cop right behind me! He pulls over and doesn't know what to make of the whole thing. I'm lucky he didn't shoot me. He just starts yelling 'Ma'am…Ma'am…what is happening?' Can you believe he called me ma'am in the first place?! I'm not a Ma'am! I'm young and hot! Anyway, I start yelling that there was a bee, but of course where is that little asshole now? Gone! It must have flown out the door when I opened it!"

"So you got a ticket?" Olivia did her best not to laugh.

"No. He actually thought it was pretty funny. He even checked my car to make sure it hadn't flown back in."

"Well, then why is everyone an asshole today?" Olivia asked.

"Because that made me ten minutes late to my spin class, and because of that I couldn't find a spot. Then I had to park a mile away, and that made me miss my class altogether. So now my only options are the treadmill and the stair climbers. It's now 7:00 and you're not going to get anything then. This perky little bitch looks at me from her treadmill and just gives me that yeah right look as she ups her speed. How dare that judgy yoga pants bitch give me that look! So now I've wasted all my time, got no workout in, and have to turn around and go to school."

"So, when you say everybody is an asshole, you mean the bee and the Miss judgy yoga pants bitch. They speak for the entire nation?"

"Yes! Exactly!"

"Ohh-kay then. Well, are you on your way to school now?" Olivia got up and headed to her bedroom to get herself ready for the day.

"Yes. And I can't be late there. This one class is kicking my ass. Plus, there's a really cute boy…"

"And THAT'S why you've got the fantastic boob shirt on!" Olivia said smugly.

"Yep," Elle said confidently.

"You're a nut! Listen, I gotta run, but call me later, OK?"

After hanging up, Olivia shook her head. Elle was her favorite person in the world and one of her oldest friends. They had met at recess one afternoon on the kindergarten playground. Elle turned up in several of Olivia's classes over the years, and they developed a bond that would last a lifetime. They did what all girlfriends do—sleepovers full of sugar and secrets, talking about boys, dreaming about boys, dating boys, and getting through those really gut-wrenching heartbreaks. They had been through it all together.

There were, of course, the long breaks, especially when they both fell into a relationship. Elle was now attending college in their hometown, and between work and school, Olivia had only been home for Christmas. Elle had been up a couple of times, and they enjoyed long weekends in the city. They almost never saw each other, but it didn't matter. A day, a month, a year…Elle would call and start a conversation in the middle of the story. Olivia would always take that minute for one of her very favorite people in the world. It would never change—they both knew that.

Olivia grabbed her purse and locked up the apartment. She jogged down the steps and pushed open the building's door. She smiled. Deep breath in, *this never gets old*. It was a gorgeous June day, and it promised to be nice and hot. It had been a particularly rough winter and cold spring, so she found herself soaking up the sunshine as much as she could. She regularly used the subway because she had to be realistic, but if she had the time, she much preferred walking. It would take a long time to walk, sure, but it gave her the ability to look at the buildings that kissed the sky. She'd smile at the people passing by, and giggled at the children who were running to be somewhere fun in the city. She often wondered how anyone in a cab or car or on the train would volunteer to miss this. Walking to and from work was quite often the best part of her day.

"Good morning," Olivia greeted Dave as she let herself into the locked bank. She turned to relock the door before giving him a chance to answer.

"Mornin' doll," he said as he took his first sip of coffee and sat down at his desk.

"What's on for today?" Olivia asked.

"Not much. We've got a few overdrafts but nothing major," he said.

"Good. Is Kurt here yet?" She grabbed the keys to the vault to get her cash drawer in order to set up her station for the day.

"He should be here soon. He overslept," Dave said as he rolled his eyes.

Kurt was twenty, the same age as Olivia, but very much a wild child. He partied hard, often, and into the mornings. He was a hard worker when he showed up, but mornings were tough for him, especially when they happened on a Monday. Olivia loved him because he'd been born and raised in New York. He was exactly what she had pictured in her mind when she closed her eyes and thought of a New Yorker.

Olivia started working as a part-time teller at Twin Ridge Bank just after her junior year of high school. She loved the job, but after high school, she felt like she had to get away from small town life. And where do you run when you live in a small Maryland town? New York.

With little research, and the savings she had from babysitting and her bank teller job, she got on the bus with lots of dreams and no plans. She'd just figure it out when she got there.

As luck would have it, one of the larger banks in the city was hiring, and she was hired. And the best part of the job was learning how to deal with big city culture. Her coworkers helped her learn that.

For one thing, she learned that when you live in New York, you have two jobs: what you are, and what you do to make money. Dave was a forty-year-old bank manager who had been working at the bank since he was thirty. That's what he did to make money. What he WAS, however, was an artist. He could capture emotion and beauty with just a single piece of paper and a pencil. He was amazing, but amazing didn't put food on the table for his wife and daughter consistently. Welcome to New York!

Olivia loved that everyone who worked there seemed to identify themselves in some way other than their career at that bank. Dave was the artist. Kurt was the musician. Audrey was the dancer. Olivia's goal was to live her "larger life" like they were.

She worked at a bank—that's what she did to make money, like everyone else around her. What she WAS, though, was a student. She was taking classes part time. Sometimes she felt she only did it in order to appease her parents, but since they paid her tuition, she didn't mind that at all.

So far, she loved learning about money. Who knows? She could be the next financial adviser with her own television show. But that wasn't all she liked. She also enjoyed creative writing. Maybe she could be a best-selling author. She learned that she was absolutely no good at art. Everything she attempted looked better in her mind than it did in real life. She liked interior design, but she didn't have the desire to learn the architectural side of the career. And she also had a passion for travel and photography. If she ever became rich, she thought she would take a year and travel through foreign countries with camera in hand, just to one day have a book sitting on a coffee table with stunning photos in it. Oh that? Those are just some pictures I took while in Dubai. The truth is, she had no idea what she wanted to be or how to even get there. It's why she came to New York, to find out.

Just before they opened the doors, the phone rang.

"Good Morning, New York Central Bank. This is Olivia, how may I help you?" she cheerfully greeted the customer on the line.

"Hi," her brother, Connor, said.

"Oh, hi. What's up?" she asked as she continued processing the night deposit bags from the weekend.

"Liv, I've got some news."

Her hands slowed. She and Connor kept in touch quite often, but he rarely interrupted her at work.

"What's wrong?" she asked in a quieted tone.

There was a silence that sent a cold chill down her back. One…two…three…

"Connor?" she stopped what she was doing completely when his sigh came through the line.

"Mom and Dad." Another sigh. "There was…an accident. Late last night. They're gone, Liv."

She was in shock but somehow managed to ask about the how and the where. Her brother told her the police had knocked on his door just a few hours ago and informed him about the accident. Apparently, their parents had been out past midnight on their way home from a real estate seminar and another car had crossed into their lane and hit them head on. He said the police think the other driver had fallen asleep, but no details were in, except the fact that everyone was dead.

Olivia stood at her desk. The phone trembled against her ear, and she remained silent as her brain tried to process everything Connor had told her. Dave walked in front of her and smiled, unaware that her world was being torn apart. It was time to open, and he unlocked the door to let the first customer of the day in.

A man walked in as Dave went back to his desk. He was tall and well built. His dark hair, though trimmed, possessed an unusual combination of imperfect perfection. As he walked up to her station, Olivia slowly made eye contact with his deep brown eyes, and the remainder of the color that she had left in her body drained out in an instant. Was he real? She nearly reached out her fingers across her station to touch him. He was the ghost who had been haunting her dreams for the last two years.

"Dean's here," she heard herself saying to her brother.

"He's there for you, Liv. You need to come home."

Just like that, her whole world changed.

Two

Olivia 8, Elle 8, Connor 13, Dean 13

"Are you sure we're allowed up here?"

"Yes," Olivia said as she started to climb the ladder up to the tree house.

"But this is the neighbor's tree house," Elle insisted, climbing up behind Olivia. "It's not even your yard."

"It's Dean's tree house, and Connor's, and mine," Olivia said as they reached the top and stood. "And yours now."

"Who's Dean?" Elle asked.

"I'm Dean." A tall, lanky boy walked across the lawn from the house directly in front of the tree house.

Elle watched him take just a few strides across the lawn and then haul himself impressively up the rope ladder attached to the side of the platform she was standing on.

"Who are you?" he asked.

Elle sized him up. His hair was cut skater style, leaving his dark locks longer on top and his head shaved underneath. He was tall…really tall. He had to be at least five and a half feet, Elle thought. That's how tall her mom was, and he was at least her height. He was wearing a black T-shirt with the sides completely cut out, and his frame was thin, but his muscles were starting to take shape. He wore a black backpack that had seen better days, shorts, and his sockless feet were shoved into scarred and scraped work boots.

"People call me Elle," she quipped. She stood as tall as she could, almost on tiptoe, as if she had to defend her right to be on his property.

"Hi…Elle," he said. His voice, which had started to lower just that fall, made him seem older than he really was. He then turned to Olivia.

"Are you planning on playing dolls or something? Connor and I have business today."

"No." Olivia scrunched up her nose in defiance. "We're gonna paint our nails."

"Whatever," said Dean. He dumped his backpack on the floor.

Olivia grabbed Elle's arm and pulled her into the tree house. She started moving the little wooden furniture around so she could set up a table for their nail polish. As Dean saw her grab a chair, he grabbed a table and sat it down in front of the widow for better light. He grabbed the other chair and motioned to Elle to have a seat.

"Hey!" Connor yelled as he ran up the steps leading to the platform and into the house. He stopped when he saw Elle sitting in her chair, her brown hair pulled up in a ponytail and wearing short blue shorts and a light green top with a sparkly shamrock on it.

"They're painting their nails," Dean informed him, and then motioned to the floor. "We're here."

"Cool," Connor said as he put his backpack down and pulled out the contents. He turned his attention to Elle. "Hi, Elle."

"Hi," she returned.

Elle watched the boys as Olivia set up their nail polish and other supplies. Connor was the complete opposite of Dean. He was wearing a red polo shirt and clean blue jean shorts. His boat sandals had hardly a scratch on them. He pulled a black binder full of plastic sleeves out of his backpack as Dean pulled an old shoebox out of his own backpack. Baseball cards. They were organizing, trading, and labeling their baseball cards. Despite the fact that Dean's cards were in a box, Elle noticed they were well cared for, and he had everything in little file pockets. Connor had his in a binder with sleeves, most likely in order of name or lineup or something OCD like that.

"Dude, I can't believe we got Ripken to sign our cards at the game," Dean said.

"I know. I want to get the whole team," Connor said, referring to the Baltimore Orioles. "Dad said he'd take me to a few more games this year. I've already got Anderson, Gonzales, Tettleton, and Worthington."

"I can't believe this card says fuck face," Dean announced as he held up a Billy Ripken card.

"Dean!" Olivia scolded.

"Sorry, Mom," Dean offered mockingly. He held his head low after thinking better of her little ears and offered a more genuine "Sorry."

The girls continued to paint their nails, freely chiming in on the boys' conversation every now and again. Over that summer, they spent a lot more time in the sacred tree house of the brotherhood that was Connor's and Dean's. The boys may have minded a little, but they didn't seem to care too much. Dean built a few more shelves for the wall and left them empty. Olivia eventually moved some of her things there for permanent storage, and Elle followed suit. She hung some dream catchers and brought a carved wooden triquetra protection symbol.

"What's this?" Connor asked.

"It's Celtic, to protect the space. It's got a lot of meanings, but the one I like best is past, present, and future. The circle around it is for protection. Can you hang it above the door?"

Connor ran his hands over the three intertwining leaf shapes. In the center was a circle with a scroll pattern burned into it. It looked like witchcraft, but Elle was rather insistent that it needed to be there.

"You're weird," Connor said as he nailed the symbol to the door.

"I try to be," Elle said. She smiled as she looked at it hanging above the little door. "Now it's home."

They passed through the city rather quickly even though it was morning rush hour. And because they were headed out of town, they had clear roads ahead. As they made their way onto the highway, the city's skyline filled the passenger side mirror. Olivia looked at the outline of those tall buildings that had become her home. It was far more her home than the town she had spent the first eighteen years of her life in. Going back to Rising Ridge was going to be weird. She would be a stranger in a strange land. She closed her eyes and laid her head back on the seat.

Her parents were dead. Her parents. She felt an immeasurable emptiness, and she knew it would never get better for her. She loved them, and they loved her. She had no doubt of that. But their jobs were always their first loves. Their lives didn't stop or slow down when they had kids. The children's lives had already been determined by their parents, but Olivia never felt comfortable living a life she had been assigned at birth. Anytime she told them she wanted something different in life than they wanted for her, they would tell her it was a nice thought, but those were dreams for other people, not her.

When Connor left for college, she felt more restricted than ever by those bonds. She quietly decided she just needed to break free of their mold. She packed her things and informed them she was going to be leaving for New York City the day she graduated.

They thought she was being silly. They thought she was wasting time and money. They wanted her to find a nice boy and settle down. This fantasy just wasn't for her, because flying high above the ground was great, but only for other people. They agreed to let her go find herself as long as she was a student. In their minds, they were OK with a small adventure if it was part of a preapproved goal. A daughter attending college at NYU while working at one of the largest financial institutions in the world was something they could work with. It looked great in the Christmas newsletter. A daughter taking a few classes here and there while living in a shoe box so she can find herself was not so Christmas newsletter worthy. She left, and they loved her still, but they did not understand her need. Now they never would. They would never see her fly, and her relationship with them would never be better.

She closed her eyes and cleared her mind, then turned to look at the man driving. She could feel the storm of emotions brewing within her. The sudden loss of her parents was trumping everything, but she could feel pangs licking at the edges. Especially now, sitting so close to him. She took a deep breath in, trying to pretend he was just Dean, her older brother's best friend. Dean, the boy who had lived next door her whole life. Dean, the family friend who was just being a good person by coming to get her. And nothing more.

"You cut your hair," she said. It was the first thing she had said out loud since he'd walked into the bank to get her.

He was the most handsome man she had ever seen in her life, and he had been that way for as long as she could remember. As it turned out, he finally stopped getting taller at six feet six inches tall. He was always outside, always enjoyed physical labor, and as a result, kept his body fit and firm. It seemed the last two years had not changed that. He was dressed in jogging shorts and a T-shirt. In fact, she wondered if he had been jogging when he got the news. Why had he come and not Connor? Nothing made sense to her; she looked at her small hands and wiggled them. Maybe she was dreaming.

His gaze never left the road. He didn't know if he should look at her. He didn't know what to do. The space between them might have been only two or three feet, but it felt more like two or three thousand feet.

"It was time," he finally said. A slow and polite smile spread across his face and was gone before she blinked.

"It looks nice," she said. She returned her stare to the highway.

"I'm sorry, Liv," he offered.

When he had walked into the bank, she was on the phone, and he knew Connor was on the other end. He wasn't surprised she turned white as a ghost when she looked up at him. He felt so guilty about that. He was anxious about being near her to begin with, but it was something he had to do for her. For Connor. For everyone.

That morning started out as innocently as any other. He was jogging on his normal route, and as he passed Connor's house and saw the police car in the driveway, he immediately went to the door to find out if everything was all right. He knew it wasn't, though. It was four in the morning—nothing good happens that early.

When Connor opened the door, Dean knew immediately it was bad. Connor told him the police were there because his parents had been killed in a car accident. Dean sat with him until the police left, and he stayed through the minutes of silence as Connor rocked in his chair staring at nothing. He had no idea what his best friend needed, but whatever it was, it was going to be done.

"Olivia," Connor whispered. It was the only word he could muster.

"You can't just call her. Somebody has to be there," Dean said.

"You're right. I need to go," Connor said. He stood and moved in erratic circles as he searched for his wallet and keys. Dean could tell he was rattled beyond measure, a rare sight.

"Connor, stay here. Take some time to process this. I'll leave now and I will get her. Give me time to get there and then call her." Dean wrapped an arm around his friend.

"You can't do that Dean. That's an all-day trip."

"Which you are in no shape to take," Dean said firmly.

Connor wanted to go get his baby sister, he needed to. He needed to wrap her up in his arms so he knew she was safe. He needed to fall apart, and he wasn't going to do that until she was with him. Dean was right though, he was in no shape to make that trip. And he had no idea how Olivia was going to take this news. *Why does she have to be in New York?*

The ride to New York had been uneventful, since he arrived well before rush hour.

With a few hours in the car, he had time to plan his entrance. He wished he had taken five damned minutes to shower. Connor had driven him back to his apartment and he grabbed a few things and headed out in his black pickup. It wouldn't have killed him to take the five minutes, but he felt it would have been selfish. This was not about him, this was about them. This was about being a good friend. What was he going to say? Would she want to see him? Was this going to make things better, or worse? How was the ride back going to be? Would she come with him? Would she punch him in the face? He had no idea. His nerves were already shot. This was going to be a day he'd have to wrap up with a good stiff drink. He just needed to get to the end of it first.

She was beautiful. The late morning sun danced off the edges of her dark blonde hair. It was shorter than the last time he saw her, as it barely swept her shoulders now. She was dressed for the June weather, but one of the things he knew to be true about her was that she was always dressed for June, even in December. She wore a white top with spaghetti straps and a formal sheer overlay that made the shirt look like a dressy, flirty tank. From what he could see, it looked like she wore just a bit of lip gloss and a touch of makeup to tone down the freckles on her nose. It had only been two years since he had seen her last, and he didn't expect her to look any different. But for the brief five minutes he stood and watched her from the window before the bank opened, she had looked different. She looked free. Happy. Then he watched as she picked up the phone. It took just a few seconds for this new life to drain right out of her.

Now in the car, the girl sitting next to him was the girl he knew from the past. Small and hopelessly lost.

"Thanks," she finally said to him. "Thanks for coming to get me. I'm not sure when I could have gotten the next bus out…or if I could have really handled all that."

"It's not a problem," he replied. He smiled to assure her he was telling her the truth. He really didn't mind.

"I don't understand what happened. I don't even think I processed anything Connor told me."

It was all one big blur. After hanging up the phone with Connor, she locked her drawer and walked into Dave's office. She closed the door and sat down in front of him. She couldn't even remember if she said anything at all to Dean before she went into Dave's office.

"My parents died." It was all she could manage to say.

Dave immediately got up and gave her a big hug. He asked what he could do, and she pointed to Dean through the office window. She never even identified who Dean was—it was just, "Dean's here. I have to go home." Dave took her key, kissed her on the head, and told her to take all the time she needed. He told her to call him when she was ready to let him know anything, and he promised she'd still have a job when she came back.

Before leaving the city, Dean drove her to her apartment. He looked like a giant awkwardly standing in a dollhouse while he waited for her to collect a few things. She also had to leave a note for Debi. She went into the bedroom as he waited in the living room, and very absentmindedly threw about a week's worth of everything into a suitcase. When she returned to the living room, he took the bag from her, and they started on their way back to Rising Ridge, where they had grown up together.

Olivia sat in silence as she pieced together the last hour of her life. "Well," Dean said, "I was jogging this morning, and Connor's house is on my route. I saw the police cars, so I knocked on the door. When he opened it, he looked much like you did when I walked into the bank—colorless. So I sat with him and the police. From what they gathered, the accident occurred somewhere between one and three o'clock this morning. There were two cars. Your parents and the other driver. They think the other driver fell asleep at the wheel, but they are going to do a toxicology on him. He crossed over into your parent's lane and they hit head on at fifty miles an hour."

"And everyone died," she sighed.

"I'm sorry, Liv," he said and patted her leg with his hand before returning it to the wheel.

"Go on…" she pressed.

"They were taken to the hospital." He paused. "Are you sure you want to hear the rest?" He knew the rest, and his heart hurt for having to tell her.

"Yeah," she sighed. "I want to know everything."

"The policeman said it looked like your dad died on impact." He paused and took a deep breath. She did too. "Your mom…she held on for the ride to the hospital, but she had been bleeding internally. There was nothing they could do. She died before they got her out of the ambulance."

"Oh, God," Olivia said. She was going to be sick. Her eyes threatened tears, but she refused to let them come. A single tear escaped and slipped down her cheek, but she quickly wiped it away.

"How's Connor?" she asked.

"He's like you, I think. Just trying to process the whole thing. The first word out of his mouth was your name," he assured her. "He didn't know what end was up. He stood up and walked in circles…I don't think he could have gotten it together quickly enough. I couldn't let him get in the car and come get you, and I didn't want him to just call and lay this on you when you have nobody here for you."

"I have people," she blurted.

He looked at her. Her nose crinkled every time she stood up for herself. He'd seen it a million times, but it was always so cute how quick she was to defend herself.

"I'm sure you do. Your boss seems real nice, and I'm sure your roommate is great, but they're not family."

There was silence once again. A million words ran through Olivia's mind. The longer she sat in silence, the more uncomfortable Dean got. Maybe this was all a mistake. Maybe he should have just stayed out of it. He didn't want to add more pressure, but he knew he inevitably would be. He wanted to do the right thing, but the longer she sat there saying nothing, the more he wondered if he knew what the right thing was.

"You're a good friend, Dean," she smiled for the first time. "Connor is very lucky to have you."

As if somehow knowing he needed to hear it, she added, "You did the right thing. Connor and I both appreciate it. Thank you."

"Any time. I'll always be here for you guys," he said.

The town she had grown up in had not changed one bit in the two years since she had left. It was in full swing with midafternoon summer happenings. The world stops for no man, she thought. They left the rush of the highway behind and she watched people happily shopping on Main Street as they drove through. She saw Dean wave a few times to folks; some she recognized, and some she didn't. Main Street had been kept fresh and nice. There was a lot of town pride, but many choices that gave it a small town old-fashioned feel. Instead of power lines and big, square lights, the streets were line with old-fashioned streetlamps. Black iron benches had been placed every few stores, and she knew there were a few older people who would sit on them for hours just people watching. Most of the stores were the same as they had always been, with friendly widows welcoming customers. When they turned onto Oak Crest, Olivia saw her brother standing in the doorway of his two-story red brick house.

She had not actually seen the house in person. He'd purchased it just a few months ago, right after he got out of college. It was a fixer-upper, but Connor always liked working with tools and didn't mind having a few things to fix up, especially if it could bring a profit. He favored their mother more than their father, with the exception of his height. He always kept his dark hair trimmed neatly and dressed the same as always—like he'd come out of a J. Crew catalog. He'd been sitting by the window with a cup of coffee when he saw Dean's black truck coming up the street.

"Connor," Olivia said as she opened the truck door and ran into his arms.

"Hi," he said softly. He wrapped his arms around her.

Dean quietly got out of the truck and grabbed her suitcase. He stayed back to give them a few minutes with each other. When Connor's gaze lifted over Olivia's head to him, they nodded to each other, and then all three headed into the house.

Three

The funeral was on a Saturday morning at the end of June. Olivia had made the arrangements with the family church and contacted all the family members, while Connor took care of more logistical matters like arranging the burial and going to the bank to collect the will the knew they had in a safety deposit box.

It was a nice funeral, as they say. There was a good turnout of family, friends, and business associates. Her parents had run a small real estate firm, where her father focused on finding cheap properties they could flip and her mother focused on the people buying or selling a home. They made a great team. Connor had his own ambitions for his career, but he did see how much money they sometimes made on a flip, so he kept his eye on the market and had made a few bucks already on one house. She knew he was looking to do the same with the house he was living in now. Olivia was not surprised by how many people came to pay their respects. It was a small town, and everyone had known everyone else pretty much since birth. Her parents were no exception. They had met in high school, and James started his business soon after graduation. Maggie was happy to be his biggest cheerleader and strongest asset. They had been together thirty years. Their business was well respected in the town. Maggie was insistent that Connor get his real estate license to bring in some money and stability as he was working toward opening his custom-built wood shop with Dean. He did have his parents' full support, but it made her feel better to know he could come work for the family business anytime he wanted. Just in case.

Connor and Olivia were now guests in their own home as Elle and her mother saw to the family gathering after the funeral. Elle had dropped everything when Olivia called her. Elle attended a small, but well-established, liberal arts college in a neighboring town, so she still lived with her parents in Rising Ridge. Elle's mom, Rose, had been friends with Olivia's mom, Maggie. Their friendship had been established when Elle and Olivia became joined at the hip in kindergarten. Rose was the complete opposite of Maggie. She was a stay at home mom who knew every move Elle made but gave her the freedom to make those moves all on her own. She always decorated her house with a million trinkets to celebrate every holiday, and she seemed to have a good handle on what was happening at school. Whether gossiping or talking about academics, it was clear to Olivia from day one that Elle talked to Rose. They were friends. Olivia wasn't sure if she and Maggie were ever friends.

"Can I get you something to eat sweetie?" Rose checked on Olivia, who was sitting on the sofa in her own parents' house.

They had chosen to have the reception after the funeral in their childhood home, which was only a few miles from Connor's house. It was a larger house, and definitely in better shape than Connor's fixer-upper. 3317 Maple Avenue had been their home since Connor was in preschool and they knew Olivia was on her way. That was when it was time to buy their forever home. The large brick house sat on a corner lot and had a lovely manicured lawn. Bright flowers always reflected the season; right now pink and purple Zinnias grew happily in the late June sun. Her mother had decorated each room meticulously, and the house could be featured in the latest home and garden magazine at any given time. Connor's room was always whatever Maggie wanted her "boys' room" to look like. Everything matched, blues and browns mixed throughout in that catalog sort of way. Connor was so easygoing, he lived where he was told. If his room was decorated in bright yellow and pink clowns, Olivia suspected he would have somehow made it work. She loved him for that. Olivia's room had a bit more of her own personality than that, but was still very much predetermined by Maggie. Olivia had once liked dolls. So her room became a white and pink lacy oasis with rows and rows of porcelain dolls. Pretty flowers lay in small jars around, too; a sweet little girl's room. When Olivia had expressed interest in a more grown-up room, there had been a few changes. The dolls came down, but not much else. The walls remained pink, and the bed remained a white lacy five-year-old's dream come true. A few art prints on the walls tied all the colors together, but nothing Olivia would have picked out for herself. Teenaged girl, designed by Maggie. Once she and Connor moved out, Maggie quickly changed their rooms into quaint little guest rooms reflecting Maggie and only Maggie. She hadn't even asked their permission, because to Maggie, it was her house, so why would she ask? It never dawned on her Connor or Olivia might have considered their room to be their own personal space. Maggie packed up the things that are inevitably left behind when a child moves away, stuck them in a box with the children's names on them, and then they went into the basement. Their entire childhood seemed to have been erased from the house within days of them moving out.

"I'm fine, thank you." Olivia looked up and smiled at Rose.

"Now, Livy…you can lie all you want to anyone else in this room but not to me. You are not fine, little girl," Rose said as Olivia welcomed her to sit on the couch.

"I will be. We will be," she said as she looked up at Connor, who was chatting with a cousin across the room.

"That Connor is a fine young man," Rose reflected.

"Yeah, he is. He's the best big brother in the world." Olivia smiled at him.

"And you're the lucky girl who gets to call him that," Rose agreed. "That boy, and Dean. They were just a couple of knuckleheads a minute ago. Now look at them. Connor's fixing up that house, he's a college graduate, and he's opened that shop on Main Street. Dean, I thought he was a lost soul for so long. He's got that broody bad boy thing down pat. But he's a good man. He is so talented, and has quickly become a respectable name around here. Hell, I replaced my kitchen table last year; I have a Dean Winston original."

As she mentioned Dean's handcrafted solid wood table, she made the hand gesture of puffing up her hair in that fancy way. Olivia smiled, looking at Dean grabbing two beers from the fridge. No doubt he would be walking one of those over to Connor.

"Your parents loved you, you know," Rose said seriously.

"I do know."

"They were proud of you," she informed.

"They didn't understand me," Olivia sighed.

"No, they didn't. Your drum beats so much louder than your mother's ever did. But I think she admired that about you. You are not afraid of anything, where Maggie was afraid of everything that wasn't already happily settled into her world. And your father, he was a businessman. No doubt about that. But when you talked to him, he would be the first to tell you his two kids were going to take over the damn world."

"Ha," Olivia said with an affectionate sarcastic tone.

Her father was a dreamer. He ran a business, but he imagined that one day it would be an empire. It wasn't enough to just put dinner on the table; he had to tell them as they sat around that one of these days they would have servants bringing them their meals. He dreamed of a six-figure kind of life with a blue-collar paycheck. He treated their small office staff well, and he gave one hundred and ten percent to his clients. His work was top quality because at the end of the day, he had a brain that could work out even the most complicated of puzzles. He was so smart, but he just kept passing up what he had in his hands to pursue what was next. He missed the fact that both of his children would have been happy just having what was.

"Yeah, me and Connor. Taking over the damn world." She smiled at the memory of the dreams and stories her father used to fill her little mind with at bedtime. He did tell the best bedtime stories—when he was actually around to tell them.

"Well, cheers to that," Rose said as she picked up her cup of Sprite and kissed Olivia on the cheek.

"Cheers," Olivia agreed.

The family members all gave hugs, and friends all offered words of encouragement. There was enough food in frozen casserole form to feed a small army in the freezer and refrigerator. Connor held his ground so well, Olivia thought. He smiled, chatted, and made sure to make his way around the whole house, saying hello to every single person. Olivia just sat on the couch and kept conversation with whomever sat down next to her for a few minutes. Everyone meant well, but what do you to say? They loved you, they were proud of you, it will all be fine. Times one hundred. Eventually, she started to feel like she could not breathe. What do you talk about when all you want to do is leave this place and go back to the safe haven you've built for yourself in a city two hundred and thirty miles away?

"Hey," Elle walked up to Connor and Dean. "How you guys doing? Do you need anything?"

"Seriously, Elle…you've done too much already," Connor said. "Liv and I could have done this, but not this." His hands gestured widely toward the organized tables of food, drinks, and everything else he had no idea went into an event.

"Hey, it's what I do," Elle said referencing her party planning business. It wasn't what she wanted to do with her life, but it paid the bills while she was in school and it was flexible and weekend heavy, which was good for a student.

"You do it well," Dean complimented her.

"Thanks."

"How's our girl?" Connor asked her, looking at the spot Olivia had not moved from all night, but this time seeing an empty place.

"I don't know. I don't know if she's in shock or what. She's just sort of…on pause or something. Still, silent," Elle admitted, feeling bad for her best friend.

"Yeah. I should never have moved out when I went to college," Connor said, blaming himself for the disconnect between Olivia and her parents. He had always been the peacemaker between them.

"Connor, you were eighteen years old. You had a scholarship. You needed to go and live at the dorms. You needed to live irresponsibly for a little while. You're so…perfect," she said, for lack of any other way to describe him.

"I'm not, but thank you. I just feel like I abandoned her. She just sort of shut down after that," he reflected.

"Again, thirteen," Elle chuckled. "I think that was going to happen whether you were here or not. It's biology. Girls are weird."

"Yes they are," Dean chimed in.

Elle playfully smacked him.

Dean looked around, but did not see Olivia anywhere. She had sat in the same seat all night long, politely talking to everyone who sat next to her but showing no signs one way or another of how she was feeling. She had always been so stoic in front of other people. She never wanted to accidentally show her human side. He chatted with Connor and Elle for a few more minutes and then excused himself to throw away his empty beer bottle. He went to the refrigerator and grabbed a Sprite, some mint, and a lime. He stood at the counter and made two mock mojitos, then he quietly slipped out the back door and walked across the expansive yard into his own parents' backyard.

The tree house stood silently in the moonlight as it had for the past thirteen years. It was a summer project his father had brought home for him. Connor's father, James, and Dean's father, Henry, designed the house one evening, and had to be talked into a more logical and budget friendly design after presenting the idea to their wives. They had to be reminded the tree house wasn't actually for them. It turned out to be a nice midsized house. It had a door with a small pane of glass embedded in it, windows on each of the side walls, and a ladder leading up through a chimney that served as a lookout. A small porch with a railing wrapped around it, and the house had multiple entrances. You could climb the wood planks nailed into the tree, you could pull yourself up on the ropes hanging down, or you could walk up the steps they had built for the sole purpose of parents being able to get up there in case of emergency. No need for them to break their necks getting to a hurt child. It was large enough to hold five or six eight-year-old boys in the height of a backyard adventure day…and as it turned out, quite often two little girls as well. Dean and Connor had helped in its construction, and it was probably the most well-built tree house there ever was. It had seen many adventures in its time. He sighed as he looked at the ladder and the ropes. They seemed smaller and smaller every year.

"Knock knock," he offered to the cosmic void around the house. There was a heartbeat of silence.

"It's your house. You don't need my permission to enter," Olivia said, peeking out one of the windows.

"Liv, if you want some alone time, it's yours. If not, I've got drinks." He smiled as he shook the glasses.

"Come on up," she said.

He took the stairs and handed over the drinks as he tried to fold his six foot six frame into a four foot door.

"This used to be bigger," he said.

"You used to be smaller," she retorted.

He looked around. He hadn't been up in this space once in the last couple of years.

"Liv, I'm not sure if we're alone up here," he said as he looked around at all the dark corners.

"I did a creeper sweeper," she said, using their term for checking for animals. Being in rural Maryland, most of the time the tree house was fine. But on occasion, there would be a snake, raccoon, or squirrel inside. And Henry knocked out at least one hornet's nest every few years. The kids got used to checking with a flashlight and a small broom they left up there for just that purpose. It was actually something they all secretly wished for, with shrill screams and running around in attack or fear mode (depending) when they did find something.

"We are alone," she assured him.

He handed her a drink. She accepted it, took a deep sip, and frowned into her cup.

"This is Sprite," she said.

"You're still not twenty-one," he replied.

"Oh, for fuck's sake, Dean." She laughed as she continued to enjoy her favorite mock-tail. "I'll be twenty-one in a handful of days."

"None of which are today," he insisted.

"Is yours alcohol?" she asked as she tried to grab his cup.

"No. I've had my couple of beers. This is Sprite too. Sorry to disappoint you," he said, attempting to sit down in the middle of the floor next to her.

When they were kids, they could lay down in the middle of the floor and have a perfect view of the night sky out one of the windows. That window had spent time being a window in a rocket, a pretend telescope, and the only escape from the high seas flooding the area. Olivia could still lay there, with her legs propped up on the wall. Dean could too, if you cut him off at the knees.

"This floor used to be wider," he said as he propped himself against the wall.

"You used to be smaller. How did you know I would be up here?" she asked him.

"It's the only place I thought you would be," he said.

It was her spot. She was only three when this house went up, so she never knew a time where it wasn't a part of her memories. And she never remembered a time where Dean wasn't the boy next door. All of her life, the lines between their yards did not exist. It was one big backyard. Dean had lived there since birth and was very excited that a boy his age was moving into the house next door. There were many play dates and sleepovers, and when the boys expressed an interest in sleeping in the backyard, Dean's father thought it was high time for a tree house. Once the major construction was done, the boys got to add their own personal touches. They painted it, put stickers on it, and tacked on a No Girls Allowed sign on the front door. Olivia always ignored that sign, and in turn, so did Elle. There were times Connor went there to get some man time with Dean. Get away from his annoying baby sister. There were also times Dean would find Olivia in there by herself. She would be coloring in a coloring book or listening to her Fisher-Price radio, or just playing school with some dolls she had hauled up the steps.

The first time she ran away, she was seven. She packed her little bag with two nightgowns, five shirts, and one pair of pants. She grabbed some pudding cups and plastic spoons and headed out. Good-bye, forever. After several hours of a panicked search by her parents and all their friends, Dean had gone out to the tree house after seeing flashes of light in it from his bedroom window. She had managed to hide from everyone all day long, but being alone up there at night was freaking her out. Twelve-year-old Dean marched out to the clubhouse and asked her what she was doing there.

"I live here now," she informed him as she was trying to get herself comfortable on the hard, cold wood floor with only the blanket from her bed and her pillow.

Dean had told his father, who called her parents. Her mother had done something completely surprising that evening. Rather than scold her daughter, she came up the steps to the tree house with sleeping bags, a small light, and some snacks.

"You can run away, but you have to take me with you," she whispered in her daughter's ear. And they both slept in the tree house that night. It was one of Olivia's most treasured memories of her mother.

The timing of the children being five years apart worked out really well. Dean and Connor moved on to cars and girls, and the tree house became vacant. Olivia and Elle took it over. They redecorated, but only with items that were temporary, for while they were there. They would haul up pretty blankets to sit on and small tablecloths to cover the wood tables Henry had made for them to play on. All things they could and would easily pack back up and take with them when they went home.

"Thanks, Dean," she said as she raised her glass. "I just needed some space."

"It's your space, Liv. It hasn't been mine for a very long time," he said truthfully.

Olivia sat her drink on the table and laid back down on the floor to stare at the moon again. Dean crossed his legs and tilted his head so he could see the same view.

"That window used to be bigger," he said.

"You used to be smaller," she giggled.

They sat in silence for a while. Dean was good at that; he had always been good at that. At first, Olivia was so thankful for it. Her parents were always talking at her. What to do, where to go, what to wear. Their pursuit of the perfect children seemed relentless. Connor had always wanted to just help her do the things they asked her to do, and Elle was ready at a moment's notice with an escape from life plan. Somehow, whenever she was looking for something that fell in the in-between, Dean was always the gentle hand holding her steady.

Now, the silence was maddening. Somewhere along the line, she realized he would always be there for her if she reached out to him, but she wasn't sure he really wanted to be. She made him that. Just like her parents, she gave him a role he did not ask for and that does not fit.

What frustrated her, what caused the abyss of silence between them, was she knew if she reached for his hand right now, he would take it. If she laid her head on his shoulder, he would rest his head on hers. If she put her hand on his chest, she would feel his slow and steady heartbeat begin to quicken and lose its pace. She put him in the role she wanted him to fill, but he let her. It was moments like those when she wasn't sure if his were the arms she would be safe in, or if they were the arms that would dance her to the furthest edge of a cliff and then let go. She hated herself for the itch she felt in her fingers to reach out for his hands, only inches from hers, and she hated him because she knew he would allow it if she did.

Two years. She had put two years and a few hundred miles between them, and it was all for nothing. She had fooled herself into thinking that she was over him and had moved on. She didn't think of him in her life in New York. It was true that she had not dated, but she was giving herself time to get to know the Olivia who had never gotten a chance to live. She was happy there, and had the promise of everything she had ever dreamed of. She looked at him as he sat silently looking at the stars, and realized she had never gotten over him. It was just a room in her heart where she had turned off the lights and closed the door. It was still there, in the darkness, as big and complicated as it had always been. She sighed.

"Whatcha thinking?" he asked, turning his attention to her.

"Feels like yesterday," she stated simply.

"What does?" he asked, curious where her mind had wandered off to.

"The last time we were up here." Her face had not given away any emotion. Though her heart was racing a million miles a minute, her face remained unchanged.

He took a deep breath and turned his attention back to the stars above them. She could see the muscles in his square jaw tighten. She imagined a million thoughts running through his mind. What she did not know, what she may never know, is if the memories of their last encounter were comforting thoughts that warmed the evening, or if they were the chill in the air that passed through.

"It's funny how something can seem like just yesterday in one thought, and a lifetime ago in another, I suppose," he finally said.

A lifetime ago. That's where she was to him; she was a lifetime ago. She wanted to scream. She wanted to cry. She wanted to feel his arms around her so bad that she almost couldn't breathe.

I am going to have to deal with this, she thought, I've got to find a way to let go. As the thought of letting go of him completely filled her mind, her hand moved closer to his. She was unable to breathe. Looking down, he felt her fingers on the edge of his hand and he gathered her hand up in his. She closed her eyes and took the deep breath she needed so badly. He pulled her closer, and she laid her head on his shoulder. As she knew he would, he rested his head on hers. The role of Dean, as told by Olivia. A tear slipped down her cheek. She knew she had to find a way to free him from this room in her heart.

Mistaking her tear of heartache for him as one for her parents, he pulled her in even closer and whispered the comforting things he always had. The gentle hand that held her steady. She would surely go mad before she got herself back to New York. She was beginning to wonder if New York was far enough away.

When she fell asleep, he quietly crawled out of the house and went into her childhood home once more. He told Connor they were having a sleepover. When Olivia woke up the next morning, she was stiff as a board but there was a pillow under her head and a blanket on top of her. Elle was sleeping quietly next to her and Connor and Dean were curled up in sleeping bags on the outer edges of the house. They had taken all the furniture out and the four of them took up every inch of floor space.

Olivia looked at these people and finally broke down. Tears streamed down her face as she freely mourned two people who had their issues, but she had nonetheless loved with her whole heart. She shook her head at the fact they had all crammed themselves into the tree house. Oh, this place. Oh, these walls. The silent backdrop of her life, and quite often its own character.

Four

"So, what's the plan?" Elle asked as she cut up the chicken sandwich she had ordered from the small vintage coffee house where she met Olivia before her evening class.

"Well, we got through the funeral. Now we have to get through the wills and all their stuff. I have no idea how long that will take. I called in to work to check in, and Dave assures me he's got everything covered. Called Debi, she's fine. As long as I have my half of the rent, she doesn't mind having the whole place to herself. I am thinking a week. Maybe. I don't know. I need to get back to work though if I want to pay that rent," Olivia said as she picked through her chicken salad.

"And the will stuff seems pretty straightforward?" Elle asked.

"Yeah. Connor went and got the wills. As far as I know, everything is in a trust belonging to him, so yeah, straightforward."

"What about you?" Elle asked, surprised that everything wouldn't be split 50/50.

"Honestly, I don't know. I don't know when they last updated their will. I could have been a minor. Connor's only twenty-five, and I'm only twenty. He hasn't said anything about being shipped off to some weird relative in Nebraska I've never heard of, so I assume I am safe. I'm assuming they left everything up to Connor and trusted he'd take care of me. He will; I'm not worried." She smiled as she took a sip of her water and looked across the street to Connor's store.

Rising Ridge Designs had been open exactly six months. It was a small store in what had been an old-fashioned candy shop until the owner retired and it was closed. Connor went to school for business and marketing, but his passion and hobbies were building and tinkering. He was the perfect combination of both his parents. Dean went to school for art design and woodworking. He never really wanted to bother much with the business end of things, he just wanted to build things like his old man did. Henry Winston spent his entire career as a carpenter, and ran a rather profitable construction company. With his professional experience and a little financial seed money, he became a silent partner in Rising Ridge Designs. It was the perfect marriage, as Connor loved the facts, figures, and salesmanship of it all. Dean just liked to build stuff.

Olivia noted the blue and brown arbor above the store window. She giggled. Her mother must have painted that. In the window, she could see two handcrafted rocking chairs with a small table between them. Magazines filled a large wicker basket next to one chair and a fake dog lay curled up next to the other. It was a sweet little window, giving the image of a slower life. She had not made it into the store yet; it was on her list of things to do today.

"Well, if your parents were secretly rich and you never have to worry about another thing in your life, don't forget the little people," Elle offered up a silly grin.

"I'm going to head over to the store after lunch. You want to come with?" Olivia asked.

"Sure. I've got...fifteen minutes before I need to go."

After paying the check, they walked across the street and pulled open the door to the store. A small bell chimed and the soft smell of handcrafted wood welcomed them. Elle had been in the store many times over the months Connor and Dean had been open. Olivia had only seen pictures; it was lovely to see it all in person. She had planned on visiting to see it sometime over the summer, once her classes wrapped up. The front of the store held the chairs and table, and behind that was a wall of shelves holding small handmade trinkets and treasures. A glass counter with some more expensive items in it was on the other side of the store, along with a large holder where they could display one of a number of binders they had behind the counter. No doubt pictures of their larger pieces, things they had built over the years.

"Good afternoon, ladies." Connor smiled as he came out of the back room to greet his customers.

"Hi. I heard you opened your own shop. Thought I would come check it out," his sister teased him.

"It's about damn time," he said as he opened his arms wide to show off the store. "What do you think?"

"Connor, it's great. The pictures you sent are fantastic, but seeing it in person is so much more. You and Dean did really good. I'm proud of you both."

"Thanks, sis." He smiled genuinely.

"We were just across the street having lunch. We were discussing her inheritance," Elle chimed in as she examined the smaller boxes and paperweights along the wall.

"Making plans already?" he asked.

"No," Olivia quickly corrected. "Elle's worried that I'm going to be out on my ass."

"I did not say that," Elle corrected, but remained fascinated with a small trinket box with a large tree of life carved in the top. She took it off the shelf to examine it closer.

"You didn't have to," Olivia said to Elle, and then returned her attention to her brother. "I'm sure as long as I don't wind up under the physical and financial care of some relative in Nebraska that we've never heard of, I'll be fine."

"Nebraska, huh?" Connor looked at her inquisitively. "I think you'd like Nebraska. It's nice."

"Sure it is, for…other people. Who are not me," she said.

"It will all be fine, Liv. We'll talk to the lawyer Wednesday. By Friday we will have all the balls that need to be rolling, and you can go back to living that big city life you like so much a million miles away."

"Two hundred and thirty," Olivia corrected him.

"Same thing," he assured her.

"I also told her not to forget the little people if you two wind up rich," Elle said as she brought the box up to the counter. "I want this."

Connor looked down at the item she placed on the counter and smiled. She had picked up a trinket box that he had designed and made himself. It was a recent addition to the inventory, but the design was something he had wanted to work into something for quite a while.

"Rich, who's rich?" Dean's voice carried into the room from behind the large box he was carrying to the front of the store.

"We are, apparently," Olivia said as she watched him set the box down. "Hi."

"Hey," he said to the group a little breathlessly. "This is the fire pit Cat wants installed at the Inn. I'm going to go deliver it now. But hell, if you're rich, I say we pack up for the day and go fishing."

"Sorry buddy, not today. Worker's gotta work," Connor said as he packed up the box Elle had picked out and rang it up for her, noting the friends and family discount of twenty percent on the ticket. He was nothing if not a sharp businessman.

"How's Cat doing? I haven't seen her at all since I left. She's been so busy," Olivia said.

"She's really good!" Elle informed her. "The Inn has really taken off. I see advertisements for town events hosted there all the time. Been to a few, too. She's running a tight ship; it's good."

"I need to get up there before I go home," Olivia said to herself.

"I'm going up now. You can come with me. I have to install this so that will give you about two hours, and then I'll bring you back," Dean offered.

"Um…" Olivia hesitated, but only enough for Dean to notice. "Um, my schedule is kind of clear right now so…maybe? Elle brought me here; I would need to get back to Connor's. They didn't build a subway system in my absence, did they?"

"We should be wrapping up the day by then, so just come home with me," Connor said as he was flipping through some papers by the register.

"Yes, then?" Dean asked.

"Yes. We can go. I guess I will be back later, Connor. I'm going to walk Elle out. I'll meet you at your truck."

The girls walked out of the store, Elle with her small bag in hand. They went back across the street to where Elle had parked, and the men watched them as the girls exchanged smiles and hugs before Elle got into her car.

"It's good that she has Elle. It's good they are still them, you know?" Connor reflected.

"I can't believe you charged her for that box," Dean said as he eyed the women.

"I gave her the appropriate discount," Connor defended himself.

"It's kind of a crappy deal to charge the girl who inspired the design," Dean quipped.

"What?" Connor turned his full attention to his best friend.

"That box. That was the tree of life box, right? That's got Elle written all over it," Dean said as a statement of fact.

"Why would you think that?" Connor asked.

"You didn't?"

"I…" Connor felt that little tug in his gut, knowing she was exactly who had been on his mind when he'd come up with the design.

"Yeah, that's what I thought," Dean said smugly.

"It's a good product," he defended himself. "Lots of people like that new age hippie dippy stuff."

"I didn't say it wasn't. It is. It just happens to be that that box showed up on the shelf around Elle's birthday last year."

"Shut up. She's an interesting person; I just had her on the brain that week because you know how she treats her birthday like a damned national holiday. It was being talked about, that's all," Connor grumbled.

"Mmm-hmm," Dean wasn't going to let this one go. "We'll see you later."

As he picked up the fire pit once more and took it out the front door to his truck parked in front of the store, he chuckled. His best friend was in love and didn't even know it. With Elle, of all people. He shook his head as he loaded the pit in the back of the truck and secured it. He met Olivia at the passenger door and opened it for her.

"My Lady." He bowed in a grand cartoon-like gesture.

"Thank you." She met his ridiculousness with a curtsey.

When he climbed into the driver's side, he offered her a smile. He had relaxed around her quite a bit since the night of the funeral. He wasn't sure if there would be any tension between them, but she seemed to be the same Olivia he had known nearly all of his life. If their past wasn't going to bother her, he wouldn't let it bother him. He felt quite a bit of relief, as the infinite silence between them had been deafening for the last two years.

"So, how you doing?" he asked, not sure what to ask.

"Good. I mean, I'm going to be sad for a while I guess. It's hard because Mom called me every Sunday night just to recap the week with each other, and last night, even though I was sleeping on Connor's couch, even though we just buried them, I still expected to hear the phone ring."

"Understandable," he said.

"It'll be good to see what Cat has done with the Inn," she said, changing the subject. "I hope she doesn't mind me just popping in."

"She won't. It's what her business is built on, actually." He smiled.

"Yeah," she agreed.

They had driven down Main Street through Rising Ridge, and past the busier streets surrounding the middle of town. The buildings gave way to expansive fields that would have corn by fall. Hills that seemed to roll as far as the eye could see. This was mostly still a farm town. Many of the homes, most of the homes in fact, were well over thirty years old. Only two or three major developments had been added over the last twenty years, and there were always bidding wars when a property went up for sale. Most of the people who lived in the town had either lived there all their lives already, or were planning on living there from here on out.

Aside from the farms still monopolizing most of the town footprint, there were also four vineyards. They all prided themselves in being Maryland's best. People in town were quick to have a favorite one for the party, a favorite one for the property, a favorite one for the wine tour, and finally a favorite one that produced the best wine. Which vineyards were assigned to what varied wildly from person to person. Olivia watched the rich green fields swaying gently in the early summer breeze. She did love this view. She always imagined what it was like to live and work in one of the large white houses standing on any given farm property. Getting up early to feed horses, chickens, or cows. Making pies in a kitchen that was two hundred years old, with a fan whirling away the summer heat. Watching the sunset pour into a field of growing vegetables.

The Inn's main entrance was marked by two brick pillars with six-foot-long walls flanking the long drive up to the property. They had old-fashioned black lampposts on the pillars with summer flowers freshly planted all around. The drive to the main house was lined with large cherry trees. Cat had been in the same class as Connor and Dean in high school and was part of the crowd of faces that seemed to always be around during their teen years. Dean and Cat even dated for one summer. She was attracted to his leather jacket and black truck, and he was attracted to her endless miles of legs. The Inn was a long-standing business in town and Cat had worked her way up, starting as a maid at the age of sixteen when she went out for her first job.

She had been running the place as manager for the last three years, after the owner expressed interest in stepping out of the day-to-day and easing his way into retirement. She made that very easy for him, as hosting the tourists and sometimes regular guests, too, turned out to be something she loved doing. She had lived in Rising Ridge since she was a freshman in high school when her parents had settled there after a few tours overseas, but you'd never know she wasn't born there. She knew every inch of the town, and made it a priority to link up business at the Inn with every business in town. She had also started regularly inviting not just guests of the Inn, but the entire town up for special occasions and holidays. The property, twenty acres in all, certainly had enough space for such events.

Dean passed the main entrance and parked his truck at the delivery door located behind the main building. He grabbed his clipboard with her order on top, and hopped out of the truck. Olivia watched him walk around the truck and smiled. He was always such a gentleman, for as much of a bad boy as he was. He opened her door and then closed it behind her.

She followed him up to the door of the building, which he again opened for her. She noted he ignored the sign reading *Please ring bell for deliveries*. They entered a small vestibule that was clean and wide, with a very large black rubber mat on the floor. There was no sign of anyone, but there was the distinct sound of a busy kitchen very nearby.

"Follow me," he instructed her.

He wiped his feet on the mat and walked in the direction of the sound, stopping in the wide doorway to the expansive and bustling kitchen. Olivia looked around and saw two large restaurant grade stoves; pots and pans on the burners had delicious smells wafting from them. An enormous island sat in the middle of the room, where two well-dressed teenagers were collecting plates and organizing them on trays to take out. The Red Hot Chili Peppers song "Give it Away" poured out of the stereo in the window as a young woman, who was at least six feet tall with a mass of fiery red curls tucked in a bun on top of her head, chopped vegetables into a salad. A man, equally as tall, stood with his back to the door as he stirred a pot of steaming soup.

"Hey, Dean!" The red head looked up, spotting the pair at the door, and stopped chopping vegetables. The man at the stove looked at her, annoyed.

"Keep chopping, I've got this. You know how to read, right?" he asked Dean as he put a lid on the pot and turned the burner down.

"I do," Dean offered.

"Then why do you ignore the signs for deliveries?" the man asked as he walked over to them, giving Olivia a friendly smile but returning to Dean with a smug stare.

"Because it pisses you off," Dean replied, deadpan.

"Oh, I see. OK. Good luck to you on poker night, my friend. I will be after blood," Rohan said as the two men exchanged smiles.

"I've got a special delivery for Cat today," Dean said. "This is Olivia. Olivia, this is Rohan. He runs the kitchen and is the head chef here at Chez Snooty Plates."

Olivia coughed back a giggle. She extended her hand to him.

"Hello," she said politely. "I'm an old friend of Cat's. Well, my brother is, but she likes me too."

"Who's your brother?" Rohan asked.

"Connor. Connor Reynolds."

Rohan smiled genuinely, which made Olivia happy. He obviously had a good opinion of her brother.

"Wow, that sorry SOB has a beautiful sister. Who da' thunk it. Well, welcome to Archer's Inn. Are you hungry?" he asked.

"No, just ate. Next time." She smiled.

"Yes, for sure. I'll grab Cat. Maya, you get that soup dished out," he directed the young girl behind him. "Dean, I assume you have something else?"

"Fire Pit," he informed. "Just need somebody to sign for it and then I will get on installing it."

"Carson can do that. Check the front. Olivia, follow me."

Olivia followed him down the hallway to a white door with a frosted glass panel in a floral design. He knocked on it.

"Come on in."

"Dean brought a special delivery for you," he said to the tall blonde behind the desk. He turned to Olivia and said, "It was nice to meet you," before returning to his duties in the kitchen.

Cat broke out into the biggest smile and jumped out of her chair.

"Livy!" she exclaimed as she grabbed Olivia in a warm embrace. "I heard you were back. How are you? I'm so sorry about your parents."

"Thanks." Olivia smiled. "I'm good. Except for feeling like maybe I've become Alice, and this is Wonderland. I feel very small around here."

"It's on the applications. Must be over six feet tall and totally smoking hot to work here. It works out well for me," Cat teased as she watched Rohan walking down the hallway to the kitchen. She might be married, but she did appreciate the way his chef's uniform clung to his muscles.

"It seems to have worked out really well, from what I've seen. Things are running great, everything looks wonderful," Olivia said as she sat in the chair opposite Cat's desk.

"I'm lucky. Mr. Archer still owns the place of course, but he's been pleased enough with my work that he just lets me do whatever I want. I'm proud of everything we've done here. We've got a great team."

"I'm sure you do," Olivia agreed.

"How long will you be in town?" Cat asked. "Where are you staying? We've got a room free."

"Oh, I'm with Connor, but thank you. I'm staying the week, for now. We go for the reading of the will on Wednesday. Then it'll take a few days for everything to be sorted out."

"Well, how's life in the great N-Y-C?" Cat asked.

"It's good. I'm working at a bank. I really love it, my coworkers are great. Even though none of them are six feet tall or totally smoking hot, we get by."

"You have an apartment, or rent a room, or however it works there?"

"Apartment. It's small, in a Brownstone that was converted to four apartments. Very New York. I've got a roommate, Debi.

She's awesome. It's a one bedroom but it's fine, because we are both out a lot. We wanted to be smack dab in the middle of everything, and this was the way to afford it. I love it." Olivia smiled.

"Amazing. I am so totally going to take a vacation one of these days and come up for a weekend. How's Connor doing? I'm sorry I didn't come to the funeral. I was out of town trying to secure the fireworks company for the Fourth of July party," Cat said.

"He's doing OK. He did a really great job with all the funeral arrangements. We had ourselves a good cry. I think when we deal with their stuff it's going to be hard."

"I can imagine. They will be missed. They were much loved around here," Cat said. "Well, do you have time? I could give you a tour."

"Yes I do, I came with Dean. He's installing the fire pit you ordered," Olivia said as they got up to head out.

"Oh, goody! Yay. We should have time then," Cat said, looping her arm in Olivia's. "Let's have a tour of the old place."

The ride back into town was peaceful. The visit with Cat had put Olivia in a good mood, and for just a few seconds, Dean thought she seemed content as wisps of her dark blonde hair escaped her ponytail and were flying wildly in the wind from her open truck window.

"So…" she said, but kept her gaze on the road ahead of them.

Dean didn't say a word. He knew enough about women to know that when a conversation started with the word so, it was not going to be a fun conversation.

"Are we OK?" she asked.

"What do you mean? You and me?" he asked, surprised at how she was going to start the conversation they had not been having for the last several days.

"Yeah. I mean, there's been no time for us to talk. I just…I can't lose you too," she said quietly, and mostly to herself. "I'm sorry, Dean. I know that's selfish of me to be thinking right now."

At her words, Dean pulled the truck off to the side of the road and put it in park. He turned to face her, and for a few minutes just looked at her. She honestly looked scared to death, and was having a hard time looking directly at him.

"Livy, first of all, it's not selfish. I've been wondering myself if you and I are OK. Wondering how you feel, thinking to myself that I'm selfish for even thinking I might be on your mind at all at a time like this. One thing I can tell you without question is that you're never going to lose me," he assured her. "As far as anything needing to be said…we just, we went in different directions. It's OK. You…needed your space. I needed mine. We're good. I promise."

"So, it doesn't have to be weird?" she asked, finally facing him.

"No. It doesn't have to be weird. We're friends. We will always be friends," he said. "I'm never not going to be there for you if you need me, Liv."

Five

Olivia 12, Elle 12, Dean 17, Connor 17

The sun was relentless. Maryland was experiencing a heatwave, and the temperatures had not dipped below ninety in the last two weeks. Olivia loved it. She was OK with winter; it was fine for a day, or even a weekend, but she didn't care for the months of winter. Summer—summer made everything magic. The days were longer, the nights were warmer, and only fun things filled the in-between. She seemed to always have a swimsuit and shorts on, and at some point in the day, she and Connor made it over to the neighborhood pool. Since Connor was seventeen, he could go to the pool by himself. And her mother told her that if she listened to him, and he agreed to watch her, she could go with him this year. The idea of being at the pool without her parents made her feel so grown up. She was almost a teenager, and the taste of a promise of freedom was sweet.

"Oh, I like her suit," Elle said.

Olivia opened her eyes and shielded them from the blazing sun. The girls were lying on chairs by the pool to work on their tans. It was something

Olivia had wanted to do, not to be tan, but to be a girl lying by the pool getting her tan. She followed Elle's gaze to a tall blonde walking toward the deep end of the pool; she was wearing a one-piece suit with the sides cut out. Her firm, golden skin peeked out to reveal the soft curve of her hips. She was wrapping her hair up into a bun, and then dove into the pool and surfaced just in front of Dean. Olivia could not hear what she was saying, but she was able to see Dean's slow smile forming and watch him turn to give this girl his full attention.

"That's Missy. I've seen her before," Olivia said.

"What do you think they're talking about?" Elle asked.

"I don't know. She walks by our house sometimes, and stops when Connor's out in the garage. She's always asking him to do stuff for her, because she just doesn't know how," Olivia said, raising her voice to mock Missy's flirtatious bravado and sitting up to toss her own hair.

"Do you think Dean's cute?" Elle asked, out of the blue.

"I…" Olivia began "Dean? I don't know. I never really thought about it."

The girls focused their attention on the boy Missy was so busily vying for attention from. He was tall; he had grown quite a lot in the last two years. Just that winter he seemed to tap out at six foot five. His baby fat had thinned out, and he had started working out and jogging, leaving him with firm arms and legs and a tight stomach. He tanned easily, and his dark brown hair had been recently shaved, leaving a clean buzz cut. He was leaning against the wall of the pool, smiling at Missy with his perfect teeth. She had worked her way so close to him she seemed to be tucked up into his armpit. He was good-looking, Olivia supposed. She knew that lately, when she saw him, she got little butterflies in her stomach like she did whenever Michael Winchester from her class talked to her.

"I guess he's cute. I don't know; it's Dean," she finally said.

"I wonder if they've kissed," Elle said.

"Who? Missy and Dean?" Olivia brought her attention back to her best friend.

"Yeah. Or Missy and Connor," Elle noted as Connor swam up and joined Missy and Dean. Missy seemed to give him equally flirtatious attention. "I want to kiss William."

"William, like in our class?" Olivia asked, surprised.

She and Elle had never really talked about boys like this before. She had started to notice boys more and more this year, and she found herself suddenly getting nervous jitters anytime Michael passed by her and said hi. She noticed Elle had started talking to boys more and more, where before she never really had.

"Yeah, he's cute. He did just get braces, but he's still cute." Elle smiled as she got up and stretched. "I'm going to get in. I'm too hot."

"Good idea," Olivia said, getting up to join Elle in the pool. She continued to keep an eye on Dean, studying him with a new perspective. She had known him for as long as she could remember. She had watched him grow from a long-armed, long-legged, little-bit-pudgy eight-year-old boy into the teenage version of Superman. She had seen him with girls before. Connor too. Last summer, Dean dated that girl Cat, and she was always around. Olivia saw them kissing and sneaking off to be alone. She had been fascinated enough to watch them have those personal moments, but they always sort of made her stomach hurt and she'd get nervous and shy away.

"How did everything go?"

"Good, no surprises," Connor told Dean as he was walking into the shop, wearing the suit he had worn to the lawyer's office.

"Are you rich?" Dean teased.

"They were smart. Really smart. We're not going to be hurting for anything, except them, of course. I can pay off my half of the loans for this place."

"Wow. So, that's good, right?" Dean asked.

"Yeah. They put everything into a trust the day I turned eighteen. So the house is mine, no red tape. They both had life insurance, which covers more than enough," Connor said as he pulled off his tie, unbuttoned the top button of his light blue shirt, and hung up his jacket in the back room. He rolled up his sleeves and checked where they were on parts for an incoming order on the computer.

"That's awesome. What about Livy?"

"Well, turns out, when she turned eighteen they added her name to all the bank accounts."

"Ahh…" Dean said. "So, she's the rich one."

"I'm sure there is a decent nest egg, yes. She just wanted to go back to my place and to bed after the lawyer. Losing one parent is hard enough, but losing them both…she just…we both…well, you know. We need to go to the bank to find that out," Connor said. "And I have the house. We also have the direct orders to share and switch as we see fit."

Dean stood in the door of their small office, looking at the man he had called his best friend since he was eight years old. Connor was such a stoic guy; Dean knew this had to have been much harder than Connor was letting on. Dean really liked James and Maggie Reynolds. He knew Olivia had her differences with them, and Connor let way more roll off his back then he really should have, but they were still nice people. The shock of it all had to be tearing their kids apart.

"You gonna sell the house?" Dean asked.

Connor said nothing. There was nothing he could say. You don't expect to be dealing with packing up a life at the age of twenty-five. He was just starting his. He didn't know if he wanted to keep it, but for now, he sure as hell wasn't going to sell it.

"No. I mean, I don't know. I thought we would, but they wrote us letters. There was a letter for me and one for Liv. I guess Mom was just in that mindset of what would she say if something happened since they were putting together wills. This whole thing is just…"

"I know. How you dealing with it?" Dean asked.

"It sucks. I've gone to call Dad twice this week. Stupid things. Little things. I'm never again going to laugh at my mother's Baltimore accent. Hear her complain about her warshing machine or eat her mashed batatas. I think there's been so much to deal with, I went into business mode. I even made myself a goddamn action item list for the funeral," he said as he lifted up his phone to show Dean the ridiculousness. "I can't gauge Livy at all. When the lawyer handed the letter to her, she just kind of looked disconnected. She politely said thank you and tucked it in her purse as if he had just handed her his business card. But then she kind of held it, without opening it, all the way home. She said she just wanted to be alone. I left her sitting on the deck in the backyard. I don't want her to go back to New York. I know that's unrealistic, but it's just too fucking much. She's so young, and now she doesn't even have her own mother. A girl her age should have her mother."

"I know. I'm sorry," Dean said as he patted his friend on the back. "I've got one more delivery to make. My parents, actually. The cabinet I've been working on for my dad is finished. You want to grab a beer after?"

"Nah, man. I just want to go to bed tonight. Tell them I say hello. I hear they're taking a cruise to celebrate his retirement in the fall."

"Yup. Seven day cruise to Bermuda. Mom hates boats, but she loves Dad…should be fun." Dean smiled.

The drive to his parents' house wasn't long. Rising Ridge was a fairly small town, with only nine thousand people spread across a little more than twenty-six hundred acres. He had lived here all his life, and planned on staying for the rest of it. People were friendly, the pace was slower than most towns, and they still had things like Bingo at the fire hall. He wanted to travel, and see the world, sure. He just knew exactly which spot on the map was home.

His mother had insisted on feeding him dinner. He didn't mind, she was an excellent cook. His father asked him about the business. Henry generally liked to remain a silent partner, and he was very proud of the way Dean and Connor were handling things, but he was still a partner. Some of his early retirement was wrapped up in the success of Rising Ridge Designs. As Dean was helping his mother dry the dinner dishes, his attention was drawn to the backyard. Daylight had faded and there was a small light coming from the tree house.

"Mom, can I go outside and play?" he asked his mother as he bent down to her very tall five foot nine frame and kissed her on the cheek.

"You're a little big for that, don't you think?" Sophia smiled up at her boy. He had grown taller than her the summer he turned fourteen.

"I'll be in the backyard for a little bit, going to get a few things out of the shed, and then I'm going to head home. Don't stay up too late. That's an old man you've got out there."

He said his good-byes and quietly opened the patio door to the backyard. The heat of the early summer day had dissipated with a rainstorm earlier and a nice chill was in the air.

"Hey, Moneybags!" he shouted up to the tree house.

"What are you doing here? How did you know I was here?" Olivia's voice carried out.

He did not answer her. He walked up the steps, and once again found himself folding his body to get into the door that she could still just duck a little to very easily walk through. He sat down on the floor, mimicking her crossed legs, and joined her in staring up at the stars.

"You've always been scared of the dark," he said as he grabbed the small lantern she had brought with her. "I saw the light, I was over for dinner. I would have invited you in had I known you were out here. My parents would have fed you. Have you eaten?"

Olivia answered him by pointing to a small lunch bag with remnants of leftover something or other. She continued to stare.

"She said that I'm brave, and strong." Olivia said as Dean noticed she was holding an open letter in her lap. Must be the letter from their parents that Connor had mentioned.

"You are," he agreed. He knew she was talking about Maggie.

"She said that she admired me."

"She did," he assured her.

"They left me their money so I could have the freedom to follow my dreams, whatever they may be." Her voice caught in her throat.

Dean wrapped his arm around Olivia and pulled her closer. She folded her small body into this safe space, covered her face, and began to cry. His hand brushed her hair and he kissed her forehead. She wrapped her arms around his neck, and pulled herself into his lap.

"You're OK. It will all be OK. Isn't it a good thing that maybe she understood you a little more than you thought?" he whispered as he rocked her.

Her breathing calmed and she wiped the tears from her eyes.

"It is, but why did she never say that to me? I want her to be here. I want him to be here. I'm sorry," she offered.

He brushed her hair out of her face, his fingers tracing the edges, and tucked it behind her ear. He smiled at her, and for the first time in a long time, they really looked into each other's eyes. She offered him a smile as he wiped away one last tear. She looked exactly the same as she always had to him. Her blonde hair had darkened over the years, going from the sunny bright white of her childhood to soft golden tresses that swept her creamy shoulders. She had never been one to deep tan, but her skin was always sort of sun kissed. Her eyes were blue, the sweetest light blue or the deepest dark blue, depending on what she was wearing. He had never once complimented her on them, because he knew it bothered her when people did. Blue eyes were just what she came with; they said nothing about the person she was. He did love them though, so clear. It made him happy when she would get excited over something and they would just sparkle. It killed him when she looked scared or hurt. He could get lost in them.

"Better?" he asked quietly.

"Yes. I'm sorry," she said.

"It's OK to be human, Olivia. It's OK to cry about this."

She looked at him; he was such a good man. He had always been a good man. It had been a long time since they had spent any time together, and her heart began to ache as it did when she was a teenager. Did he see it in her; could he feel what he did to her? She tried so hard not to be in his way, but when he was this close to her, she slipped so easily out of her place. Her heart began beating harder, and the sound in the air became a soft buzz. *Why does he always have to look at me like that?*

"I should go," he said as he politely lifted her a bit and sat her back down on the floor. "Do you want a ride back to Connors?"

"I'm fine. I can get back," she said, not sure what else to say. What to do, how to act. Embarrassment had replaced the butterflies in her stomach and she wanted to be wherever Dean wasn't. Some things never change.

He quietly walked back down the steps, through the space between their parents' houses and out to his truck. He never even looked back. As he climbed into the truck, he closed his eyes and sank down into his seat.

"Ugh!" he said in frustration as he hit the steering wheel.

He should have just let her be. He was trying to give her space, and not invade her privacy. She obviously had a life plan, and he just stood in the way of that. He didn't want to, but what sort of defenses did he have? He could still feel her body sitting in his arms.

As she watched his truck high tail it down the street, she felt the red flush reaching her cheeks. How could she have been so foolish? He obviously would rather not explore that road with her, and he had been nothing but good to her. She was once again forcing him into a situation he didn't want to be in.

She climbed out of the tree house and walked through the yards to her parents' house. As she passed the garden, she reached under the little iron bench with the little iron children reading a little iron book and retrieved the magnetic hide-a-key. She opened the back door, and silenced the alarm with the same code they'd had since she was tall enough to reach the panel. Nine, eight, nine, one. The exact amount of miles that Falkor flew Atreyu during his ten thousand mile quest in The Neverending Story, a movie Olivia was obsessed with at the age of seven. She never had the heart to change the code.

She walked up the steps and stood for a second in her parents' silent bedroom. The house had been cleaned, and the beds had been made. Her parents were here just a week ago, living their lives. A magazine sat on her father's bedside table, still folded open to the page he had last been reading. A book her mother had every intention of reading but had not gotten to was on her nightstand. The remote to their TV on the dresser. Life, interrupted. She walked over to her mother's side of the bed, unfolded the covers, and tucked herself into her parents' bed. She found herself in the middle, closing her eyes and wishing they were there.

Six

Olivia 15, Dean 20

On the eve of Olivia's sixteenth birthday, she was brushing her hair and staring at her own reflection in the mirror. Elle was laying across Olivia's bed scanning the pages of a fashion magazine.

"What are your parents getting you for your birthday?" Elle asked.

"A computer, I think," Olivia said absently as she pouted her lips at her herself. She evaluated her face, pulling at the last bits of baby fat that were lingering.

"Too bad it's not a car," Elle noted.

"Did you get a car that I don't know about?" Olivia stopped brushing her hair and looked at Elle in the mirror.

"No, just saying it's too bad." Elle tossed the magazine on the floor, rolled over, and fixed her gaze on the ceiling. "I'm not complaining about the emerald earrings they gave me. They're beautiful."

"You're a good daughter," Olivia commended.

"Yeah, well, if I want to get my license it's yes ma'am and no ma'am for a while," Elle joked.

"I think my parents can't wait until I get my license, then they don't have to worry about my schedule. Not that they ever did," Olivia reflected. "So what's up with you and William? I saw him yesterday at the quick mart and I know he saw me but he just up and ran out of the store."

"We broke up," Elle informed her.

"What? When?" Olivia was shocked that Elle would break up with her first boyfriend and not tell her.

"Yesterday. He wanted to go all the way and I wouldn't let him. Tiffany Taylor did though." Elle narrowed her eyes at the thought.

"Oh, jeez, Elle. I am so sorry. Why didn't you tell me?" Olivia asked.

"I'm still processing. It sucks, but I'm just not ready," Elle said honestly.

"You! Ha! At least you've kissed a boy."

"Lots of boys like you, Liv, you just have to let them know you like them back. Which boy can we pick?" Elle asked, her mood perking up at the idea of making magic happen.

Olivia said nothing.

"Michael," Elle stated. "You still like him, don't you?"

"No. Well…maybe…kind of? Oh, Elle," Olivia said as she threw herself on the bed next to Elle and covered her face with her hands.

"Oh my God, you still like him since middle school?"

"He's cute."

"Yeah, he is. And by the end of the week, he will be yours. I am totally going to make that happen," Elle said with full confidence.

Olivia had never had a boyfriend. It was true that she did like Michael. She had liked him from a distance for a couple of years. She's just never had the confidence Elle seemed to have been born with, so she just thought he was cute…from afar. One of her parent's rules was that she couldn't start dating until she was sixteen, and the idea of going to school the next day and being able to say yes…to Michael of all people, made her stomach do some serious flips.

After Elle had left for the evening, Olivia went to sit on the patio swing in the backyard. It was her favorite spot in the yard because it didn't face the house. It was tucked in a quiet little garden corner and faced a farm across the road. An endless field, where the sun would set and shine amazing colors over the grain. It was time she caught up with the world.

"Hey there, kiddo," Dean said from the neighboring lawn. He had been out putting a fresh coat of paint on his mother's Adirondack chairs.

"Hi Dean," she said, but made no motion to move or turn to face him.

He watched her for a minute, sitting quietly and swinging slowly. She was obviously lost somewhere in her mind. He could only imagine, as he never could quite keep up with her randomness. She was getting pretty, he thought. Over the last two summers, he had watched her go from a gawky little girl with combination skin and braces to a lovely young lady. Her hair had darkened a bit, turning more gold, and was just inches above her thin waist. Her braces had come off and she was fair skinned, with a sprinkle of very stubborn but cute freckles above her nose. As he watched the sunset frame her silhouette, he thought about how she was making the transition from cute to pretty.

"What's on your mind?" he asked her as he set his paint cans down and walked across his lawn into hers.

"Getting old," she sighed.

"You sure are getting up there," he teased her as she steadied the swing and he sat next to her.

"I'm going to be sixteen tomorrow."

"I did get the party invite," he teased.

"Oh, my mother. This isn't my party, it's hers," Olivia said. "You're coming, right?"

"Yes, ma'am."

They sat for a bit. His feet touched the ground from the swing so much easier than hers, and he set a slow pace for the swing.

"I've never had a boyfriend." Her voice broke the silence as they watched the sun setting.

Oh boy, here we go. Dean cleared his throat and sat up a little straighter.

"You've got all the time in the world for that," he said.

"I've never been kissed," she said, keeping her gaze straight out at the field ahead of them.

"There's time for that too," he said quietly.

"Dean?"

"Yeah?"

"Am I pretty? Like Elle is?"

A very big sigh.

"No, you're pretty in a completely different way," he said as they turned to face each other. She didn't seem to be all together happy with his answer.

"First of all, don't compare yourself to anyone. Elle is cute. She's perky, she's fun, she's loud, and she's a little crazy. That's her. You're a beautiful girl in your own way. You're much more reserved, you're curious. You've observed life so much more than you've lived it. That's you. If I were a sixteen-year-old boy, Elle, as pretty as she is, would be invisible standing next to you."

She blushed, smiled softly, and lowered her eyes. Boy did she have that down, he thought. He'd told her the truth. Elle was pretty, and always would be. He had no doubt that she would have a steady and constant line of boys following her. But Olivia would be the kind of beautiful that haunts people. He could already see it.

"What do I do? Elle's got it in her mind that she's going to set me up with this guy and I'm terrified. What if I'm not good at the stuff?"

"What stuff?" Dean smiled

"You know, kissing. Flirting. Being all…Elle." Olivia threw up her hands in frustration.

"You'll be fine. Just be you." He smiled a sweet crooked smile to reassure her.

"Six—teen, Dean!" She emphasized the word six. "I need to know how to kiss a boy."

"*Olivia, you'll know. It's just something that you figure out when it happens. Your body will know what to do.*" *Am I really giving her the birds and the bees talk,* he thought.

"*What if I suck at it?*" she said, all of a sudden lost in a thought again. "*On the first day of school, Lindsay Aero told everyone that David Piper was the sloppiest kisser ever.*"

"*Well, I'm sure you're going to kiss a few frogs.*" He smiled. "*But if it's the right kiss, with the right guy, it will be fine.*"

She looked at him. He was so handsome. She had gotten used to the tickle in her stomach when he spoke to her in these very rare moments they spent alone together. He was off at college, just like Connor, and rarely ever home. She knew she had a crush on him, but she just looked at it like he was a movie star. Unobtainable. He was a man. A real man. She wanted him to kiss her, right here, right now. The thought of it all of a sudden overwhelmed her.

Be Elle. Just jump.

"*Howdoyouliketobekissed?*" she asked so quickly, all the words ran together.

"*Excuse me?*" He was surprised.

"*How do you like…to be kissed?*" she managed to say each word independently.

"*Olivia,*" he said, clearing his throat.

"*Elle said that if you want somebody to kiss you, you have to just go for it.*" She turned to him. "*Move in, little by little.*"

What is happening? Why is she looking at me like that? Alarm bells were ringing loudly in every corner of his mind.

"*Um, yeah, well…*" His voice lowered as he focused on the inches she was closing in on him.

"*Focus on the lips,*" she whispered as she focused on his and licked her own.

Dean got lost for only a second, then he slid as far away as he could get without falling off the swing. His heart raced, and he mentally begged her to stop talking.

"*That's not appropriate. You know that,*" he said seriously.

"Why? It's you. It's me," she said, *though her heart had begun to spin out of her chest at the fact she was actually having this conversation with him. Out loud.*

"Well, for one, because it is you. And it is me. And I am not sixteen," he reminded her.

"Come on, Dean." She swallowed the lump forming in her throat. *Sweat was beading on the palms of her hands. "Who better? I know I can trust you."*

Before she lost her nerve completely, she stood up and placed herself directly in front of him. She closed the distance between them so that she could lift her hand and rub it through his hair. Her body was touching his knees. He grabbed one of her hips with one hand, took his other hand, and gently placed it on the wrist of the hand that was in his hair. He could feel the tiny but furious beat of her pulse.

"Olivia, I can't kiss you," he said gently. *He did not push her away, but his hands were keeping her firmly in place.*

"How will I learn how to fly if I don't jump every once in a while?" she asked quietly as she took the final step that closed all distance between them.

"Olivia, sto…"

She never gave him the chance to finish the word. She found his lips, and offered hers. They were soft and warm, so wanting yet so giving. He momentarily got lost in the feel of them. He opened his mouth and gave her the warmth that she craved. Her body exploded, his hands found her hips and held to them, and then gathered the material of her shirt up into his fists. She leaned into him closer and a soft moan escaped her throat. The sound woke his brain up to the reality of what was happening to his body. He gently pushed her back and stared at her, his mind swimming on overload. He closed his eyes and put his head down on her shoulder.

"Shit. Shit," he whispered. *He pushed her back a few steps and stood.*

"Did I do it wrong?" she asked him. *That wasn't the reaction she'd hoped for.*

She was hoping for a fairy tale, and what she got was exactly reality. A fifteen-year-old girl just made some very serious moves on a twenty-year-old man. She began to fold into her own embarrassment.

He looked at her standing in front of him. Her lips were red, and her pale skin a little raw looking from his touch.

"Oh, God, Olivia, why did you do that?" he asked, not necessarily to her.

"I did do it wrong," she said, more to herself than him, and sat back down, defeated.

"What? No, you didn't do it…that's not the point." He shook his head, how was he going to fix this?

"You didn't do it wrong," he began. Think, think. Come on blood, go back up to the brain he commanded himself. "You…I…it…Uhh! It was a good kiss. You did everything right."

She smiled a little at his assurance.

"Did you like it?" she asked.

With that he stood. He needed to be far, far, far away.

"Olivia, This. Can. Not. Happen. You are fifteen."

"Sixteen," she corrected.

"Tomorrow! I'm twenty! I could get arrested for this. Connor would kill me right now if he saw this. I would kill me." He laughed at the insanity that was happening.

"Sorry," she offered honestly. "I just, I wanted to know what it was like to be kissed."

He stopped pacing.

Her first kiss. That was her first kiss, one she would remember for the rest of her life. Damn her for doing this to him. He sat down next to her and gathered her hands in his.

"How do you feel?" he asked.

She smiled. She blushed. She leaned her head on his shoulder and started to laugh.

"Olivia," he said as he laughed with her. "You're going to make some kid a fine girlfriend. Kid, as in sixteen. Now, get in the house and go to *bed." He kissed her on the top of her head and walked quickly away from her.*

Later, when he was alone in the shower, he let the steaming water beat down on his back as he leaned his head against the wall. He had scrubbed his skin nearly raw trying to get the smell of her off. He had no idea if she would remember the details of her first kiss, but he sure as hell knew that he was not ever going to forget them. He was hard just thinking about it, and furious with himself.

Damn her. She was only sixteen…tomorrow.

His hands slid up the side of her body from her knee to her waist. She could feel the soft kiss of her cotton T-shirt part from her body at his touch, the familiar feel of his hand came to a rest on the curve of her hip. He pulled her closer to him; she felt his body behind her, the whisper of his breath on the back of her neck. She had been here a million times, where he had found her in her sleep. She arched her body, pressed into him as his hands slid up her stomach to her firm mounds that were free and aching for his touch. She felt his reaction to her, hard and wanting. He pushed away her soft blonde hair and his kiss rested sweetly, but deeply, on her neck. The gentle tickle of his fingers, followed by the deep warmth of his mouth was enough to send her flying over the edge. Her whole body ached for him. He pulled her toward him and she turned to face him, her hands climbing into his dark brown hair. They looked into each other's eyes but said nothing; there were never words for this space. Smashing Pumpkins' "Tonight Tonight" filled the quiet air. Impossibilities and impossible moments were within her hands here. He had his life, and she had hers, but somehow there was this space that existed only for right here and right now. She settled onto the pillow as he removed his own shirt, and he returned to her, finding the space that had only ever been his, ready and welcoming. As his body, hard and willing, touched hers, she could hear heavy footsteps somewhere in the house. His voice called out her name. He was so close, but it was only a whisper. The feel of his touch became lighter and the music faded away into the distance.

Olivia's eyes flipped open and her body ached from the dream she had just been jolted from. Her heart was pounding, her chest damp from sweat. As she gathered herself out of her dream and tried to settle back to sleep, she heard what had woken her. Footsteps. Heavy footsteps that were nearing the closed door of her parents' bedroom. Fear shot through her and she bolted off of the bed. Her brother's old Nirvana T-shirt she had rummaged out of a box in the basement hung loosely on her, just covering her white cotton underwear. She looked to the end table across the bed where the phone sat. Too late; whoever it was, was now at the door, and she would not be able to get around to the other side. She ran to the bathroom and shut the door just as the intruder opened the bedroom door. Her heart pounded as she backed further and further into the room. She felt around in the dark and grabbed a small decorative lamp sitting on the counter. She took the shade off and unplugged it. As the door to the bathroom swung open, she swung the lamp, base first wildly and high into the air. She felt the contact with the man's body.

"Ow!! Livy?! What the fuck?" Dean's voice rang out over the adrenaline that had been rushing through her.

"Dean?" she whispered as she dropped the lamp and backed up even further from the shadowy figure in the doorway.

"Yes. Jesus Christ. What the hell?" he asked as he grabbed the counter top for support. She had connected with the side of his face pretty good.

"Dean?" She said again, but this time running toward him and wrapping her arms around his waist. "You scared the crap out of me. Why are you here?"

"Hey…" He turned his body toward her and wrapped his arms around her. He could feel her shaking. "I didn't mean to scare you. I've been calling your name, didn't you hear me?"

"Sorta. I thought I was dreaming that," she said as she let go of him. Good thing it was still dark because she could feel her whole body flush as she remembered exactly what he was doing in her dream.

"What are you…" he stopped as he felt wet liquid on his cheek. He was bleeding. "I think I'm bleeding. I need to turn on the light."

He reached to the wall and flipped the switch. His eyes first met hers in the mirror; her hair was tousled in a small, cute mess, and she was wearing a black T-shirt with a familiar slightly drug induced yellow smiley face and Nirvana written in yellow letters above it. He recognized it from his youth; it had been Connor's. Her sleepy confused eyes widened in shock, he focused on his own reflection and saw the blood dripping down his cheek from his eyebrow.

"Damn, Liv. You got me good," he said as he studied the cut.

"I am so sorry. I thought you were a burglar. It's the middle of the night," she said, then stood still for a second before she opened the bathroom cabinet under the sink and pulled out the first aid kit her mother had kept there since before she could remember. "Wait, why are you here?"

"You never went to Connor's. He woke up at some point to get a glass of water and found you not there. He called your phone, which you did not answer. "

"Ohhh…tree house," she said, realizing she had climbed out of the tree house hours earlier without any of her belongings.

"Yeah. Well, Elle didn't answer her phone either, so he went there and I went out to the tree house because that's the last place I saw you. Your parents did just die in a car accident. We both kind of panicked."

Guilt hit her immediately; she should have realized that going missing would make him panic.

"I need to call him," she said as she moved past Dean to grab the phone. "Sit down on the toilet and I'll clean you up."

"He knows I found you. I texted him when I saw your shoes at the door. He said he's going to kill you."

"Did he make it to Elle's?" she asked as she studied the cut and started to clean it up. "This bled a lot, but I think you're OK. I'm sorry."

"It's OK. What the hell did you hit me with?" he asked.

"That lamp." She pointed to the lamp on the floor.

"Who the hell puts a lamp in the bathroom?" he asked.

"My mother," she quipped.

"True. Good thinking on your part," he said. "Yeah, I'm not sure if he got there before I texted him and told him that I found evidence of you here. Your stuff is all still in the tree house, but I saw the kitchen light on."

"How'd you get in?"

"My parents have a key, and your mom's code. Like I said, I called for you. I looked in your room first."

"You mean the garden room?" she asked.

"It's still your room," he said.

"I know," she said. Her hand stilled and she studied his face. The tips of his hair was wet from where she had washed away the blood around the cut. Even though he sat, he was nearly face to face with her as she stood in front of him. "All patched up. I'll get you an ice pack. Maybe you should stay just in case you have a concussion."

"I've got a headache for sure," he said honestly. "But I don't think I should stay."

"Why not? It's the middle of the night, Dean; there are lots of empty beds in this house."

"Yeah, but…" he said as his hand reached around and covered the one she was using to put a small bandage just above his eyebrow.

At his touch, her whole body warmed in the chill of the night.

"But what?" she whispered.

"This is…not a good idea," he answered her honestly, despite the fact he found himself wrapping his arm around her and pulling her closer to him.

Their lips met quietly. The temptation was too overwhelming, finding themselves in the quiet of the night. Dean's hands slid up the backs of her legs and under the Nirvana shirt. A soft moan escaped her throat, the same small sound he had heard once before. And just like that time, it snapped him into reality.

"I'm fine, really. Just a cut. You're safe, get back to bed. I'll let myself out," he said, standing and pushing her back several steps.

She watched his truck pull away from her parents' bedroom window and cursed the fate she seemed stuck with. She loved him, she always had. But she was just Connor's little sister. Connor's little sister who was always throwing herself at him. He was trying to be a gentleman, she could see it. That did not change the fact that she wanted to scream. She was going to have to get over him…she just didn't know how.

Seven

Elle stopped by the grocery store on her way home from her morning classes. She was running low on staples like the ramen noodles that hold together a college kid's monthly budget. She walked through the aisles, loading up her cart with fruits and veggies, and singing Nine Inch Nails' "Kinda I Want To." As she picked up a box of Pizzelles, a treat she never could resist, she heard a familiar voice behind her.

"You and Livy, and those damn Pizzelles." Connor smiled at her.

She turned around and saw him standing there dressed in a white dress shirt, black belt, and khakis. He was holding a small hand basket with a salad from the salad bar and a prepared portion of baked chicken.

"You look nice," she commented.

"As do you," he noted as she twirled in her blue jean shorts and black tank top that read I solemnly swear I am up to no good.

"Thank you." She smiled. "Lawyer stuff?"

"Nope, that's all done. I had a business meeting this morning. I just popped in to grab some lunch." He held up the small basket.

"Yeah. I'm stocking up on a few things. It's hard to cook dinner for one. My parents are out of town," she said as she looked through the selection of frozen meals.

"Especially when you can't cook," he teased.

"I cook." She scrunched her face at him.

"Can't. I didn't say don't. I said can't," he smiled.

"Whatever," she said as she teasingly smacked his arm.

"No, no…you're right," he giggled. "Everyone loved that pineapple upside-down cake you made in that special pan."

"I was sixteen; I had no idea that was a broken pot lid! I've come a long way, I will have you know." She stood as tall as her little five foot frame would allow.

"I'm sure you have," he said, plucking the package of ramen noodles out of her cart and shaking them at her. "I'm just teasing, dear."

"Yeah, yeah," she smirked at him.

Making their way through the store, they chatted about the meeting that Connor had. He was up at the Inn that Cat runs. She had contacted them about building a gazebo, digging out a small pond, and adding several pavilions. They had never really done that big a project before, but when she contacted him, he and Dean talked about expanding their horizons.

They went to the cash registers together, and Connor checked out first since all he had was his lunch items. The young girl behind the counter smiled brightly for him.

"Good afternoon, Mr. Reynolds. How are you today?" she asked as she scanned his items, keeping steady eye contact with him.

Elle saw the puppy love written all over the young girl's face. She herself had invented that look on this very same boy about a decade ago. She was ten, he was fifteen, and there was just something about the way his lean body was starting to become that of a man. It grabbed her attention like it never had before. When she began to daydream about falling in love, she found him at the center of her fantasies.

"Hi, Abby. I can't complain. How are you doing today?" He smiled sweetly back to her.

Elle could all but see the girl hanging on Connor's every word, and knew the poor girl wasn't hearing a word. She was lost in whatever little fantasy she had going in her own head. Elle smiled and looked at Connor; he was completely oblivious. He was handsome in a classic way. His dark hair was always kept neatly trimmed. His clothes always looked nice, even when he was casual. And you could tell his look was always intentional.

"Oh me?" she blushed. "I'm fine, thanks. Are you taking your lunch break?"

"Yeah, think I might go eat in the park," he remarked.

"It's a beautiful day today." She smiled, not even remotely moving her eyes from his gaze as he shifted to look out the windows at the warm spring sun shining in the sky. Elle watched them as she loaded things onto the conveyer belt. Abby could not have been more then sixteen. Must be her first real job.

Connor waited for Elle to be done with her purchase and Elle noted Abby's immediate and abrupt change of attitude toward her. Abby was cool and professional, but very inquisitive. Who was she? How did she know Connor? Were they together? Elle knew she was getting the third degree because Abby was jealous of whoever she might be.

"Elle, this is Abby. Abby's father works with us on our larger projects. He's a hell of a craftsman. We will certainly be using him on this upcoming project once we get all the details hashed out."

"Hello," Abby said quietly.

"Hello." Elle smiled, a little bit wickedly.

Whoever she was, Connor was waiting for her. That, in Abby's mind, made Elle a foe. Elle was very gracious and answered Abby's every question, really playing up how she and Connor had known each other forever. He had been a big brother to her most of her life. The more she talked, the more it irritated Abby. Elle knew it. Abby knew it. Connor was completely oblivious to all the things that were not being said very loudly between the girls.

When they got out to the parking lot, Connor walked with Elle to her car and picked up her bag to load it into her trunk. She shook her head at him and laughed.

"What?" he asked.

"You are a moron," she announced.

"Huh? What are you talking about? Is this how you thank a man who offers to put your groceries in your car for you?" he asked, and stood straight to look at her.

"No, I'm talking about Abby," she answered.

"Abby in the store, Abby? Did I miss something?" he was totally confused as he closed the trunk and stood closer to Elle.

"She's in loooove with you," She smiled as she stretched out O sounds.

"What? That's ridiculous. She's a child. I work with her father."

"She's what, sixteen? You're a tall, dark, and handsome older man, Mr. Reynolds," she reminded him.

"I'm a dinosaur," he said, "She's actually told me that before when she walked into the shop and Faith No More "Midlife Crisis" was streaming on my computer.

"You're not that old. Under the ten year mark is totally doable; she just has to wait a couple of years." She smiled. "And that girl is In. Love. With.You."

She moved to get into her car, but Connor didn't want her to go just yet.

"Join me for lunch?"

"No, thanks. I've got some things I need to work on. Besides, I think if you're hard up for a date, you should have just picked her up in the checkout line." She gestured at the window of the grocery store where she could clearly see Abby staring at them. Abby immediately got back to work.

"Stop it. Just…stop," he said as he waved good-bye to her and headed off to his truck.

"Yup," Elle said to herself as she watched him climbing into his truck in her rear view mirror. "You wouldn't know a sixteen-year-old girl in love with you if she fell into your lap."

At home, Elle put away her groceries and decided on a whim to pack up her schoolwork after she ate lunch and head back out. It was a beautiful day, she should be outside. Maybe the sights and sounds would be inspiration for her creative writing class. She headed toward Rocky Point park, one of the larger parks on the outskirts of Main Street just before the land turned into crops.

Maryland winters could be easy to get through, but every couple of years they would have what seemed to be months of gray skies when they'd get pounded with snow and ice. Usually by April, the snow and ice were gone, but it was still pretty cold if the wind kicked up. June was always gorgeous in Maryland. School had just let out, and the park was full of children enjoying their first days of freedom.

She settled herself under a big tree on a large hill facing the majority of the park, then pulled out her laptop and turned it on.

"I will write amazingly awesome crap today, so mote it be," she said out loud with her eyes closed, praying to whatever god chose to listen to her.

"St. Francis de Sales." Dean's voice floated into her head.

Elle opened her eyes and saw Dean standing in front of her, dripping with sweat. He was wearing a gray running shirt and shorts with his iPod strapped to his arm and his ear buds resting on his neck.

"Hi," she said, craning her neck to look up at his tall frame from the ground. "What?"

"The patron saint of writers. That's who you need to be praying to," he informed her as he sucked down the remainder of his water bottle and then laid down on the blanket next to her. "Hi."

"I just ran into Connor not that long ago, now you. Don't you people have to be open to make money?"

"Dad's babysitting the store today. Connor had a meeting up at the Inn. I had a bunch of phone calls to make, numbers to crunch. That is Connor's thing normally, not mine. I needed a break…so I'm running."

"Oh. Saint who? And why do you know this?"

"Francis de Sales. Because I am a good Catholic boy," he said, winking devilishly at her.

"At this point," she huffed, "this sinner will entertain the idea of a saint."

"What are you writing?"

"A short story about gods and demons and fairies," she informed him.

"Oh, so an autobiography?" he teased her.

Elle had always been in touch with the other side, even when she was a small child. She saw things other people didn't, felt things other people didn't. Dean had a very vivid memory of an eight-year-old Elle sending a cold chill down his back in the tree house when she brought along her Ouija board one night. The rest of the group were playing a child's game, and there she sat, little as she was, channeling whatever full on crazy vibe there was in the air.

He personally had never experienced anything like that, nor had any of the others, but there wasn't one among them who doubted there were shadows in the corners if Elle said there were.

"What are you doing here?" he asked.

"Same thing. I just needed…outside," she said.

They sat for a few minutes just looking out over the town they had both lived in forever. The landscape had changed and grown over time, but it was careful growth and development. It remained a small town, something they both really liked.

"How's she doing?" Dean's voice broke Elle's thoughts.

"I think she's fine." Elle knew he was asking about Olivia. "She's talking more and more about going back. She's going to leave soon."

"I know. I know she doesn't live here anymore and she is happy where she is, but I just can't help think she is running away again," he admitted.

"She never felt like she fit in here, and I don't know why," Elle said. "She's so dumb. She's the glue and she doesn't even realize it."

"She's the glue?" Dean asked.

"Yes. She's my best friend, and if she's not here, I don't hang out with you and Connor as much. Her parents didn't really venture out much over the last few years because she wasn't here to push them out the door. She was always the one asking to go to far off places for vacations. Hell, for the last two years they considered their trips up to New York their adventure for the year. I know we are all growing and getting older and stuff, but I feel like when she left, there was a shift in the world."

"You're not wrong," Dean said.

"She's lost. She's looking for home and it's here. It's fucking here. It's not the house she grew up in, sure. But this town…with us."

"It's her journey," he offered. It was all he could ever offer; Olivia was meant to wander. He felt the ache in his chest that wandered with her always, and to the ends of the earth.

Eight

"Five hundred thirty-two thousand, six hundred seventy-five dollars and forty two cents."

"I'm sorry, what now?" Olivia was surely hearing things.

She and Connor sat in the bank manager's office while he read the number from his file for her again.

"Looks like five hundred thirty-two thousand and change when all is said and done. Plus, of course, the life insurance policies that were quite generous," said the branch manager, Timothy Greenfield, according to the nameplate on his desk. "Your parents were wise investors. Slow and steady with some things, and fast and furious with others. The way it should be, if you ask me."

"Looks like we're about even." Connor smiled at his sister who was still silent in her chair.

She knew they were careful, and she knew they were focusing on retirement, but she never really gave thought to an actual dollar amount. She had hoped it would be enough to help get through her classes and maybe get her own apartment once she figured out what it was she wanted to do with her life.

"What do you mean?" she finally asked him.

"I had a realtor look at the house, who said we can put it on the market for five fifty. I know they left me the house and they left you the bank accounts but I am sure they would have wanted us to even out if need be."

"Are you going to sell the house?" she asked.

"Well, I would never make that decision without you of course. I don't know. What do you think we should do?"

"I don't know. I just…" she looked off into space again. "Five hundred and thirty-two thousand dollars."

"And they paid off the house, my college, and were paying for yours outright, Liv," Connor said.

"Wow," Timothy chimed in. "Yes, this is the textbook scenario where everything goes the right way. There's no red tape. Your name is already on the accounts, we just need to get you to sign a signature card. Then we'll have their names taken off the account, and it's all yours. If of course, you want to continue on their plan of financial investing, here is the phone number of their adviser."

"Um, thank you," Olivia said, taking the card from him.

When Olivia and Connor got back to his house, Connor looked at the ongoing construction and thought things over.

"I don't think this is my house," he said.

"Huh?" Olivia asked.

"You should just feel it. When I found this house, I was thinking investment. Clean it up, sell it for a profit. I don't see me here, with a family."

"Connor," Olivia smiled at him. "Are you thinking about settling down?"

"I guess. It's the order of things. Graduate college, get married, house in the 'burbs."

"Get married. You have to get married. Who are you going to get married to?" she asked.

"The missus is still T-B-D, but what would you think if I just kept our house? Would you be mad?"

"No, of course not. Connor, it's a great house. It's just not my house. You have always been Mister Rising Ridge, so it makes sense. It's a good house, and some girl is going to love it one day." She smiled at him.

"So now that you know how much money there is, what are you going to do?" he asked. He was a little bit terrified to hear her answer.

"I guess I am going to go back home and figure it out. I would love my own place, but I don't want to leave Debi hanging. So that will take time. Maybe I can find a bigger place for the two of us, with two bedrooms and she can pay me the same rent."

"Maybe," he agreed. He did like the idea of her not being alone.

"Maybe I will travel. Take a year to breathe," she said.

"Olivia, that's all you've been doing, kid. That's what the last two years have been, you breathing. It's time to figure out what you want to be when you grow up."

"Yes, sir," she sweetly mocked his serious tone.

Too damned much to deal with. These were the only words swirling around Connor's mind as he sat in the silence watching the wind dance on the pond. He had woken up this morning as he had every morning, and eaten a sensible breakfast, taken a shower, and dressed for the day. Only on this day, rather than going to work, he had spent the day dealing with the paperwork of life, or death, as the case may be.

He had a dozen or more things he'd added to his to do list, and had realized that maybe it was time to make different lists.

One for work stuff, and one for his personal life. His parents were gone, and he was still having a hell of a time dealing with it. How can they just be gone? I just saw them. He had found himself picking up the phone several times to call his father with questions about the business. He ached just thinking about the holidays, how were they going to deal with Christmas?

And Olivia, what the hell was he going to do with Olivia? Sure, he was happy that she was doing her thing in New York and seemed happy. But somehow, when he sends her back to the life he ripped her from, it will be another loss. She might as well be a million miles away. And if she had her way, she would be a million miles away. She wanted to take off and see the world, and he just wanted to tie her to a damned tree in the backyard. He knew it wasn't fair, and he was trying to remain fair. At least the estate was in order, or so it seemed. His mother had kept him up to speed on things, letting him know when they made any major changes. He knew that they had their ducks in a row exactly the way they wanted them to be, but right at this moment, he could not have cared less.

He looked at their names on the paperwork signing everything over to him officially. Initial here, read through this, sign there. As the day tick-tocked away, he found himself more and more stressed. He got jumpy. He was going to explode at some point…very soon. He dropped Livy back at home with the excuse that he had a few more errands to run. Rather than run them, he found himself pulling into the parking lot at the local park. He walked up the hill and past the playground. He stopped for a second and ran his hand around the gazebo Dean's father, Henry, had built some twenty years before. He walked to the edge of the small pond and sat on a bench. He had come here a few times on his own, to think. Thankfully, this evening, the pond was quiet.

"You know, yelling is good for the soul," a voice behind him offered.

He jumped, the voice cracking the silence, and turned to find Elle standing not twenty feet behind him.

"It is?" he asked.

"Yep. According to accent Chinese wisdom, letting out that much air puts pressure on your lungs and gets them pumping blood with greater expectancy. In Japan, yelling is breathing with strong energy, and here in the good ol' US of A, according to Miss Piggy, you get better at martial arts if you yell 'Hai-yah!' first."

"Miss Piggy?" He smiled and scooted over on the bench for her to join him.

"She's a credible source," Elle assured him. "You should just yell."

"Excuse me?" he asked.

"Go ahead. Yell. There's nobody around but you and me, buddy."

"How is there even a you and me around? How did you know I was here?" he asked.

"Oh, I didn't. I was driving back from a gig and saw your car in the parking lot. I thought, being that it's eight p.m. and all, I might want to check to see if you had drowned or something."

"Eight?" He checked his watch. "I've been sitting here for two hours. Good God. I need to get home. I just needed to breathe a little."

"Did you?" she asked seriously. "Did you breathe?"

"I don't know," he answered honestly. "It's all, this has all been…"

"I know," she said. "I know."

They sat in silence together for several minutes, looking out on the sunset kissing the edges of the water. It was a local park, and the pond was stocked for fishing. He had been here a million times with Dean and Dean's father. He had even gotten his own father out once or twice, and they had caught a few fish to take home.

Elle didn't like the way he looked. Connor had always been stoic. In all the years she had known him, she had never seen him face a challenge that he didn't excel at. He was smart, thoughtful, brave, and strong. Last week, his world was turned upside down and she watched him try so hard to be the Connor everyone expected him to be. To be the Connor he had always been. She could see the stress behind his eyes, knew his brain was probably not shutting down properly at night. She watched him dealing with things properly, no matter the cost.

She looked out onto the water, where the sun had disappeared just moments ago, and took in a deep breath.

"Ahhhhhhhhhhhhhhhhhhhh!" she yelled.

Connor sat silent for a second, keeping his eyes focused on the water. He had not so much as moved an inch when she yelled. A bubble of laughter slid up his throat and a smile formed at his lips. He began to giggle, and then laugh. He wrapped his arm around Elle and kissed her on top of her head.

"Thank you," he smiled.

"Good for the soul." She smiled. "That felt so damned good. Your turn."

"I'm not going to…" he began.

"Yes, yes you are." She poked his side.

He sighed, smiled at her, and then looked back out at the water. He cleared his throat. She was a nut. He couldn't just yell, that was lunacy. But seeing that silly little smile on her face had inspired him. He cleared his throat once more and let out as much yell as his lungs would allow. And damned if she wasn't right. It did feel good. The sweet little smile she was wearing turned into that of a woman who knew she had just been proven right. She pulled her legs up on the bench and crossed them like a child. She patted his leg.

"Told you so."

"Holy shit," Elle said as she stared at the paper Olivia slid across the table. "Well, I guess you're set for a little while."

"Yeah. My big worry was school. It's amazing how I didn't want to take any classes in the first place, but it was my first bubble of panic," Olivia said.

"Do you want to go back full time?" Elle asked.

"I don't know," she admitted honestly. "I think I just want to go somewhere and think."

"Um…isn't that what you're doing in New York?" Elle asked.

"That's what Connor said!" Olivia pouted.

"He's not wrong, Liv. I mean, I know we're only twenty, but this is your chance. Pick your direction and go."

They had decided to have lunch at the Inn, and the air buzzed with people running all over the place getting ready for the Independence Day celebration happening in just a few days. Cat had popped over to say hello, and they had since seen her several times at various spots on the lawn talking to workers. It looked like it was going to be quite the celebration.

"Looks like this is going to be quite the show," Olivia said.

"Yeah, they pretty much took over last year. It was their first party like this, and Cat just did everything right. Local bands, local wine, corn hole contests, kids' games, vendors, and all the food. I think I ate my weight in funnel cake. It was like one huge family cookout."

"Sounds nice," Olivia said as she spotted Rohan walking toward them. "Hello again."

"Well, hello ladies." Rohan smiled. "Came up for lunch, huh?"

"We did," Elle said. "Nobody can do chicken nuggets like Maya."

"Chicken nuggets?" Rohan lifted his sunglasses up off his face to more closely inspect Elle's plate. "She better not have…"

"I'm kidding." She smiled "I totally had a hot dog."

"I'm sure you did." He saw she had the remnants of his signature chicken sandwich with homemade mayonnaise.

"I wish I would have known you were coming up, I would have made something special for you. I was at the fish market all morning, making all the bribes to ensure I get first pick on Saturday."

"We were just talking about that. Tell her she needs to stay for this," Elle urged.

"Oh, yes, you must. You have to. I cook an amazing spread. I mean, I love the holiday season with all the traditional stuff, but summertime and everything you can do with a grill…man, people just don't understand what you can do with a grill. It's a shame. It's a travesty," Rohan informed her.

"I'll stay," she conceded with a smile.

"Really?" Elle sat up in excitement and clapped her hands.

"Really. I might as well enjoy one last weekend, and apparently I need to know what I can do with a grill."

"What are you doing tomorrow?" Rohan asked.

"I was going to pack, so now nothing that I know of," Olivia said.

"I'm working the dinner shift. What would you think about coming up here at nine and I will teach you a few things."

"If I can get a ride. I don't have a car. I'm a New Yorker."

"You're staying with Connor?" he asked. "I can pick you up, it's on my way."

Olivia looked at Elle for some sort of interjection.

"It would be a travesty…apparently." She smiled.

"Well, we wouldn't want that. I could use a few tips, thank you."

"See you tomorrow morning, then." He smiled and continued on into the kitchen.

"Olivia, you have a date," Elle whispered.

"I do not," Olivia corrected. "That was not a date request."

"He's going to teach you a few things," Elle teased with a wink.

"Stop it, Elle. I'm going back to New York. He knows that," Olivia said.

"Yeah, well, he's really hot. Why don't you get a little hot in the kitchen before you go?"

"Finish your sandwich," Olivia said as she all of a sudden became a little uneasy about the causal meeting she'd just set up.

Rohan was very attractive. He obviously kept fit, and he was tall. He looked to be about twenty-five. She had spoken to him only a couple of times, but she liked him. Everyone who knew him seemed to have a good opinion of him. But she was going back to New York, and she had never been one for flings. Maybe it was time. Lord knows, she needed to jump off the Dean train she'd been on for the last couple of years. She really needed to get him out of her system; it wasn't healthy.

Nine

Olivia changed three times. Maybe it was a date. Damn Elle. She heard a loud motor getting closer to the house and looked out the window to see Rohan pulling up on a motorcycle. Of course he had a motorcycle. She watched him climb off, set his helmet on the bike, and walk up to the door. When he rang the bell, she waited. One, two, three, four, five.

"Hey," she said casually as she opened the door.

"Hi. You look nice." He smiled.

She had settled on black Capri pants and her Baltimore Orioles fitted T-shirt. They were her home team, and as it so happens, they were up in the games.

"Thank you. Hometown love," she smiled.

"You watch the game last night?" he asked.

"Yeah, with Connor. I love it when we crush people, but I love it even more when it's a nail biter like that and everyone is just silent…then, boom! The whole earth shakes with excitement, you know."

"I do know." He smiled. "Maybe next time you're in town we can catch a game. You ready?"

"As ready as I'm going to be." She smiled when he offered her a spare helmet.

As they took the winding roads up to the Inn, she was able to appreciate the small town in a whole new way. The views were spectacular, especially when they started to go through the valley. Rohan made a left turn, and Olivia wondered where he was taking her. She realized he was following the trail of the old railroad tracks, which went through an older part of town where it seemed more still and the properties were much bigger. Fields of grass, white fences, horses, stables. It was beautiful, and a place she rarely visited since it wasn't on the way to anywhere.

Rohan had weaved his way through some of the more beautifully landscaped areas and then slowed down, turned right on a cobblestone road, and drove carefully and slowly on a dirt road no bigger than a sidewalk. To her surprise, when the trees broke and they came to a road again, she was on the other end of the main road, nearly directly in front of the Inn.

"I had no idea that road was there." She smiled as they hopped off the bike. "I've lived here pretty much my whole life."

"I don't know how long that's been there. I think it's a dirt-bike track. When I moved to town, I took a weekend and just rode. All over. It's the only way to find places like that." He smiled, pleased he was able to show her something she had not seen before.

"Well, that was awesome. I have no reason to ever go that way, those homes and the horse farms are lovely. Do you go that way every day?"

"No, not every day. Just the special days." He winked at her. "Let's get you into the kitchen."

They had a lovely time. Rohan pulled more vegetables out of the refrigerator than she eats in a week. He filled the kitchen with music; his tastes were similar to that of her brother's…deep in the Seattle sound that was the nineties. He showed her how to chop properly, what to look for at the market, and other small chef's secrets. There were a few vegetables on the counter that she had never even seen or heard of. They made their way out to the grill with some supplies on hand. A lot of things seemed to depend on timing. Two minutes on one side, flip, one minute, sprinkle something on it, flip, three minutes, flip, sprinkle something else, four minutes.

When the food was done, they walked back into the kitchen, where he sliced and diced everything on the plate beautifully. She had a small salad and a petite steak, with raspberry sauce all over everything. He walked over to where she was standing at the kitchen island, and stood for that second too long, just looking at her, before he reached under her arms, picked her up, and sat her on the island. His gaze never left hers as he reached back, picked up her plate, and handed it to her.

"Bon appetite," he said quietly.

"Thank you." She blushed. She started to feel the heat of the kitchen.

He grabbed his own plate and leaned up against the counter in front of her, sampling his food as if the last thirty seconds had never happened. She was completely out of her element.

"So, New York, huh?" he asked casually.

"It's home…for now," she said.

"What do you do in New York?" he asked.

"I work at a bank, go to school, eat. Not at all like this. This is amazing," she said.

"Thank you."

"Where did you go to school?" she asked.

"I didn't," he offered.

"This was a natural born talent?" she asked.

"This was a nurture born talent. My parents. My dad was a chef in San Francisco and my mom was a food critic."

"Oh, did she love his food and that's how they met and fell madly in love?" she asked, already swept up in the romantic notion of it all.

"No, quite the opposite. She had asked to speak to the chef because she felt that he needed to be schooled in the art of how to properly prepare a perfect medium steak. They argued and screamed at each other, and he hauled her back to the kitchen and asked her to show him how to do it if she was such a know it all."

"Oh, lord. And they fell in love?" she asked.

"They did. They came up with that method right there." He pointed to her steak "Perfectly medium. And she kept coming back to the restaurant, and he kept inviting her into the kitchen. They got married a year later, and had me soon after that. I learned in his kitchen, on his apron strings, and with her attention to detail."

"Is he still a chef?" she asked.

"Yes, though he will be retired in a couple of years. My mom is still his toughest critic."

"That's amazing. What brought you to Maryland? Why didn't you work with him?" she asked.

"Because I wanted to know what other people thought of my food. So, I drove to the other side of the country and started looking for restaurants. Mr. Archer's Inn popped up, and I don't know…it just felt right. This is my place to really grow as a chef." He smiled.

"Wow. That's amazing," she said. "Seriously, you are lucky to have found your passion."

"What's yours?" he asked.

"Don't know yet," she answered honestly. "It seems to be the question of the day."

"Well, that's what our twenties are for, right? You've got what…" he cocked his head and smiled as he asked.

"Ten years. I'm twenty. I think I want to travel, like really travel," she answered.

"OK," he said, encouraging her to tell him more.

"I've seen a good bit of the country, but I want to see the world. I want to get lost in…I don't know…Thailand."

"So, go get lost in Thailand," he said. "It's important to make that jump. Sometimes you just have to take those opportunities that unexpectedly present themselves and see where they lead."

He stood, and closed the distance between them. Taking her plate, he set it aside and returned to her. He lifted his hand and gently swept her hair back. This was a date, after all. She took a deep breath and did what he said, she jumped. His lips were smooth and gentle. His hands held her face, and he gave her all the time in the world. Slow, sweet, amazing.

"Rohan, did we get in the…oh, shit," Cat said as she walked through the doorway. "Sorry."

Olivia's hand firmly and quickly pushed Rohan back. Her whole face went red with embarrassment, and Rohan smiled a devilish grin at her.

"It's OK, boss. Nothing has come in yet. Nothing due until about eleven." He smiled. "I'm not actually here for another thirty."

"Alrightly then." Cat smiled. "Hi, Olivia."

"Hi." Olivia gave up and just put her head on Rohan's shoulder. "Sorry."

"No big thing, babe. We do have other rooms, if you need one," she said.

When, completely mortified, Olivia popped her head up, Cat laughed. "You coming up on Saturday?"

"I've been told it's a party not to miss." Olivia smiled as she relaxed.

"It is. It's going to be our biggest party to date; it would be a real shame for you to miss it."

"I'll be here," Olivia assured her.

"Yay! Oh, and come find me sometime today. I was going to call you later, I have something I want to run by you, but it can wait. Carry on." She smiled as she off to the front of the Inn for other business.

Rohan giggled, wrapped his arms around her, and kissed her on the top of her head.

"Do you need a ride back?" he asked.

"No, you need to get ready for work. I can call Connor later. I'll go find Cat; I'm sure she just wants a little girl talk."

"Want to have dinner with me, tomorrow?" he asked.

"You know I'm going back to New York, right?" she stated.

As she stood, he closed the distance between them once again and kissed her.

"I know. I'd still like to have dinner with you. I can pick you up around seven thirty." He smiled.

"OK." She returned the smile and left him to start his work day.

Olivia went into the small lounge area of the Inn and sat down. What was happening? Her parents were gone, and life as she knew it was changing, yet all of her thoughts were swirling around one man…and now two. She had not expected to come home to any of this. She had to deal with this Dean thing. She knew she was going to have to put the whole thing to rest. He was hell bent on her leaving town two years ago; he damn near shoved her out the door himself. And now, why did he kiss her, why did she let him?

Rohan. Rohan was awesome, and sweet. He was funny, kind, and smart. He asked her out on a date. Like a man should. He kissed her, and then he asked her out. If she was ever going to shake Dean, now was the time.

She pulled her phone out of her pocket, intending to call Connor to ask if he could pick her up, but instead she called Elle.

"Hey. I need your help. Can you come get me in about two hours?"

After she secured her ride home, she went to find Cat. To her surprise, Cat mentioned nothing about Rohan. Instead, she had a job offer.

"I've seen some of your photos of New York when we were over for poker night at Connor's. They are beautiful," Cat offered.

"Thank you. I like taking pictures of the world at large," Olivia said.

"Well, that's what I wanted to talk to you about. There is a magazine we've been trying to get into. Essentially, a travel editor would come out and do an article on us, but we need to submit a write up with some photos. I was hoping you could take a few."

"I would love to. I don't have my good camera though; it wasn't on my list of things to grab for the funeral, you know."

"Oh, of course. We actually have one, but I have no idea how to use it." She walked over to a file drawer and pulled out a black case containing an older but decent Nikon digital. She handed it to Olivia. "Would you be able to work with this?"

"Yeah, I think so," Olivia offered as she eyed all of the settings and noticed spare lenses in the bag. "I can even look up the model and glance over the manual. One of the classes I took was on digital photography, so I can at least try."

"Oh perfect! Do you think you can take some Saturday? I really wanted to capitalize on the whole town event thing."

"Sure. I've got a bit of time now; I can walk around and take a few shots. Just let your staff know the crazy lady with the camera belongs here."

"Absolutely." She grabbed a walkie-talkie from her desk. "Good morning campers, this is your fearless leader. There will be a crazy lady walking around for the next few days with a camera. She's with us, taking pictures for the magazine we're trying to land. She goes where she pleases."

"That's efficient," Olivia said.

"Done. Thank you so much. I'm excited!" Cat said.

Olivia walked around the property, taking many pictures of the landscape itself. It was a beautiful piece of land. The main house was stunning in its own right. It was a fully updated nineteenth century plantation house with a white porch that wrapped entirely around the red brick building. A lovely manicured front lawn led up a small, but grand, set of stairs to the porch. There were several aged oak trees in the front yard she could take some fun photos of, and several small tables on the porch would give their guests the perfect view. The vast lawn behind the house offered a nice variety of public and private spots. Pavilions for weddings yielding to winding paths that led to a quiet swing in front of a flower garden. Further down the property, Olivia found an old red barn that was no longer in use, but shined brilliantly and defiantly in the early afternoon sun. Cat had the groundskeeper find a few out of commission tractors to tuck inside, completing the look. She happily snapped away the luscious landscape, but took some time finding those small treasures, too, like a baby duckling standing on the small pier at the edge of a pond. Cat would have a wide variety to choose from.

She saw Elle pull up and around to the service entrance. Perfect timing. She smiled and waved. Elle whistled a catcall. Olivia rolled her eyes and got into the car.

"Like what you see, honey?" she asked, batting her eyes at Elle.

"Absolutely! So, how was your date with Chef hot-pants?" Elle asked when Olivia was in her small white Jetta.

Olivia smiled and blushed.

"Really? Oh…tell me! Tell me, tell me. Tell me now." Elle danced in her seat as she pulled down the drive and headed back into town.

"He kissed me." Olivia smiled.

"OK, OK…walk me through everything." Elle urged eagerly.

"He picked me up on his motorcycle and we drive back through the Kentlands. Did you know there is a dirt-bike path that leads out to the main stretch?"

"Of course he has a motorcycle. Oh, yum! I did know about the path, it hasn't been there long, but I've seen it," Elle smirked.

"It was beautiful. We got up to the Inn and did the cooking thing."

"Uh-huh…" Elle smiled.

"Actual cooking, Elle. He was telling me about how he came here. He's self-taught, he's amazing. And we were talking about what I wanted to do and I said I wanted to travel. Go get lost in Thailand or something, and then he said to go to Thailand because sometimes we just need to jump. And then he kissed me."

"How was it?" Elle asked.

"Exactly the way you think it would be," Olivia offered.

"Hot damn!"

"He asked me to dinner tomorrow. And of course I am going to see him Saturday."

"Well, look at you, Missy. Maybe you will stay for a while then."

"I'm not staying, and he knows that. I want to go out with him, but I've got other issues right now."

"What other issues?! This is fun, Liv. You need fun," Elle said seriously.

"I know. I just, I don't know what to do. I can trust you, right?" Olivia asked.

"What? What do you mean?"

"If I tell you something, you have got to pinky-swear that it does not leave this car."

"Oh…tell me!" Elle smiled.

"I'm serious Elle, this isn't a game," Olivia said, all humor lost.

"To the end, babe," Elle quietly swore. "It's you and me, to the end."

"I slept with Dean."

With that, Elle pulled the car off to the side of the road. Of all the things that could or would have come out of her best friend's mouth, that was the last thing she'd expect. She put the car in park and turned to her friend.

"I'm sorry, what?" she asked.

"I slept with Dean. I don't know what, if anything, it means for us," Olivia honestly confessed.

"When? Why? How?" Elle asked; she felt like reality itself was being torn from her.

"Before I left for New York."

"Two years ago? Holy shit. Why am I just finding this out?"

"We weren't, we're not. I don't know. I liked him, I always have liked him. I guess I just got it in my mind that it was the perfect thing. I had kind of pictured him every time I pictured my first time…so it actually wound up being my first time."

"What? Olivia! But you left."

"I did. I needed to. We haven't actually talked about it since it happened."

"OK, wait, wait, wait. Start at the beginning. I need to wrap my head around this."

Olivia began her story with a young girl nervous about her first date and hell bent on getting her first kiss under her belt. She told Elle how beyond that day, Dean never spoke of it. She had hoped she would find him stealing glances, or standing too close on purpose. But the opposite had happened. He had made it a point to never stand next to her. He made it a point to never be alone with her, never to accidentally on purpose stand too close.

Even though she had finally gotten her first boyfriend with Michael, she was already completely heartbroken.

"I was so young. I mean, he was twenty. I wouldn't kiss a fifteen-year-old right now. I guess I was just living out the fantasy I had in my mind."

"Well, you said he kissed you back," Elle reminded her.

"He did, for only a second. It was enough."

"How did you wind up sleeping together if he never stood too close?" Elle asked.

On the side of the road in front of a field of green, as the afternoon sun began its relentless assault of heat, Olivia spoke into the world a story she had never told anyone.

Ten

Olivia 18, Dean 23

"Hello?" he whispered.

"Hello." Olivia's voice floated through the wood floorboards two feet above him.

"What are you doing up there?" he asked.

"It's too crowded in there."

"It's just about cleared out now," he let her know.

"I'm gonna stay out here."

Dean grabbed onto the rope and pulled his large body up to the floor of the tree house. As he did, he realized he had not been up there for quite some time.

"Was this thing always this small?" he asked.

"No," she answered.

He ducked his body into the small doorframe and discovered Olivia snuggled up in a large sleeping bag with a few extra blankets for padding. She had brought out two pillows and a small lantern.

"*All night?*" *Dean asked.*

"*I just can't go back in there; not tonight,*" *she admitted. She sounded so defeated.*

He looked for a spot and sat himself down at her feet.

"*I'm sorry. I know it's hard to have everyone in town celebrating you,*" *he said.*

"*It's not that, Dean,*" *she said from under the covers.*

"*No? Are you going to go with it's my party, and I'll cry if I want to?*"

"*No.*" *Olivia sat up, and was face to face with him.* "*That's not my party. That's a James and Maggie production. She's been cleaning the house for a week and fussing over the menu. She just invited whomever she wanted. She didn't even ask me.*"

"*But they all love you still,*" *he reminded her.* "*That's why they are here.*"

"*I know, and I appreciate that. I'm just done with having my life dictated to me. I mean, I don't want to ride off into the sunset with a guy on a motorcycle or anything, but I just need some space. Freedom.*"

"*Well, high school is officially over. Space and freedom come with the welcome kit to adulthood.*"

"*I got into NYU,*" *she confessed.*

"*Your mother told me.*"

"*Of course she did,*" *Olivia mocked.*

"*Are you going to go?*" *he asked.*

"*Yes…No…Maybe…I want to just breathe. I'm going to New York…like tomorrow. I'll figure it out when I get there.*"

"*That's quite a plan you've got yourself there. It will all be fine,*" *he said as he brushed his hands down her arm to comfort her.*

"*It will be. I just need to get out of here.*"

She had been so excited to be accepted into NYU. Her parents had made her apply to several schools locally, but the only one she honestly cared about was NYU. She just wanted to take a year to decide. A year to do, see, and travel. Was that too much to ask? Apparently. So the yelling and the screaming started. And then happy, shiny faces for the party, because it's a party, dear.

Dean sat with her. He felt helpless when she was like this. She always ran extreme in her emotions. Most of the time, it was enough for him to just be there. He took off his shoes, and laid down next to Olivia. She lifted the blankets so he could scoot under with her, and she curled herself around him. They lay silently until they both fell asleep.

Dean woke to the subtle smell of a flower garden. Before he opened his eyes, he could feel soft skin pressed against his cheek and felt warm, soft hands wrapped around his waist. He had attempted to untangle their legs without waking her, but as he stirred, she just made her grip tighter around him. She slowly opened her eyes, and looked up at him. The small lantern was off, so she could only see hints of his features. She realized it was a face she knew so well, she could close her eyes and picture every detail. With her arms wrapped around his waist, and his arms cradling her, she felt that ache in her heart she'd had for him since the night she kissed him in the garden.

"Dean," she whispered as she did her best to close the small remaining distance between them.

Somewhere in the back of Dean's head, a little alarm was going off saying this was wrong on every level. But he was too lost in the smell of her and in the way her warm skin felt so soft as she slowly began to explore him. Her lips found his in the darkness and he felt a deep warmth spread through his chest. Why did she taste so good? Why had it taken him a month to shake off the thought of one kiss two years ago that should have never happened? Why? Why?

"Olivia," he began, urging his brain to gain control of the war it was now having with his body. "We can't. You have got to stop doing this to me; it's not a teenage girl's game this time."

She continued to rub her hands up and down his sides under his shirt. Her kisses spread from his mouth to the bottom of his ear and then she settled on his neck. She said the only thing her mind seemed to say every time he had been within ten feet of her for the last two years.

"It was never a game," she replied honestly, more to herself than to him. "I don't regret that. I needed you then, and I need you now."

Dean tumbled further from reason when she reached for his hands and guided them under her shirt. She stopped for just a fraction of a second before she leaned in to kiss him again, as if to see if he would follow her into the madness. He lifted his head and propped it on his elbow. He looked at her and withdrew his hand from where she had guided it to her stomach. Every inch of him wanted this, but this was a line that could not be uncrossed. She pulled his hand up to rest on her heart, which was beating wildly. He could feel the mad flutter under his fingers. No turning back, he thought.

"Are you sure? We can't laugh about this later, Olivia."

She reached up, pulled his face down to her, and poured everything she had to offer into her kiss. All of the love she had for him, which was abundant. His heart must have skipped a beat; he lost his breath. He gave into his own need and returned the simmering passion. The warmth spread through her body from the tip of her toes to the top of her head. Every inch of her that he touched instantly turned to goose bumps as she arched up, giving him permission to take more. His hands found her panties underneath her pretty knee-length navy dress, and he slowly pulled them down. She released him from the buckle of his pants. He held her underneath himself, kissing her lips and neck. Then he took off her bra and filled his mouth with her as he pushed the dress over her head.

"I don't have a…I didn't expect to…Olivia, are you taking…" He struggled to keep his composure.

She said nothing; she just shook her head no.

"There's never been anyone before," she admitted.

At that reality, he started to release her, but she felt his hesitation and met it with a soft, slow touch.

"I want this, Dean," she whispered to him. "I want it to be you; I need it to be you."

She kissed him slowly and pulled him closer to her. He lost all reason. She arched her body up as he freed himself from the rest of his clothes, and carefully slid into the warm heat waiting for him. They silently climbed the passion their bodies were creating and she lost herself in the waves that tore through her. He buried his face into her hair, and somehow found the self-control to separate himself from her as his body released him into pleasure. As his heart pounded against his chest, he kissed her softly and laid next to her. She tucked herself under his arm and put her head on his chest so she could hear his heart starting to slow from its furious pace.

She was one of the most beautiful women he had ever seen, but she was so young. How did he get here? How did he just seem to lose all sense of reason around her? He turned to her, watching her as she closed her eyes and settled in for sleep. His hand trailed down her naked back, and he laughed to himself at the idea that he wanted to protect her…from himself. She had dreams, real dreams. She had been rattling on for a couple of years now that she was going to travel, see the world. She was going to get out of here the second that she could—anywhere but here.

But his life was here. He was going to school and planning on going into business one day. He loved the town and the people in it. He knew he would only be holding her back, stopping her. What if tomorrow morning he asked her to stay? She would resent him. He had to step aside and let her have that freedom she so loudly proclaimed she needed.

"Are you OK?" he whispered as he traced the outline of her naked body.

"Yeah," she answered. The love he had just poured into her with every touch was more than she had dared hoped for her first time. She had thought about when and where it would happen, and had decided that she would wait. She wanted it to be with a man she loved. She wanted it to be with a man who was good, and kind, knowing she would never look back on it and wish it had not happened. She wanted it to be with a man she could spend her life with, easily.

Dean was the one who found her in the tree house. He was the one who always found her. Her kid-sized crush turned into a one-sided love affair the moment their lips touched. He was the one thing in her world that made sense and felt right. When she heard his voice break the silence of her night, she released every bit of tension she had been holding onto the whole night. When he was around, she was somehow exactly where she wanted to be. The overwhelming need in her screamed, "Tonight! This man! This man and this night."

"Holy shit," Elle said as she sat back in her seat.

"Yup," Olivia said.

"But you went to New York. He…oh…" Elle said as the wheels started to spin.

"What?" Olivia asked.

"After you left, he kind of got real weird. He had this drive, like he had to get school wrapped up and his business off the ground. It was all he talked about anytime I saw him. He became obsessed."

"When I woke up, he was gone. He had tidied up the tree house a bit because we'd knocked a few things over. I called him. He answered and said he needed to think. I asked him if he was going to come say good-bye, and he said no, that something had come up and he and his dad had to go out of town for a job or something. It broke my heart…actually, it shattered my heart," she said, wiping a tear from her face.

"I'll kill him," Elle said as she started the car and yanked on the steering wheel, pulling it back onto the road.

"No, don't! I don't understand why he did what he did, but I can't change it. It happened. We didn't speak after that until he showed up at the bank to tell me about my parents."

"And what is happening now?" Elle asked.

"I don't know. At first, it seemed to be like my first kiss. We just didn't talk about it. He's Connor's friend and nothing more. For some reason, I just keep throwing myself at him anytime he is around. He kissed me that night you guys were looking for me and I was at the house. And then he acted like he had done something terrible and couldn't get out of there fast enough."

"Well, do you want to have a relationship with him?" Elle asked.

"I want to not lose my mind every time I'm around him. I need to get over him."

"Do you love him?" Elle asked.

"Oh, Elle. I think he might be the love of my life," Olivia said, defeated.

"What's the problem then?"

"It just seems that fate has already decided. I'm just not the love of his."

Eleven

"What's good here?" Rohan asked as he looked over the menu.

"Everything," Olivia smiled at him. "Have you never been here before?"

"No, but I've been wanting to check it out. I just had to wait for the right girl to invite."

Olivia was pretty sure she was a few shades of red as she turned her attention back to the menu. When Rohan picked her up, she was taken by how nice he looked. She had always seen him in his kitchen uniform, and tonight he was very GQ in his dark navy button-down shirt and black pants. The shirt was a bit fitted, revealing that he must spend a lot of time in the gym. It was unbuttoned just at the top, giving a relaxed but still totally put together look. She had chosen a simple black skirt that flowed loosely around her legs and stopped just above her knees. Her top was white, a bold choice for an Italian restaurant, but it looked cute on her, and she had been very limited by what she had brought with her what she found in Elle's closet. Rohan had kindly told her how lovely she looked when she greeted him at the door.

"What will we get, Mister Foodie?" she asked.

"Since it's so hot out, maybe a Caprese salad. How about pizza? Chicken and spinach?" he suggested, looking over the menu.

"That sounds delicious. Afterward, maybe we can go for frozen yogurt. I'm thinking a salty caramel, banana, and coconut concoction," she offered.

"You drive a hard bargain. I'm going to need to walk home, but it will be worth it."

The food arrived, and they continued to enjoy the low-lit casual atmosphere of the brick oven pizza place. They had chosen an indoor table, since the early July heat was hanging in the air. Lenny Kravitz's voice sang "Fly Away" somewhere in the distance.

"It's been a long time since I've been here, but not much has changed. I think the last time I was here was a few years ago. Celebrating getting my driver's license."

"Big moment, that freedom. My first car was a beat-up Yamaha motorcycle."

"Mine was my mom's old mom car. Nothing special, but it was freedom. I didn't have to depend on my parents or Connor to go places. I think Elle and I drove to the furthest stretches of Maryland to go shopping that year. Just to go, like we were being all grown up." Olivia smiled at the memory.

"You two have been friends for a long time?" he asked.

"Forever. We met early in school, and the normal things keep you together, and then apart, like now with me being in New York and in school and her being here and in school, but we hang onto each other."

"That's nice. I was more of a transient kid, moving with my parents. I have friends, but not like that. It's nice that you have that. Connor and Dean seem like they've been joined at the hip since birth too."

"They have been. I think Connor was four when we moved here, Dean was right next door. They went in different directions for college, but came back and opened the business together. They are brothers. So, you had a motorcycle even at sixteen?" she asked, to steer the conversation away from Dean.

"Yes, ma'am. A bit cheaper to buy and a lot cheaper to fuel on a dishwasher's salary." He smiled.

"I'm sure it also doesn't hurt with the ladies," she smirked.

"I did OK," he grinned.

"I am sure you had girls falling at your feet." She batted her eyes.

"I don't know about all that, but there was a girl," he admitted.

"Your first love?" she asked sweetly. "Tell me about her."

"It was high school. This girl just kind of came out of nowhere, and then all of a sudden she was everywhere. She was quiet, but smart. We got paired up for a chemistry lab, and I guess she assumed she would be doing most of the work."

"Were you a studious sort?" Olivia smiled.

"I didn't let my grades slip; I wouldn't say I was studious. My parents thought it was important that I didn't have anything standing in my way. So I was held to a standard. The chem lab was fun, cooking has a lot of chemical science and experimentation to it, so it came easy to me. I surprised her." He smiled at the memory.

"And you fell in love?" she asked.

"Yes," he smiled "Anna. Her name was Anna."

"What happened to Anna?"

"High school. I wasn't ready to be a man, the man she needed. I was just a dumb kid with a motorcycle. She was one of those who was going places. We both knew it, and loved each other enough to let each other go. I came East…and she is out there, somewhere…hopefully taking over the world." He smiled.

"You don't keep in touch?" she asked.

"No. We both needed the silent abyss for a while. I wish her nothing but good."

"You're quite the guy, Rohan." Olivia smiled.

"Well. You know about me. I want to know about you."

"What do you want to know?" she asked.

"Anything. Everything. You lived here first, your best friend since forever is Elle, you moved to New York two years ago. Fill in some blanks." He smiled.

Their pizza came, and she immediately thanked herself for letting Rohan pick. It wasn't something she would have ever picked for herself, but it was a delicious combination. They continued to chat as they ate.

"My parents bought our house when they found out I was on the way. My mom had the perfect house, on the perfect street, in the perfect town plan. Part of that plan was the boy child and the girl child. I think we would have had a dog too, except she was allergic to dogs."

"Sounds like a reasonable goal," he offered.

"Yeah, it's just…I don't know. I feel like I was born to fill a role in some weird play of my mother's life. 'You will be playing the role of Olivia.' When I was little, I was always jealous of Elle."

"Why?" he asked.

"Because she knows who she is. She's always known. She's a lover of her Irish heritage, she sees ghosts, and she says the first thing that pops into her mind. For as long as I have known her, she has lived her own life, loudly. I used to go into her room and see her personality splattered all over it. Her closet was a mess, stuffed full of weird clothes. Her jewelry, treasures, and trinkets spilled from boxes that were always perpetually strewn about. Posters on the wall, sayings taped to her mirror. And then I would go back to my house, to my room that was decorated for me. The personality that was splattered in a tidy fashion, the one that was handed to me. My closet with all my clothes hanging in neat rows, nothing weird. What kid doesn't own something weird?"

"I had a duster jacket, went down to my knees. Guns N' Roses patch on the back. It went great with my Doc Martins," he admitted.

"See?" she motioned that he'd made her point exactly. "I played the role of Olivia."

"So, New York?" he asked.

"Yeah. I just needed to go somewhere big and get lost."

"And find the unscripted Olivia," he offered.

"Exactly. Connor…Connor kind of is the role he was born to play. He's smart, and driven, and organized. He can do anything. I'm convinced that if the Apocalypse came, he would just find some piece of land and quietly set up a self-sustaining farm. It's just what he does. He was happy to flip houses with my dad, and made enough money on a few to start that business of his. He didn't even blow the money irresponsibly. He had an IRA account in preschool, I'm sure of it. I was always borrowing money from his allowance. So for him to stay here and live this life, it's what he wants."

"So, Miss New York…how's it working out for you?" he asked

"Good. Obviously, my parents weren't happy with the idea, but I was eighteen, so they really couldn't do anything about it. We negotiated. Rather than taking a year to find myself, by myself, I would go to school. I got into NYU."

"Nice, so you were a studious sort." He smiled.

"Yes, but for myself. I don't recall my parents ever looking at our report cards. I just wanted to work hard for myself. I wasn't the best, but I was decent. So at NYU, all of my classes have been sporadic. Interest driven, just trying to figure out what

I want to be when I grow up. My apartment is great; I've got the best roommate. Together, we're able to afford a shoebox smack dab in the middle of everything. My job is good, and I love the people I work with, but it's just a job. They all feel the same way. Dave is an artist. Kurt is a musician. Everyone in New York is something other than what they do for a living. It's a good home for lost souls, really," she said.

"So what has interested you the most?" he asked.

"Ummm…" she began. "I guess I'm still looking for something."

"Close your eyes," he commanded.

"What?"

"Close your eyes," he repeated slowly. She complied. "It's ten years from now. The afternoon is bright and warm and the sun is brilliant. What are you looking at?"

"Trees. Butterflies." She smiled.

"What are you doing?" he asked.

"Taking pictures of them."

"Open your eyes." He smiled, "Tell me about your photography classes."

"It's fun. It's hard, with the logistics of it being a class. History, different arts with the camera, different types of cameras. But taking pictures, just enjoying the simple pleasure of having captured a moment in time and freezing it is what I love. Freezing that feeling, or just remembering what a good place you are in when you see something amazing. That's why I kind of want to travel. I want to take a picture of something amazing and remember the feeling I had on that day, forever."

"That sounds like a good plan to me."

"I'm a work in progress," she smiled. "My parents never understood my need to look for something more than what was handed to me."

"I get that," he said. "I guess I am lucky that my parents were very supportive of me packing my whole life into a duffel bag and heading east."

"What do they think of you now?" she asked.

"They're proud. When I told them I wanted to go, I think my father thought more of me because I didn't want to start my career on his coattails. My mom said she would not make a decision before I cooked for her."

"Did you?" she asked.

He laughed. "I did. And I was terrified."

"What did you make?" she asked.

"I made her a meatloaf."

"A meatloaf?!" She giggled "That's not…why a meatloaf?"

"Because of all the fancy dishes she had eaten in all the world, when she came home and cooked for us, she always made meatloaf. It was something simple for her very complicated palate that she absolutely loved. I made the fancy sides and even followed it up with a chocolate lava cake, but I think it was the meatloaf that won her heart over." He smiled. "She told me I cook with love. That is something that can't be learned at a fancy school. You're born with it. So, go. I must go, and cook with love."

They walked from Bruno's to the local frozen yogurt shop, and enjoyed the silliness that ensued at the toppings bar. They both walked away with frozen yogurt topped with a five-year-old's treasure trove of candy. Rohan drove her home and walked her to the door. His fingers laced with hers as they walked slowly to the end of their evening together.

"I had a great time with you tonight." She smiled.

"I'm glad I met you, Olivia," he said.

His hand brushed her loose blonde hair off her face and continued down her arm until he wrapped his hand around her waist and pulled her in to close the space between them. He lowered his head to her, and their lips met in the quiet evening air. Soft, sweet, perfect. He whispered good-night in her ear and kissed her on the cheek. She let herself into Connor's house, closed the door, and slid all the way down to the floor. He was amazing. He really was. Now, if only she could get her heart to stop whispering the name of another love, the evening would be grand.

Twelve

Magnus Archer, Rohan, and Cat had dinner with Didier and they discussed his proposal of exclusively stocking wines from Choucher Du Soleil. It was the vineyard to go with, in Cat's opinion. It was the oldest vineyard in town and really focused on quality over quantity. And because Didier was French, every single bottle came with a love story. That's what people want when they come to a bed and breakfast in the middle of the country; they want a love story.

Cat adored the idea, but Rohan had more specific questions dealing with menu changes, recipes, vintages, and seasons. It was well more than Cat had thought about, which is why they had hired him to start with. He was young in his career, but he was serious and smart. He knew a kitchen down to its bones, and Cat was quite sure he would be famous one day. To think, that famous chef got his start right here at Archer's Inn.

Once business was done, Didier insisted on taking Cat on a walk. He flirted terribly, as was his nature. She took it all in good fun, as it was intended to be. He enjoyed chatting with her about all she had done to the Inn and all she wanted to do. He wanted to pass along his vast knowledge of the business world and the town he had called home all of his adult life. He was a great resource to anyone who would listen, and Cat did so with pleasure.

"My belle fleur, Cathleen, when oh when are you going to stop teasing me and run away with me?" Didier asked as she slipped her hand through his arm so they could walk through the evening gardens together.

"Didier, you are the most handsome Frenchman I have ever known. My love for you will transcend time. In another life, one where I am not under the spell of the youth and charm of my husband, I will gladly run away with you." She smiled at him.

"Ah, yes. Another life, perhaps. I will wait for you, for you are worth the wait," he said as he twirled her around in a dance, dipped her, and kissed her on the cheek.

"Oh stop. My husband will burn the place down in a jealous rage if he finds me in the garden with a lover," she teased him.

"If only, my belle fleur. I have turned into such an old man so quickly." He sat down on a swing with her under an arbor in the center of one of the small gardens.

"You are still young, Didier. You still charm all the ladies." She smiled.

"Oui, mon enfant. That is the way with the French. We come to your country and we charm all of your women right out of your arms." He smiled.

"And you, sir, have charmed one very lucky lady," Cat offered him.

She loved Didier's wife, Lorraine. Lorraine was an American who had fallen in love with a twenty-something Didier when she had come to town to visit the vineyard. Cat loved the story of how they met.

"Ah, oui. But you are wrong, belle. I am the one who is lucky." He thought of his wife.

"Tell me Didier, tell me the story," Cat asked, though he had told her this story in almost every spot on the grounds. It was like a favorite old movie or book.

"My Lorraine. She was so young then, just nineteen. She had come up with her parents for a weekend in the country. I found her standing on the top of the highest hill, watching the sunset over the fields. Never in my life have I seen such a beautiful sight. She took my breath away, and I knew that no matter how many days I would live, the image of her standing there would haunt me."

"You loved her from the first moment?" Cat asked, as she always did.

"Oui, mon enfant. From the first moment. My heart, it did not beat until she came into my life. Only on that day, in that moment, did I know what it felt like for love to run through my veins and bring my heart to life." He closed his eyes, and he could still see her standing there. She had a pink dress that clung to her as it blew in the breeze. Her long red hair was glowing along the edges as the sun sank behind her. Just remembering that moment, with his eyes closed, picturing it as if it was just a moment ago, made his heart ache in the best possible way.

"Did she love you from the first moment?" Cat asked, already knowing the answer.

"Pas! She took one look at me, dirty from working in the fields all day, and wanted to run back to her parents. I scared her. She was so innocent."

"Did you corrupt her?" Cat teased, as she had always done.

"Pas, mon enfant. She corrupted me! As she walked by me, she smiled. Every inch of my soul climbed out of my body and followed her. I knew all the days of my life would amount to nothing if they were not spent with her."

"And what did you do?" Cat asked, knowing and loving the answer.

"I followed her. I got one of our very best, most expensive bottles of wine."

"Which your uncle later made you pay for," Cat always remembered.

"A price worth paying; pennies compared to what I got in return," he always said.

"I found her sitting on a blanket watching the evening sky. I said nothing, but I poured a glass for her and sat down. I poured a glass for myself, and we toasted to the beauty of the sun and the elegance of the stars. We drank, and I told her of my life. I told her that I came to this country with hope for a good education; I had a head for business and wanted to make millions. I come to work at my uncle's vineyard and had to work from the smallest job on up. I told her that I had nothing in my pockets, no money to offer. But I tell her of what I see for the land, for the harvest, for the wine. If I work hard and I learn, one day he would leave it to me, as he had no children of his own," he said.

"And she fell in love with you then?" Cat asked, as it was always the next question.

"Pas. She fell in love with the grapes." He smiled. "She asked for a second glass. God have mercy and thank you, Lord for that second glass."

"What happened when she drank the second glass?" Cat asked, her favorite part.

"Ah. The earth moved, mon amour. She looked at me, and I could not help but want to kiss her. She was so beautiful, the most beautiful girl in the world. I wanted to have a kiss from her to go on living. When our lips met, all of the angels in heaven sang the sweetest song." He closed his eyes and smiled at the memory.

"And then she loved you?"

"And then she loved me." He smiled. "We were married just six months later. I knew there would never be any other woman in the world I would want to love. I gave her everything in that kiss. My heart, my soul. My future was nothing without her in it."

"And now?" Cat asked.

"And now, I am the luckiest man alive. She let me love her. She gave me three beautiful children and nine glorious grandchildren. I have watched her become more and more beautiful every day. I open my eyes every morning and I get to see my bride. I lay my head down at the end of the day, and fall asleep to the sound of her sweet breath. My heart only beats for that woman. As it will be all the days of my life," he answered.

"And after…" Cat prompted.

"And after, I will live that life all over again. With you," he teased.

"I can't wait," she replied as always, resting her head on his shoulder.

"Are you ready for your big party tomorrow?" he asked her.

"I think so. I want it to be perfect. Mr. Archer is thinking about really stepping back and letting me take things over full time. This will be a big step in that direction."

"It will be fine, mon amour. The day will be warm, the women will be beautiful, and the wine will be flowing." He smiled.

It did turn out to be a beautiful day with no threat of rain until the late evening. The entire staff showed up at dawn to put the finishing touches on everything. Cat even enlisted the help of her husband, Eric, to do odd jobs. Rohan had the kitchen sectioned out as to what would go out in the early afternoon, what would go out for the dinner crowd, and then what would go out for the people who wanted to party into the night. It was going to be a very long day for everyone, but hopefully one to remember.

"How was your date?" Cat asked Rohan as she walked into the kitchen with her clipboard to check a few things off.

"How did you know I went on a date?" he smiled.

"Habits of a small town, my friend. You and Olivia were seen sharing a pizza at Bruno's."

"Wow. That's kind of creepy," he confessed.

"Nah," she smiled. "I'm just kidding. I ran into Elle at the grocery store. She totally told me."

"Funny. It went. It was a nice evening. She's got a lot on her plate. She will be leaving to go back home Monday and then I think she's going to travel a bit," he said.

"Are you planning on trying to keep in touch?" she asked.

"I'm enjoying getting to know her. We will see where that leads," he said. "All the salads go out at eleven. The grills will start up at two."

"Good, good," she said, noting that he had changed the subject. "It's almost show time."

Thirteen

Connor and Olivia showed up at noon. Olivia wanted to take pictures throughout the day so Cat would have a variety to pick from for her magazine submission. She took some pictures of the crew setting things up, then found Rohan in the kitchen with the music up loud.

"Mötley Crüe, classic." She smiled.

"Hi," he greeted her, walking over and offering her a friendly kiss that lingered a bit.

"Hi," she smiled when he took a step back from her.

"So, you're here for the day?" he asked as he went back to cutting up fruit.

"Yeah, I came up early to get some shots in. I want Cat to have a nice variety of things to pick from."

"I'm sure it will be great. It's nice to see you; I had a great time last night."

"I did too," she replied honestly. "You're a great guy."

Rohan's hand stilled. He looked at her standing in the corner of the doorway. She hadn't moved.

"Oh," he offered. "I'm getting that speech already?"

"You're not getting that speech." She smiled "You are a great guy, but I'm going back to New York Monday. And then I'm going to quit my job."

"You are?" he asked.

"Yes. I'm going to jump. I booked a flight to Thailand for a month from now."

"Olivia, that's awesome," he replied, genuinely happy for her.

"Thanks. You were quite inspiring with your moving to the other side of the country on a wing and a prayer story."

"Well, I'm glad I was inspiring to you." He smiled.

"You are. You are amazing, and I had a really good time," she said.

"So I am getting the speech?"

"I don't know. I like you. I've had an unexpectedly amazing little thing here with you in this kitchen," she smiled "But New York. Thailand. That's not really conducive to a relationship, is it?" she pointed out.

He closed the distance between them and wrapped his arms around her waist, pulling her in for a lingering kiss.

"It's not, no. I like you, too. Could we just agree to keep some doors open? Enjoy for now and the next couple of days and then maybe I come be a tourist in New York for a bit. You never know."

"No, I suppose you don't. I'd like that." Olivia smiled.

Guests started showing up in a steady flow just after noon. Families came, with young children who could enjoy the games, crafts, and vendors. There would be clowns, face painting, and activities for the younger crowd. Cat knew the younger guests would be tucked into bed before the evening fireworks, so lunch would be dedicated to fun for them.

Olivia worked her way around all the vendor tables, and captured some of the local businesses showing off their wares. She enjoyed watching a clown make a daisy out of balloons for a three-year-old little girl with the sweetest pigtails. She captured the sweet victory on the face of a seven-year-old boy who had won a three-legged race with his father against other father-son teams. She spent a few minutes sitting on the porch with Mrs. Dillard. Mrs. Dillard was ninety-three years old, and was wearing a crown of red and blue carnations wrapped in ribbon that her great-granddaughter made for her for the occasion.

Elle and Dean both pulled up with the second wave of guests, around the dinnertime break, when some of the folks with younger kids were beginning to head home. The evening would be filled with a little more alcohol and a lot more fun.

Dean and Connor quickly found each and looked around for a good spot to park their belongings. They saw Elle laying on a big blanket, and walked over to join her.

"Hello boys," she said. "Happy fourth!"

"Same to you," Connor replied.

He could not help but notice her outfit marking the occasion. Blue jeans cutoffs that were a tad too short but looked fantastic on her and black T-shirt boasting kissable lips with the American flag as lipstick. Dean noticed Connor starting to wander off into his imagination and knocked into him to get his attention back.

"Can we join you?" Dean asked as he smiled at Connor.

"Sure. Want a beer? I grabbed some before I came over here," she offered.

"Yes," Connor thanked her. "Enjoying finally being twenty-one?"

"Well, really enjoying being able to have a beer—in public." She winked at Connor.

"Have you seen Livy?" Connor asked.

"Not yet. She said she'd be all over taking pictures. Plus, I think she might be hanging around the kitchen some today."

"Why is that?" Connor asked as the three sat down on blankets and watched the crowd of people milling around the vendor area.

"Rohan," she said as she sipped her beer.

"Rohan?" Dean asked.

"Yup," Elle said. Her mind quickly started calculating…maybe she could get a little pot stirred, if she was very careful.

"They went on a date the other night."

Dean's hand stilled ever so slightly on his beer, but it was enough for Elle to catch.

"Yeah, he came to pick her up the other morning, too. Then she mentioned she was going out again. I thought she was going out with you," Connor said to Elle.

"Nope. Rohan," Elle smiled.

"He knows she doesn't live here," Dean said. He could feel the heat trickle up his spine.

"Yeah. He doesn't seem to care," Elle smiled. "I think it's good for Liv. You know, maybe she will find some focus or something."

Dean stood up and excused himself, saying he was going to go check out the food. He needed to have a few minutes alone; he hated the feeling that was creeping in on him. Jealousy. How could he be jealous? He had no right. They were not a couple, nor had they ever been, really. This was insane.

Fine, if that's how she wants it to be. Fine. He didn't expect her to be a saint. He was sure she had the company of men in New York. He didn't want to think about it. Connor had never mentioned anyone, but he knew there had to be. He had himself kept the company of other women. Nothing serious, but a few regulars. He wasn't lonely. He walked over to the food table, grabbed a plate, and absently piled food onto it.

"Wow, hungry?" a voice from behind him said. He turned to find a tall raven-haired woman smiling at him.

"Hi Ceilia," he smiled.

"Hello Dean." She all but purred at him. Ceilia was older than Dean by about ten years. She had been married and divorced at least twice that he knew of. She was pretty, thin, and nicely dressed. She always seemed to be all dolled up, with a little too much makeup and a little too much perfume. The divorce from her second husband had afforded her a slightly enhanced figure to get back out into the world with.

"Enjoying the festivities?" he asked as they went through the line.

"So far. Will you be staying for the evening?" she asked, finding an excuse to stand a little closer, and then a little more closer, to him.

"Yes, I'll be here."

"Well good, maybe I'll be seeing you under those fireworks." Her voice was thick with sex and desperation.

"Sure thing," he said as he started to move away from her, but then thought better of it. "Where are you sitting?"

"Oh, over on the hill there. See the blue blanket?" she pointed it out.

"Maybe I can swing by later for a bit." He smiled.

"Really?" Legitimately surprised, her voice dropped the throaty sex act.

"Yeah, sure…why not?" He smiled at her. "I'll see you later."

As the evening wore on, Olivia took the last of her pictures and put the camera away. She found an empty room upstairs and changed from her shorts and T-shirt to a more fitted and fun outfit. She chose a cute red sundress that had crossed spaghetti straps and cut a few inches above her knees. She found Elle and filled her in on her date and the kitchen happenings. Connor and Dean made the rounds, chatting with people and enjoying the festivities but also looking out for opportunities to get Rising Ridge Designs' name out there. Cat had really done an amazing job on everything. The grounds were beautiful, and the food was all delicious. There was also a stage where a lineup of local bands played all day.

Cat kept the range wide, so the music could and would be enjoyed by everyone. There was a young woman soulfully singing the blues on stage as the small gathering of people clapped along to her rhythmic beat.

"Hi boys!" Ceilia greeted the men.

"Hi." Dean stood. "Ceilia, you know Connor."

"Of course, he built me a beautiful table a few months ago. Hi."

"Hi." Connor smiled and shook her hand.

"Dean, I grabbed a bottle of wine, so you be sure to stop by and help me drink it."

"Will do." Dean smiled at her.

"Bye, Connor." She smiled as she sauntered past them.

"What was that about?" Connor asked.

"I might go sit with her in a bit," Dean offered.

"Oh, lord. Not Ceilia again. Dean, come on man." Connor rolled his eyes.

"She's not that bad," Dean insisted. "She's actually pretty nice. She's a good listener." He was speaking the truth. Ceilia may have been very unconventional when it came to life, but she had been a regular visitor in Dean's life over the last few years. She was always up for a good time, but there had also been a few times where they wound up just sitting and he would talk. She would listen.

"Who's that?" Olivia asked Elle, noticing the exchange across the lawn.

"That's Ceilia. Married, divorced, married, divorced. Boob job. She likes all men, but she does like Dean a lot. He's given her his attention every now and again. Nothing ever sticks, though," Elle whispered back.

"Oh," Olivia said. What else could she say? Dean had a girlfriend. Or a potential. She would not fault him for that, of course, but having to be witness to it was a little tough.

"Rohan going to be joining us?" Elle asked quietly. "I thought he might sneak out during the fireworks."

"Yeah, I may sneak off to be with him for a bit. Not sure if he's going to make it out of the kitchen," Olivia said.

As the evening went on, Dean kept an eye on Olivia and Elle. They walked around for a bit, chatted with people, sat on a blanket, and put their heads together to talk the way they had when they were younger. Olivia got up, gathered her things, and headed toward the kitchen.

"Hi," Dean said to her as he made sure his random path crossed hers.

"Hey." She smiled. "Staying for fireworks?"

"Yeah, I think I've got a date actually," he said as he pointed out Ceilia. "She's waiting for me now."

"Really?" She hated the fact she felt like she had just been punched in the stomach. "Well, good. Should be a good night for it. I myself am headed for the kitchen. I'm going to see about watching the fireworks with Rohan."

"Rohan. Yeah, I heard about that. He's a nice guy," Dean replied curtly.

"That he is," she said genuinely. "Well, have a good night."

As they walked away from each other, Olivia could not help but think he had done that on purpose. His smile was casual and his tone was even…but there was just…something. It was almost like he was daring her to say something about him having a date with somebody. Was he throwing it in her face? She shook her head, clearing it of the idea that he would intentionally be mean to her. She had to being too sensitive, seeing something that wasn't there.

Connor settled on the blanket next to Elle as dusk overtook the sky and the show was about to start.

"Where is everybody?" he asked.

"Olivia is with Rohan. I don't know where Dean is."

"Oh, then he's probably with Ceilia. He mentioned about spending some time with her."

"Did he now?" Elle remarked smugly. "Well, looks like it's just you and me."

"No place I would rather be," Connor said.

Elle smiled. He really was the perfect guy; life was just so easy around him. She had been out on a date with the guy from school. He was fun. He had a nice car. He had that dangerous edginess. All things she thought she was attracted to the most. But in moments like this, she loved Connor because he wasn't any of those things. He was just Connor. He made everything calm and better. They watched the fireworks and enjoyed the cool breeze blowing in.

Olivia had found Rohan and they stood together at the door of the kitchen watching the fireworks. He had wrapped his arm around her waist and pulled her in closer. Despite the show in the sky, her eyes kept returning to the couple on the blue blanket under the tree. She had noticed that Ceilia was cuddled up to Dean as they happily watched the show. Olivia felt more and more that getting back to New York was key. She smiled at Rohan, and as the grand finale lit up the night, they celebrated with a very romantic, sweet kiss.

The rolls of thunder came in just as the grand finale was being shot into the sky. As if on cue, the heavens opened up, and the rain poured onto the crowd. Laughter and screams broke through and everyone picked up their belongings, running to their cars or cover at the Inn. Olivia stood in the rain and watched Ceilia cuddle up to Dean as they ran under the arbor at the back of the building. She took a deep breath, shook off the knot in her stomach, and returned her attention to Rohan. He was soaked through, having run into the rain to help a few people gather things and get them under cover. He came back to her in the doorframe, kissed her on the nose, then grabbed her hand and they disappeared back into the kitchen.

"Would you like to come over Dean?" Ceilia asked.

Ceilia's car was parked on the side lawn along with all the other overflow cars. As he stood with her at the car door, he could see over her directly to the back of the Inn. He watched Rohan laughing, gathering things for people, and putting them under cover. Then he watched Rohan return to Olivia who was standing in the doorway. He watched Rohan's hand slide down her arm and take her hand. And he watched Rohan kiss her on the nose. All of a sudden, he wasn't in the mood to entertain company.

"It's late, love. I'll call you," he said, and he pulled her hand up to his lips and kissed it.

"You better," she winked and walked to her car with her umbrella over her.

Dean ran to his truck to get out of the rain. The image of Rohan pulling Olivia into the kitchen like two love-struck teenagers had kicked him in the gut. He put the truck into drive and headed home. He shouldn't be mad, but he was. She was just there, in that damned little red dress. The little red dress that Rohan had his hands all over. Shit.

"Do you want to stay for a bit?" Elle asked Olivia when she found her in the main lobby of the Inn.

"I do, but I think Rohan's got some things to do. Clean up. I don't want to hold you up."

"No, no. I got this. I'll be right back, do not move."

Elle returned a few minutes later with Connor's keys.

"I'm going to give Connor a ride home and he's leaving his car here. You can come home anytime you like."

"Thanks, Elle." Olivia smiled.

"No problem, that's what friends are for. Now you have no excuses." Elle smiled.

"Yeah, yeah…" Olivia rolled her eyes, knowing exactly what voices were chattering in Elle's busy mind.

Olivia found Rohan back in the kitchen, knee deep in clean up mode. She had offered to help, but he insisted no. She had been there all day taking pictures, and he knew he was going to be up well into the wee hours of the morning. So she decided to let him be, and asked him to call her later.

Fourteen

On her way back into town, she kept seeing Ceilia all wrapped up in Dean's arms. He had barely spoken to her the whole time he was at the party. What was he doing to her? It was one thing when she threw herself at him in unrequited love a few years ago, but he kissed her. And just like before, he was acting like it was no big deal or had not happened at all. The further down the road she got, the more pissed she became. They were going to have to have this out…define their terms. She passed Connor's house and went on through town to where Dean was renting an apartment in a converted Victorian. She was not just going to keep on going, and be mad. He was being a jerk; he had seen her at the Inn. He had made no attempt to be a bit more subtle with Ceilia. Asshole.

As she pulled up to the house, she saw Dean cleaning up a few things that had been left out in the rain. It was still pouring, so he was trying to be quick about it.

"Asshole!" she shouted at him as she slammed the car door and crossed over his front lawn.

"Howdy, neighbor," he greeted her sarcastically. He dropped the attitude as soon as she got close enough for him to see her face. She had been crying. Her eyes were still full of tears.

"Olivia, what happened? Are you OK?" He put his hands on her arms.

"Don't touch me!" she screamed, knocking his hands away.

"What the hell is wrong with you? Did Rohan hurt you?" he said loudly to be heard over the rain.

"Is that what this is about? No, he didn't hurt me! You! You hurt me! You are such an asshole, Dean!" Her whole body was enraged.

"Olivia, calm down. We can talk about this," he said. "Let's go inside. We can't do this on the front lawn. It's pouring. You've got that ridiculous dress on."

"Don't tell me what to do! You have no right to tell me what to do! I don't tell you what to do with that lanky sauce pot of yours!" She had become unglued, and she knew it.

"Ceilia? Umm…I don't know what you want from me here," he said.

She was starting to shake, and he could see it. The rain had brought a cold front through, and there she stood, still in that little red sundress. The rain had soaked her through and her hair was dripping as she stood there. He took off his rain jacket and swung it around her shoulders. She started to fight with him and he ignored her and just pulled her in until it was around her.

"Get off of me!" She shoved him.

"Sorry, that dress is ridiculous! It's next to nothing, Livy. What kind of fun were you looking for tonight?" he asked.

"See! I don't deserve that, Dean. I am not the kind of girl you seem to think I am. I'm not what's-her-name with the boobs…"

"Ceilia," he answered.

With that, she smacked him in the face.

He grabbed her around her waist, threw her over his shoulder, and carried her toward the house.

"Get off of me, put me down!" She started hitting his back.

"Olivia, we don't need the whole town talking about this tomorrow, so you need to calm down. What the hell is wrong with you?" he said as he ignored her fists pounding into his back and went into the house.

As soon as they were in his apartment, he planted her on the ground, and she shoved off his jacket and threw it down on the couch.

"This is a nice dress!" she defended her selection.

"It's something, all right."

"What the hell does that mean? You need to knock it off, Dean. I have no idea what bug crawled up your butt, but you have to knock it off! I am not a baby, and you have no right to interfere with my choices!" she yelled.

She was driving him insane, he wondered if she knew that. She had been for some time, but he hadn't realized it until she came back into town. It drove him mad when he had called and called her after the night they slept together and she didn't return his calls. It drove him mad when he had to succumb to the fact that New York was everything he thought it would be for her, an escape from the life she'd had. No room for him. And she had been driving him completely certifiable with the whole being totally civil and friendly as if what happened between them two years ago was no big thing. Anger. It was building inside of him, and he was furious with her for it. He had reached his limits. He watched her standing there in her red dress. She was ready to fight, to battle. Since the moment he had met her, he'd come up against nothing but walls. Walls that had been built to protect her, but for fuck's sake, she wasn't letting anyone in. He had been good to her, and every time he felt like he was making progress, she would knock him back to the ground. It was a game, and he had become addicted to it.

"No more walls, Liv. I'm so goddamn sick of the walls with you."

He closed the distance between them and forced her back several steps. His mouth crushed down on hers in full passion, his frustration with her bringing on a raging heat. Her senses had left her body all at once and slammed back into her, starving for more. She felt his teeth catch on her bottom lip and bite. He had her completely surrounded and pinned up against the wall. Her hands that were on his chest to push him back now grasped at his shirt and pulled him closer. His furious pace had become hers, and her desperation for it had become his. She lifted her head to expose her neck and he took what she was offering. He pulled her off the floor, and she locked her legs around him.

The world was being torn at the seams. He couldn't give enough, she couldn't take enough. He couldn't breathe and didn't want to. His mind had gone blank the minute he saw her coming across the lawn in that dress. Did she know the ache he felt when she was in the room? Everything about her made him ache.

That damned dress, he thought, as he carried her down the hall to his bedroom.

Her hands slid up under his shirt and he pulled it over his head and off. He laid her on the bed and kissed her shoulders, his hands sliding down her hips and under the dress to free her from the silk panties she was wearing. She arched her hips to him, pulling him down on the bed with her. He removed his belt and pants. He covered her, gathered her up in his arms, and rolled them over so he could see all of her above him.

He slid into her, and gripped her hips to pull her closer, to go deeper.

"Touch me," she whispered in his ear.

The groan was his this time, and it was guttural. His hands found the zipper at the back of her dress and he slid it down. She leaned into him, and when the zipper stopped, he pulled the fabric apart and freed her from the only layer between them. As he touched her, she spiraled with passion and pleasure. Her body rocked with him, she leaned back, and he filled his mouth with her as she crested over the edge. When she returned to him, she dug her nails into his back, and bit his shoulder. All control was lost. This was the air that he breathed. There was no world beyond the bed they were on. He let himself fall into the spiraling abyss of pleasure as he felt his body release inside of her. Her head rested on his shoulder, and rather than releasing her, he pulled her closer.

"Dean?" she quietly whispered up to him as she struggled to steady her heartbeat.

"Yeah?" The breath of his voice tickled her ear.

"What just happened?" she asked.

"That damn dress, that's what just happened."

"I'm pretty sure that damn dress is on the floor in shreds," she said breathlessly.

"Oh, that's a shame. I really liked that dress." He smiled in the dark, and the room fell silent for a few minutes.

A few hours later, in the quiet of the night, listening to his steady breathing as he slept, she said the words she had never said out loud to him.

"I love you. I've always loved you." She kissed his arm and his cheek.

He moved just a bit, and she slid silently off the bed. She watched him for just a few minutes, feeling the ache return to her heart, where it had been her constant companion for the last two years. When he woke up in the morning, he found that he was alone. She had gone. He pulled the pillow from the now empty side of the bed and covered his face with it. When the subtle scent of her hair caught him, he screamed into the pillow.

"New York calling," he said to himself, "Fucking perfect. Doomed to repeat history."

Fifteen

"You sure you want to go back? You don't have to. You can stay at the house. Hell, we could fix this place up for you," Connor said as he extended his hand to showcase the flip property they were currently standing in.

He had woken up to the sound of Olivia packing at four o'clock in the morning. He'd thought she had planned on staying for the weekend, but all of a sudden, she seemed to be in a hurry.

"Yeah. It's best I get ahead of this. I bought a bus ticket for six thirty; I should be home and settled by lunchtime. Then I will have a day to just recoup before I get back to work."

"OK. And you're still quitting?" he asked.

"Yes and no. I don't know. I like the job, I love the people. They have already been so generous with these couple weeks. I was only supposed to be gone a week. I need to either do my job or let it go. I think a trip to Thailand and then I am really going to focus on a direction and go in it."

"Well, that's good. Just please be safe, and call me…every five minutes," he said as he stopped her from packing the small bag and hugged her.

"I love you, Bubba," she said, calling him by the nickname she'd used instead of "brother" for the first four years of her life.

"I love you, too. Does Elle know?"

"Can we stop by her place? I called her already."

She had called, almost an hour earlier, when she'd left Dean's. She told Elle she needed to get back to New York, fighting tears. Elle didn't ask why, or bother to argue. She knew that Elle would now be up, showered, and dressed, waiting with coffee; because Elle did not judge, she just loved.

"Tell Dean thank you again for coming to get me. That was very kind of him."

"I will. He didn't mind. He's a good friend."

"That he is," she agreed. "That's what he will always be."

Connor noticed that when she had mentioned Dean she became more tense, and she started cleaning up the room with a little too much enthusiasm. He never could read Dean and Olivia together; they were always a little weird around each other. Sometimes he felt like they were intentionally ignoring each other, and other times it seemed that everything was fine and he was making the whole thing up. Perhaps he was, there was certainly no reason for them to have issues now.

Connor drove Olivia over to Elle's house so the girls could say good-bye. He laughed when Elle opened the door and greeted them in her yoga clothes. Her top had a pair of praying hands and read Namaste, bitches.

"Nice shirt," he said.

"Nice sweat pants," she offered as she let them in the door. "I don't think I've ever seen you in sweat pants before."

He looked cute. His hair, usually perfectly in place, was slightly disheveled. He had a T-shirt on that she recognized from a 10K he and Dean had done the year before. His sweat pants were black, and he had flip-flops on. She could not remember the last time she had seen him so casual. This o' dark thirty in the morning version of Connor was completely adorable.

"I'll let you two do your squealy girl thing. Will it bother your parents if I watch TV in the living room?"

"No. They aren't here. Away for the weekend," Elle offered.

"Even better," Connor said as he made his way into the living room and Elle and Olivia walked back to the kitchen.

"So what's with the rush?" Elle asked as they parked themselves at the kitchen island.

"Boys are stupid," Olivia said as she laid her head on the counter.

"Dean?" Elle asked.

"Yes." Her voice was muffled by the counter.

"What happened? No, no…wait," Elle said as she poured two cups of fresh coffee and sat back down. "OK, now…what happened?"

Olivia looked back into the living room where Connor was sitting on the couch, flipping through the channels, oblivious to them.

"We slept together, again."

"You did? When?" Elle asked, wide eyed.

"Last night. A few times." She smiled at the memory.

"Well…" Elle said. "Wait, when I left, you were going home with Rohan. What happened to that?"

"He was busy cleaning up stuff, so we said good-night and we agreed that we would chat once I got back to New York and see what's what. And then as I was driving back to Connors, I don't know, I just got pissed."

"About what?" Elle asked.

"That woman Dean was with at the Inn," Olivia admitted.

"With the boobs? Ceilia. They aren't going anywhere, Liv," Elle said.

"Well, the thing is…we kissed the other night. And it's not like the other times where I threw myself at him. This time he kissed me," Olivia said, jamming her finger on the counter punctuating the last three words.

"Well, that's good…right?"

"I don't know. I kissed him when I was sixteen, and he really didn't want to kiss me. Then I basically threw my v-card at him. I don't regret that it was him, but I do regret how pathetic it all sounds now."

"Hey," Elle said seriously. She turned Olivia to face her. "It's not pathetic. It's the most romantic thing I have ever heard in my life. My first time was in the back of Jake Thompson's mother's Oldsmobile. The Offspring "Self Esteem" was playing…I will trade you any day of the week."

"Did you wake up alone?" Olivia asked.

"No."

"I did. He left; I didn't even say good-bye to him. He called a few times, but I just didn't know what to say. I felt so pathetic."

"Do you love him?" Elle whispered.

"I…" Olivia hesitated.

"Don't lie to me," Elle said.

"Yeah. But he doesn't love me back."

"Well, what happened last night?"

"I just lost it. I was thinking about that kiss and sleeping with him two years ago and the fact that he was sitting there on that blanket with her as if none of that ever happened. I've tried to take his cues. He wasn't talking about it, so I wasn't talking about it. I mean, for fuck's sake Elle, I lost my virginity and never even told you."

"True. I didn't see that one coming," Elle admitted.

"So I found myself driving past Connor's and straight through to Dean's. He was out on the lawn putting stuff away, and I just started screaming at him that he's an asshole. And then he picked me up and carried me into the apartment."

"He did? Oh, and it was raining. It was raining hard. You were all wet and the rain was dripping all in your hair and you were yelling at each other in the rain and he carried you inside?" Elle's voice got lost in her romantic vision of how the evening played out.

"It's not a movie, Elle, but yes. I was soaked. We get inside and he makes some rude comment about my dress."

"That was a sexy dress," Elle informed her.

"That is a trashed dressed. He ripped it off me. Thank God I had my change of clothes from earlier in the day in the car."

"It is like a movie," Elle exclaimed. "So why are you leaving?"

"Because, it just hurts. I feel like for some reason he's just giving in to my wants. My needs. I need to grow up and move on. So, after we had sex…and sex again…I just left."

"Did you say good-bye?"

"No. I just need to get home. So I'm leaving. I need to become an adult. Elle, there hasn't been anyone but Dean."

"What? Really, not even in New York?"

"No. I've been out on a few dates, but for a while, my focus was to just be free of my parents. I didn't want to commit to somebody else before I knew who I was. And now…now it's time for me to do that. Maybe Rohan."

"Rohan's hot," Elle said, which made Olivia giggle and blush.

"Yeah, he's not bad. And he's super romantic in that completely unintentional way."

"Are you going to try to make it work out with him?" Elle asked.

"I didn't make any promises, but we agreed not to shut any doors," Olivia reflected.

"Well, good. Maybe he is what you need."

"Yeah, maybe. Thanks, Elle. I'm sorry I had to come home for this reason, but it's so nice just to be with you."

"Yeah, the universe is sucky sometimes. I'll let you know if I hear from your parents," Elle smiled.

"That's all we need, my mother haunting you. Elle, sit up straight dear." Olivia patted Elle's back in her mother's tone of voice. "I gotta go. I love you."

"I love you, too," Elle said as they hugged.

"Take care of Connor."

"Always have," Elle smiled.

The bus ride home was quiet. Her brain was on overload. Two weeks ago, she was a carefree singleton in New York. As she watched the sunrise, she was a ghost of that girl. Her parents were resting side by side in a cemetery, and she'd left her brother alone. She had a gazillion options now that she had a bigger balance in her bank account. A gazillion more than she wanted. Then there was Dean. She knew she never really got over Dean, and she was fine with that. Some people, you just love. But now, all of those feelings that she had tucked away were out and once again raw. She closed her eyes; it was all too much. She was exhausted. New York—it was just a heartbeat away. She closed her eyes, and sleep took her the rest of the way.

She slipped back into work fairly easily. She was missed, Kurt told her all about a show he had played in some basement club. He was excited, as it was his band's first paying gig. Debi had finished another grueling round of exams and was one step closer to getting her nursing license. She found herself circling outside the door of Dave's office.

"Something on your mind, Olivia?" He asked. "Come on in."

"Well, I know I just took two weeks' vacation," she began sheepishly.

"But…you want more time off?" he asked, a little surprised.

"One of the things that I've always wanted to do is travel. My parents were all about the status quo. We went to the lake house, the same lake house, every summer for as long as I can remember."

"A lake house sounds nice." Dave smiled.

"It was," she offered. "But it was also annoying. They never really entertained the idea of international travel. My mom was terrified of flying. So they left me some money, and I want to do something. Go somewhere. I booked a ticket to Thailand."

"Thailand?" Dave said. "What's in Thailand?"

"I don't know…that's kind of the point. But I want to go. And I am going to go. For two weeks, at the end of this month. I don't expect you to continue to just hold my job."

"Olivia…this is New York. I would be a fool and a hypocrite if I told you this job should be your priority. Hell, I wish I could be twenty again and do it all over. Go. Do. Be. See. It's your time to do it. We will miss you terribly, we have missed you these last couple of weeks."

"Kurt's paperwork is a mess," Olivia noted.

"Yes, it is. But that is OK. We will be OK. We will also be here, should you want to come back. Just don't worry about it. Go travel. Take your pictures. See what you can do, baby."

"Thank you." Olivia stood and rounded the desk to give Dave a hug. "You're amazing."

"You going to stay for the month? Maybe we can whip Kurt into shape and get Audrey on the computers."

"Sure, I can do that," she smiled.

Sixteen

"So it's a done deal?"

"Looks like it. It'll take thirty days for the paperwork. I'm almost finished all the work, and the buyers were comfortable with taking me on my word and the plans I showed them for the rest. I just have to get it done, which should be no problem. We're low on the 12 gauge angles," Connor said as he went through their monthly inventory checklist.

"Check," Dean said as he added that to the list of things they needed to order. "You going to do anything to your parents' house?"

"A couple of major things, but mostly minor ones," Connor said. "It's a good house. It was my parents' forever house, and I can see why they picked it. But it's outdated. This is the perfect chance to really do something with it."

Connor had put his house on the market the day after Olivia left. The summer market was coming to an end, and he knew that if he wanted to sell before spring, it would be now or never. Turns out it would be now, as a newly pregnant couple contacted the real estate agent about the house just three days later.

"Let me know when you need some help, man," Dean said.

"I will. I think my house is fine, just all finishing touches. The parents' house is going to be a haul. I've blocked out Caesar's crew for all of next week."

"Did Dad give you the family discount?" Dean asked.

"He did," Connor assured him.

"We're all going to be busy between your house and the Inn. Cat wasted no time getting me a list of things that Archer wants. Dad went up yesterday as some of the bigger projects are well out of our wheelhouse. Looks like it's going to be a family affair for the next little bit."

"As long as we're keeping the lights on," Connor said.

"Well, you need to work up an estimate for her by Friday, but I think we'll keep the lights on and maybe be able to buy a few more while we're at it. This is going to be good for us; it's our first really big showcase."

"No pressure," Connor smiled.

"Helllllllooooooooo?" A voice carried into the back stock room. Connor handed Dean his clipboard and headed out to the front of the store.

"Hi," he said as he saw Elle standing in the middle of the store. She was wearing a black sundress that had hints of blue bathing suit straps at her shoulders. The sandals on her feet were flat, but had straps that wrapped around her ankles and all the way up her slim calves. Her hair was pulled up into a small ponytail that sprouted wildly at the top of her head. She looked like a fairy who was on vacation.

"Hey. Going to the pool?" Connor asked.

"The beach, actually. My classes are done, and I am going to go and soak up the glorious nothingness that is today. I'm going to lay in the sand and not read books all day. It's going to be awesome," she informed him.

"Sounds like it," he agreed as he started to clean up some of the open magazines on the counter.

She leaned up against the counter and turned one of them around to face her so she could study it.

"Building a house?" she asked as she noticed that all the magazines seemed to be focused on house design and room structures.

"Sort of. I have a buyer for my place," he said. "I've decided to keep my parents' house, but I'm going to change a few things, update it. Getting some ideas."

"Really? Wow. I'm jealous. I need to find my own place. How can I preach to Livy about being an adult when I'm still sleeping in my childhood bedroom?"

"There's nothing wrong with that, Elle. You're in college. It's not like you're a freeloader," Connor assured her.

"I know. But I just need to find something that's small and I can come and go as I please, and that works well with my shoestring budget. It's time," She said. "This is cool."

Connor focused on the magazine she had in her hand. The page displayed a small arbor nestled under a large oak tree in the corner of a yard. The arbor had lanterns strung on the corners and a candle chandelier in the center. A table set for four sat beneath it, with vintage chairs welcoming you to sit. More candles glowed on the center of the table and goblets were filled with wine.

"You would live in the woods if you could," Connor said.

"I really would. Do you think Dean's parents would rent out the tree house? I could be happy there," she smiled.

"Alas…no bathroom."

"Sad but true," she agreed. "Anyway, I came in because I found your sunglasses in my bag of stuff. I must have picked them up and thrown them into my bag at the Fourth of July party. Sorry."

"That's where they went!" he exclaimed as she handed them to him. "I've been looking for these. Thanks."

"Well, there they are. I accidentally stole them." She smiled.

"Have a good time at the beach today. Anyone joining you? Livy mentioned something about a boy at school."

"Oh. That's Shawn. We went out, it was cool. He's got a badass car, and he was all sorts of sexy. But he knew it. I just caught him looking at his own reflection one too many times. He'd be the sort of guy who would have silk sheets and a mirror on the ceiling." She scrunched up her face in disapproval.

"Not your thing?" Connor asked.

"Not really. I'm all for a guy bringing some hot and spicy into the bedroom, but I will not be competing with his own ego for attention," she said as she placed her hand on her hip. "I should be the main attraction in the bedroom."

"Absolutely," he said a little quietly. He shook his head, cleared his throat, and adjusted his stance, all of a sudden feeling flushed. He started stacking magazines, putting things away. Anything to not be looking at Elle.

A hint of a smile tugged at the corner of Elle's mouth. She lowered her hand and watched him just for that split second. *Did I just make Connor Reynolds out of sorts? Hmmm...interesting.*

"Well, now he's alone in that bed of his. I'm just going to enjoy some alone time today. The voices in my head have missed me. They need my attention."

"Well, you and your imaginary friends have fun." He smiled.

"We always do," she said as she pranced out the front of the store.

Dean watched the exchange between the two and tried to remember exactly how long ago he'd realized that his best friend was in love with Elle. Her birthday had just passed, so it was at least a year. Connor had come into the shop with that little box in hand. He had worked on it for a week, making sure the design was just right on the tree of life, its roots spreading and intertwining along the bottom and hearty leaves on the branches above. At first, Dean thought it might be a special order that Elle placed because as soon as he saw it, he thought it matched her personality so well. Or maybe it was a gift for her. Then Connor had brought in five more, and set the display piece on the shelf in the store.

Over the last year, Dean started to notice all the little things that people miss. Connor wasn't one to drop what he was doing, but if Elle called and asked for help with something, he tended to drop things for her. He also stood a little taller, but somehow relaxed a lot more around her. Elle was the total opposite of Connor. She was wild and free, and believed in the world having more than one realm. Connor was traditional, had his feet planted firmly in the belief of one God, and had the sort of attitude that if something needed to be done, he would find a way to do it himself. Build it, grow it, make it, and invest in it. He was a flipping Boy Scout and she was going to the beach…to spend time with her imaginary friends. Dean continued on with the inventory, smirking to himself. They were perfect for each other.

Seventeen

The construction on the Inn and the demolition on 3317 Maple Avenue happened almost simultaneously. Connor found himself handling things at the shop with their smaller furniture customers so that he could keep a close eye on the demolition going on at his house. He had put all of his parents' things in storage so he and Livy could go through it at some point, together. It was already enough to stand there and watch them pull down wallpaper, paint over walls, and actually knock a few down. His parents were being erased; his childhood home was going to be a memory in the matter of a month. It comforted him that their things were safe and sound in a storage unit. His mom's plastic fruit and ceramic pies were in a box somewhere in that unit, labeled "Fake food—Kitchen," and that made him feel better. Dean had been working hard, in coordination with Henry, up at the Inn. All the final plans had been arranged and the ground had been broken on projects. Henry invited the boys for a weekend fishing trip to celebrate the end of a long, hard workweek.

"This was a great idea, Dad," Dean said as he secured things from the driver's seat for them to sit a while and fish.

"Yeah, thanks Mister W," Connor offered as he stood and just enjoyed the view of the Eastern Shore waters that lay all around them.

"Connor, I've known you nearly your whole damn life. I've put Band-Aids in places on your body I would rather not talk about. You think you're ever going to call me Henry?"

"Never gonna happen," Connor smiled. "Your wife would wash my mouth out with soap."

"You got me there, kid." He smiled. "So I hear Livy is headed to Thailand."

"Yeah. She is sending me all sorts of e-mails with places she wants to see. Looks like she is going to pack in every second."

"That's good. She's always kind of had that desire to get out there and see the world, but just never did anything about it. It didn't surprise me at all when she took off for New York. I talked to her a bit about that; seems like she's got a happy life there."

"Depends on your definition of happy," Dean said quietly to himself.

"What did you say, Dean?" Henry turned his attention to his son.

"Nothing."

"Stop fooling with all the buttons and let's get our lines out. I want to talk to you two about something," Henry said as he started handing out fishing rods. "This is my last big project, and then it's the Bahamas."

"It will be a good trip for you and mom," Dean said.

"It will be. As far as the business goes…" Henry started and then put up his hands as soon as Dean started to interject.

"No, no, let me say this. As far as my business goes, I'm happy to go out on top. I've done well for myself, and I had hoped I could hand a thriving business down to you. Hell, I'm retiring at sixty. That's the dream. But you two boys really have surprised me this last year."

"Thank you," Connor said. "We had a great example."

"It was my pleasure to help you boys get off the ground. And I am proud of what you have done. I've given this a great deal of thought, and although I am ready to not be the man in charge, I think Sophia really would prefer me not to be her full-time babysitting job just yet. I was thinking we could dissolve some of my business clients into your business. You can pick and choose, and run the show, and I can just consult every once in a while. Like at the Inn. That's a bigger job than you're used to, and a smaller one than I am. I see lots of potential opportunities on that level of business."

"Dad, that's a solid idea," Dean agreed. "What do you think, Connor?"

"I think it's a good idea, as long as we get to balance it with what we do now. I believe we can find a way to have this be a complementary thing. There's going to be a void for some projects with your retirement. We can take a look at your client roster, take the ones we would be interested in continuing relationships with, and send them a mailer with our information as a suggested replacement for you. I mean, we are a brand new business, but the response has been really, really good. It certainly can't hurt to add…conservatively."

"Ever the constant businessman, Connor," Henry smiled.

"It does pay the bills," Connor offered as he sat back in his seat and propped his feet up to pay attention to his fishing line.

"There is something else, Dean," Henry said.

"OK…" Dean's eyebrows raised. Lord only knows what his father was cooking up.

"Our house. I think it's time for your mother and me to sell it."

"Wow, you're full of surprises today. You are all right, aren't you? You and Mom are healthy?" Dean asked.

"Oh yes, yes. Nothing like that. It's just time. It's a big house, a house to raise a family in. A house we raised a family in. Sometimes I feel like we raised two," he said as he patted Connor on the back.

"You certainly did," Connor agreed. "Liv and I have a lot of memories in that house."

"You sure you want to sell it, Dad?" Dean asked, feeling his stomach turn at the idea of his childhood home being turned over to strangers.

"Your mom and I need something smaller. Her knees aren't what they used to be, and me, well, I selfishly want to hop off the maintenance train and not have a mile-long list of things to do in my later years. I've worked hard. I kind of just want to sit and be a lazy bum for a while. I've never done that. We're looking at that little retirement neighborhood by the library."

"Oh, that's a nice place," Connor said, "Market value is strong there. And honestly, if you want to sell, now is the time to do it. Winter makes it very hard."

"Well, Mom and I wanted to see how you felt about it first, Dean," Henry said.

"It's your house, Dad. I'm not thrilled with the idea, but I understand. I am certainly not going to stand in your way. I agree, it's a great place for a kid to grow up."

"Or three." Connor smiled. "Remember that one time we wanted to see if we could actually climb out of the window using the sheets tied to the bed?"

"All the sheets, we had to use all the sheets. And we broke the bottom of the bed." Dean smiled.

"Oh good lord, I found you on your backside in Sophia's roses." Henry laughed.

"The thorns. Oh my God, did that hurt." Connor made a painful face as his hand touched his lower back at the memory of where most of those thorns had stabbed him.

"You had at least ten that we pulled out of your pasty white…"

"I remember, I remember." Connor held up his hands in defeat.

"That foot for the bed was the first thing I ever fixed," Dean said proudly.

"So you owe your entire career to my pasty white ass."

"You're going to wind up in that water, Reynolds." Dean shoved Connor playfully. "It's your house, Dad. We've got a lot of memories there, but selling the house isn't going to change that. You and mom do what you need to do."

"I appreciate that. Connor, I was going to ask Maggie to put it on the market for me. Do you still have your real estate license?"

"My fallback career…yes," he affirmed. "Mom was real insistent that I keep things up to date for at least the first couple of years, just in case. I can list it for you if you want."

"I would appreciate it. It's been so long since we've done this, I have no idea how to go about it."

"Well, we will get you a good deal on that house, and I'll make sure you get a good deal on whichever house you pick in the retirement neighborhood."

"Deal. Now, enough with this business talk," he smiled, "let's catch us some dinner."

Eighteen

Cat–

Greetings from NYC! I'm settled in back at home, and have had a chance to go through all these photos and pretty them up. I wanted to make sure you have the best pictures to represent the Inn, and now they are all red eye free. Flyaway hair free. Weird random fat guy staring at me a little too intensely as I take pictures of a duck swimming in a pond free. True story.

Anyway, I am sending you a disc with all the photos. Please excuse the first several dozen photos…I was just testing out the camera in all of the different lights and different settings. I wanted to make sure I knew the camera's little quirks. I mixed up the discs and I have the one with just the Inn photos and you will get the one with all the tester shots plus the Inn photos. No big deal, I don't need them back.

– Olivia

"Good morning, Carson," Cat greeted her concierge.

"Morning, Cat."

"All well this morning?" she asked.

"I think so. Mr. and Mrs. Abernathy called this morning to extend their stay to four days. They want to check out a bit of the town after seeing the brochures we put on the tables about local businesses."

"That's what I like to hear." She smiled as she continued on to her office. She popped into the kitchen and looked in the fridge for some yogurt. Locating the big container, she pulled it out, then got herself a small bowl.

"You want some fruit with that?" Maya asked her as she was getting things prepared for the breakfast buffet.

"What have we got?" Cat asked.

"Do you like blueberries? And peaches? Oh, and honey? And granola?" Maya asked, thinking up a yummy combination.

"I like all of those things. Do your magic," Cat smiled.

Maya gathered up all the supplies and grabbed a mason jar. She layered the yogurt and then the fruit, more yogurt, a little granola, honey, yogurt. She topped it with fruit and granola. Cat was impressed.

"That looks beautiful."

"Thank you," Maya smiled.

Cat took the jar and walked down the hallway. She took one bite and stopped in her tracks. She walked back into the kitchen.

"I don't recall seeing this on our menu."

"It's not, I just made it up for you." Maya smiled.

"Well, make one of these up for Rohan. See what he thinks. This is awesome." She winked at Maya, who was thrilled at the idea of something of hers being on the menu.

She continued into her office and turned on her computer. There was an organized pile of mail Carson had put on the desk for her. She could not have been more pleased with the staffing choices Mr. Archer had let her make over the last couple of years. The place was really starting to turn from an old tucked away Inn that got the occasional city slicker longing for a weekend in the country to a fun oasis for all kinds of people. And out of town guests still very much enjoyed the charm of country living. Response had been good on the wine tour she arranged with the local vineyards, as well as the other packages she had put together with some of the local businesses for adventure weekends and crafting weekends. Locals were starting to consider it a gathering place. Over the holidays, they opened their doors for the first time to the general public and not just guests who were staying with them. Everyone really enjoyed the visits with Santa and the snowman building competitions. Kids flocked to their first ever Easter egg hunt this past spring. Thousands of eggs—they had hidden literally thousands of plastic eggs. She remembered the lawn mowers having plastic egg parts in them for weeks afterward because not all had been found. She smiled at the suggestion somebody made of sticking little trackers in the eggs so they could be found. The adults even got in on the action, looking for one golden egg containing a free weekend stay gift certificate. The Fourth of July celebration was the biggest and most successful event to date. Cat knew this would be the linchpin for Mr. Archer. For the town businesses. It was everything she had been working toward and it worked. They had a full house the week leading up to the event, and half the town showed up on the day of. In the week since the event, they had seen a triple increase in bookings. She logged onto her e-mail account and saw the file Olivia had sent. She then looked through her mail, and sure enough, there was a manila envelope with her name on it. Overnight delivery, perfect timing. She opened it and slipped the disc into her computer.

The first several images were of a tree house she recognized from Dean's house. Images close up, on the inside. Small little table, small little chairs. The pictures invoked the feeling that children had been there, somewhere…shadows of the past. It was beautiful. She had several shots of what Cat assumed was a backyard, flowers, and trees. Butterflies on leaves. There were many of Rising Ridge as a town. Several pictures of life on Main Street. Cat came across one of Didier, sitting with his wife Lorraine on a bench in the middle of the park. They were surrounded by their grandchildren, and Lorraine's smile had been captured as Didier stole a kiss from his bride.

"Oh my God," Cat said out loud.

"Oh my God, what?" Rohan asked, as he happened to be walking in from the back of the building with some fresh vegetables he had picked from the garden that morning.

"These photos. Olivia sent me the photos I asked her to take. She sent me a whole bunch. I haven't seen any from the Inn just yet but she took some around town, and Rohan, come look at how sweet this is."

Rohan rounded the desk and pulled up one of the guest chairs to join Cat. They continued to look at Olivia's photos. Many of them were locations around town at different times of the day.

"She gave me the wrong disc. She was only testing out the camera with these shots, but look how sweet some of these are."

Images of Didier's vineyard came up, with sunset hitting an endless field of grapes. Wine barrels, inside and out. There were photos of a lake, kids running off a dock and jumping in.

"She's got an eye for things, that's for sure," Rohan said.

"This is what she needs to be doing. You should see the photos she has of New York. It could easily be a coffee table book. I've seen them at Connor's. Here they are," Cat said, as she was able to locate images of the Fourth of July happenings at the Inn.

"What do you think you're going to send in?" Rohan asked.

"They asked for no more than ten, and I will have to write up something to go along with it. I'm going to try to highlight the grounds, the gardens, and the peace you can get while you are here. I will hopefully find a gem in here that evokes a party all night feeling for those who want to come for the festivities. Of course, we will highlight the food." She smiled.

"She's got a few shots of actual dishes, too. She took some while I was cooking for her," he said as they continued to flip through the images.

"So you guys, are you a thing?" Cat asked.

"I like her, a lot. It was a terrible way to meet somebody, with her parents dying, but I am glad that I met her. We certainly enjoyed some time together while she was here."

"Mmm-hmm," Cat smirked. "Says the hot and spicy chef in the hot and spicy kitchen."

"Sorry about that." He smiled. "She called me when she got settled into her apartment. We've made no promises, but we both agreed that we will just see what happens. New York isn't that far away you know…once she gets back from Thailand and all."

"That's going to be amazing for her. I'm a little jealous."

"Well, I am sure she will have loads of pictures to share. Hey, can you make me a copy of this disc? I'd like to take a look at some of these at some point. You know, do a little research on Olivia." He smiled.

"Absolutely," Cat agreed. "In fact, you can have this one. I'm going to sit here and go through these and pick out the ones I want to work with, then I will leave this in your inbox."

"Works for me," He agreed.

"Great. Oh, hey, Maya made me this," she said, pointing to her three-quarters eaten yogurt. "It was excellent. I told her to talk to you about it going on the menu."

"What was it?" he asked.

"Yogurt with peaches and blueberries and honey and granola. It was the perfect filling, but not heavy, breakfast," Cat said.

"Good. Sounds good. I'll make sure she brings it up in conversation."

Nineteen

Connor–
Hey, Bubba! How goes the destruction of 3317?
Hopefully well. Just remember to get some sleep here and
there. I worry about you with everything happening at the
Inn...make time for sleep. I sent over the photos I took for
Cat; hopefully she will find something she likes and the Inn
will get the article.

Three weeks down, and one to go! I've already
packed...and unpacked. And packed...and unpacked. What
do I take? What do I not take? Do I drink the water?

I'm going to have a one night in Bangkok story...what
will it be? I hope you don't have to bail me out of a Thai jail!
Love you.

Connor pulled onto the curbside of his childhood home.
Most of the major demolition had already happened. The house

was traditional, with many rooms on the main floor. It had a formal living room, a bathroom, a formal dining room, a kitchen, and a family room. They had spent the last couple of weeks tearing down all the walls and leaving the main floor an open concept with arches and beams instead of walls. The beams would be stained a golden oak color, and eventually a darker wood floor would be put down throughout. The upper level would remain structurally untouched, but the hardwood floors would be put in and the three bathrooms would get overhauls. He planned on putting pocket doors between the Jack and Jill bathroom that he and Olivia had shared as children, and would be adding a rain shower to the master bathroom.

"Hey!" Elle yelled to him from her bike.

"Hi!" What are you doing?" he asked as she pulled up beside his car.

"Can't you tell? I'm going to go get doughnuts. I ride my bike to the shop to feel less guilty about it," she smiled.

"Nice outfit," he remarked.

"Well, they make this stuff with me in mind," she said, climbing off the bike and twirling around in her pink biking top with swirls of blue and gray and a white skull laughing into the air. "How's it going in there?"

"Do you have time to look?" he asked as he got out of his car.

"Of course! Yay!" She smiled. "It's going to be weird, I bet. What have you gotten done? Wait, wait…don't tell me, I want to be surprised."

Connor opened the unlocked door to what was now essentially a great room. The stairs to the second floor were just off the foyer. It opened to large archways that framed out a living room space directly in front of them. To the left of the foyer was a large kitchen with two walls of cabinets and a cut out for a large island. There was another set of archways that led into a small dining area looking out onto the backyard.

"Wow!" Elle said as she walked around the dust, drop cloths, and construction workers milling about.

"Mostly wall changes on this floor; changes the flow. It's a little hard to see now, but…" he began.

"I see it," she quickly interrupted him. "Oh Connor, this is going to be amazing."

"Dean and I are doing a lot of the work on this floor. The beams will be stained, and I'm going to order cabinets, but I may do something for the doors. Furniture…obviously. I will be keeping some basic things from my parents, but a lot of it will not come back into the house."

"What color are you going to stain? What will the floors be?" Elle asked.

"I think on the darker side for the floors. Not black, but on that darker side. The stain on the beams will be a golden oak finish."

"And what goes here?" she asked as she moved into the spot on the floor in the kitchen.

"An island. It will seat four across. And the stove goes here. I've got a big six burner coming," he said. "Figured if I'm going to do all of this, might as well make it family sized now."

Of course. Connor was always the planner. He probably would paint one room pink and one room blue upstairs for efficiency. Elle smiled at him and patted his face.

"What?" he asked.

"You're perfect. Don't ever change." She smiled and stepped away from him.

"Thanks, I guess? Well, it will be a work in progress for quite some time. I'll continue to live in a half-finished home."

"Are you going to do anything with that back wall?" she asked as she pointed to the wall that stood in front of the backyard.

"Wasn't planning on it, why?" he asked.

"Oh, you could do something fun! You could make the whole wall windows, or get a nice big patio with French doors opening out." She continued as she went over to the existing small window and pointed out, "And then you could expand the patio here and have a garden and just see it every day while you're having your morning coffee. Or open the doors and bring the outside in. That would be great!"

"Yes, I'll make it a big tree house," he smiled.

"Exactly," she said. "Livy called me yesterday. She's all packed and ready to go. I wish I was going with her. I feel like I could get into some fun trouble in Bangkok."

"You too? I'm going to have to stop construction and save my money to bail you two out of jail."

"As her older brother, it is your job. Oh, speaking of jobs, how's it going at the Inn?"

Connor never could keep up with the madness that must be the inside of Elle's head. She would leap wildly from one subject to another without anyone around her being the wiser. He stopped trying to connect the dots a long time ago, and just tried to keep up with her.

"It's going. Dean is up there most of the time now. I am dealing with this house. As it turns out, I'm our biggest customer at the moment. And then we have all the regular small and medium orders coming in."

"When will you be done here?" she asked.

"This was the major change. I am thinking another month and then it will be time to do some furniture buying."

"Ohh…what are you going to buy?" Elle perked up at the idea of buying things.

"Um…a couch, a coffee table, a bed. Things I need," he offered.

"Connor, you need to make this your home! It's not home unless it has the things you love in it. Don't just buy a couch, a coffee table, and a bed. You have to feel it, deep in your soul," she said, poking him in the chest with her finger.

"In my soul, huh?" he asked and his hand folded over hers. He had done it just to stop her from poking at him, but the instant that his hand touched hers and felt the warmth, he became all too aware how close they were standing, and the subtle scent of her. Her dark chestnut hair smelled like lilacs. Heat raced up his back and he cleared his throat. She looked at him as their hands connected and never wavered from his eye contact. She grinned at him, and if he didn't know better, he would swear it was the type of grin that said sweet, but screamed scandal.

"Yeah, right there," she lowered her voice. Her green eyes sparkled with gold flecks that were almost daring him to not let go of her hand. She was making no effort to pull away from him. How long had he been standing here with her, like this? A second, a year? He somehow was no longer sure of how time and space worked.

"Yeah, well, OK." He shook his head clear and abruptly let her hand go. "I'll let you know when I get to the furniture buying. Can't have me buying the wrong couch for my soul."

"Good idea," she said slowly. She waited just a heartbeat, and then took one step forward, putting herself squarely into his way too personal space. "A couch, a table, and a bed. You shouldn't sleep in the wrong bed, Connor."

She walked away, back to her bike parked on brick path that led from the sidewalk to the front door with quite the devilish grin. She didn't have to look back; she knew he was standing where she'd left him, watching her. *Did that just happen? Did Connor finally see me?* Oh, this is going to be fun.

Twenty

The drive to the Inn was the only quiet he seemed to get these days. In the seven months that Rising Ridge Designs had been open, business had been good. Slow and steady. Dean had already built quite a few pieces for his father's clients as a teenager, the odds and ends jobs that kept gas in his truck and money in his wallet for taking a girl out. As a result, they already had a regular client list to depend on when the doors opened. It was also a small town, and he had lived there his whole life. The week they opened, the mayor even had a ribbon cutting ceremony. "Home Town Pride Shines on Main Street," the headline in the local Gazette offered just two weeks after they opened. Everyone in town ordered something, even if it was as little as a key holder for the wall.

Dean had expected that, and was pleased that the town did come out to support them. He had never had a desire for living a bigger life. He had his one-bedroom apartment in the Victorian that served its purpose. It was small, but functional. He had a good, sturdy truck that he would have until it fell apart. He had friends, and there had been a handful of women over the years. Some of them on the more serious side, and a few that he just enjoyed a night or two out with. Why did he seem to be stuck on the one girl who never wanted to be part of this little world?

Looking back on it, it seemed like she'd been tangled in his life for as long as he could remember. In the furthest reaches of his memories were snapshots of a pink blanket bundled up in Maggie's arms, little hands wiggling and Olivia's newborn lungs screaming out to her mother. A four-year-old with pigtails sitting quietly and playing with a handful of Legos Connor had given her when he went over to Connor's house to play. A seven-year-old standing at the door of the tree house in complete defiance of the No Girls Allowed sign. The thirteen-year-old who was terrified of being left alone with her parents, clinging to Connor when he left for college.

And then it happened. He was just about to head back to college; the days of summer dwindling. He was in the yard, doing a few odd jobs for his mom before he headed back, and he saw her sitting there in the moonlight. She was small, but her legs seemed impossibly long in her shorts. Her silhouette reminded him that her frame had changed, there were soft curves that he wasn't sure were there the last time he'd seen her. Her clothes clung comfortably to the new frame. Her face was lovely; the baby fat gone and little sprinkle of freckles on her nose somehow highlighted her creamy soft skin. She looked so lost, sitting there. She looked like a picture.

She'd kissed him. Why did she kiss him? His initial reaction was to protect, from him, from herself…he wasn't sure. Both? He'd put his hand on her hip to push her away, but just for a second, he felt the curve of her in his hands. It felt different. Her lips were so soft, and the air filled with the gentle scent of the floral perfume she had been wearing. Just for a second, the person who stood before him was someone he was not familiar with at all. The soft moan that escaped her throat slammed him back into reality, hard. She was so young. She was his best friend's little sister. He was an adult. This could not happen. He did what he could; he stayed with her, and talked to her. About boys. About life. About everything. Anything she wanted to talk about.

She wanted to be free, even then.

Over the next two years, he saw her very regularly as he came home for the weekends to do laundry and then over all the holidays and summers. She was polite, and never once mentioned that night in the moonlight. He found himself looking at her differently from that point on. Were her legs always that long? Was her skin always that soft looking? Was her hair always that beautiful? Were her lips always that…God, he hated himself. Connor was his best friend, so his path crossed with Olivia's all the time, and he tried to be polite and kind, and way on the other side of the room from her.

As he turned his truck onto the drive that led up to the Inn, his mind filled with the memory of her on the night of her graduation party. He had seen her at various times throughout the evening, politely talking to people in her navy blue dress. Then, as he had taken out a trash bag for Connor's mother, he noticed movement in the tree house. When was the last time he saw Olivia? It had been quite some time. There she was, doing what she always did, crying at the injustice of the restraints put on her by her parents. As he laid down next to her, and heard her slow, steady breathing, his heart did nothing but pound. I should not be here. She shifted, and her body leaned against his. He found himself sighing and opening his arm up and around her, tucking her into his side. Her legs wrapped themselves around his. *I should really not be here.* Her steady rhythm of breathing slowed his, and soon his eyes closed for just a second and he was off to sleep. He had no idea how long he had been asleep, but before he even opened his eyes, he knew he had to get away from her. He tried so hard not to wake her.

Her body stirred, and held on tighter. The smell of her had become intoxicating, and feeling her warm body there in the darkness, soft and sweet, was too much for him. Within seconds, he had gone from being desperate for the air so he could breathe, to being desperate to hold her closer because he couldn't breathe without her. They made love. It was soft and gentle, and he was so careful to attend to whatever need she had. He knew it was her first time, and it was really important to him that no matter what his feelings were on the matter, he respected that. She chose him, and it was a gift. Why? Why was she doing this to him? He felt so torn between exploring this with her and the guilt he felt about it being this girl.

As she laid in his arms in the silence that came after, he trailed his fingers up and down her naked back. Sleep was no longer an option for him; his heart might have steadied, but his mind was flying through all of the possibilities at the same time. Would she stay? Would she go? Would she resent this one day? Resent him? What if she stayed, for him? His mind raced to ten years from now, with her sitting in the moonlight, that same look of lost desperation on her face that she'd had when she was fifteen. It killed him. She needed to go and be free in New York. She needed to find her path, all on her own. She needed to breathe the air she so desperately wanted. His life was here. He was helping with his dad's business, and he and Connor had just started talking about making a business out of all of these little side jobs. She had to go.

But he just couldn't breathe if he watched her go. Looking at her, sleeping sweetly in his arms, hopelessness filled him. If he stayed, she would be doomed. If he left, he would be. She'd hate him. What kind of person just leaves in the middle of the night? He sighed. He had to. He would rather the doomed one be himself than her. He could not be the one standing in her way.

He gently pulled himself away from her, tucked her in, and left her there. She was leaving, her bags were already packed. He went into his childhood bedroom, gathered all of his clean laundry, and packed to begin the trip back to the University of Maryland a few days early. And like an idiot, he found himself under a tree in the neighboring parking lot as he watched Olivia, with her suitcase, hugging her parents good-bye. Then hugging Connor and Elle good-bye. He watched her board the bus and take her window seat. He watched her face as she sat, looking out into the sky. She looked a little sad, but when she closed her eyes and took a deep breath in, he saw it. Freedom. Nothing was standing in her way; he was not standing in her way.

He called. He just wanted to make sure she was OK. She never answered. He never left any messages. He wasn't even sure if he had anything to say if she did answer. What was there to say? She was living her life, and he needed to let her do it. And that was his plan, until fate had intervened and he found himself in New York City at eight o'clock in the morning last month. It didn't matter what stood between them, his best friend needed him. His best friend's little sister needed him, too. So he did what he did, he sucked it up and went to get her.

She was pleasant, she was friendly. And just like the kiss that they shared on the eve of her sixteenth birthday, she was silent. The only mention was when she asked if it was going to be weird between them. No, he didn't need to do that to her. Her parents had just died. Good idea; let's just put this all behind us because this was not about us. But then she had hit him with that damned lamp, and his mind drifted from the reality of her standing in front of him in the bathroom and the memory of her standing in front of him in the moonlight in nearly the exact way. His memory thought of his hand raising up to hold her hip steady and keep her from coming closer to him, and the reality of his hand wrapped itself in that Nirvana shirt and pulled her closer. The memories of her lips mixed with the feeling he had as he kissed her in the quiet of the night. Last, but not least, that damned red dress. Seeing her in it, standing in the kitchen doorway of the Inn watching the fireworks with Rohan. Watching his hand rest comfortably around her waist. Watching him pull her in for a stolen kiss. Watching her disappear with him to God knows where…imagining him putting his hands all over her. Share a bed with her. It had made him sick enough that he had ended his evening with Ceilia early. Then, from out of nowhere, there she was. Standing in front of him in the rain. In that damned red dress. Something inside of him snapped, and he lost all control. He couldn't breathe with her around, and he couldn't breathe without her. He couldn't get enough of her, realizing that he had been starved for the last two years without her.

Alone; he woke up alone. This time it was she who left. This time it was her who didn't say good-bye. Back to the life that she had fought so hard for, the one where he was just a memory. Obviously, her life in New York was her real life…and she needed to get back to it.

He parked the truck and sat for second, gathering his frazzled nerves and cursing himself that with all this soul searching, just the memory of those nights with her had his body hard and aching.

"Life goes on," he said, bringing himself back down to reality to get on with his day.

Foo Fighters was streaming though the kitchen; the air smelled like pancakes and French toast. Maya stood at the counter chopping fresh fruit and tossing it together for a salad. Rohan heard the back doorbell ring, but ignored it as he flipped the pancakes and continued to sing along with Dave Grohl's voice.

"Rohan, can you grab the door? I've got a guest up here," Carson's voice came over the phone intercom.

"Always doing everybody else's job." He smiled at Maya and handed her the spatula, teasing her quality skills. "Flip when you see golden brown around the edges. You can do it, I have faith."

Maya took the spatula from him. She had hopes of becoming a second cook for the Inn, and had quite a bit of skill. Rohan usually let her run the show once a week, just to let her stretch her wings in running a kitchen staff. Being able to cook and being able to run a kitchen were two different things.

"I got this boss," she teased. "I'll try not to burn the place down."

Rohan washed his hands quickly and went to the back door. He was surprised to find Dean standing on the other side.

"Hey." He opened the door for Dean.

"Hi," Dean said firmly. "I've got Cat's chairs that she ordered for the porch, just need somebody to sign for them and let me know where she wants them."

"Was the door locked?" Rohan asked, confused at the fact that Dean rang the bell. "Did you actually ring the bell for delivery?"

"Looks like it," Dean offered coolly.

"I'll grab Cat. Come on in."

Rohan went into the kitchen and grabbed the walkie-talkie sitting on the table by the phone.

"Cat, we've got a delivery of chairs here. You want to come and have a look or do you want me just to sign for them?"

"I'll be right up; I'm down by the pond. I want to see them; five minutes," Cat's voice answered.

"Affirmative, Roger that. Ten four, over and out…" He smiled into the walkie-talkie.

"You're so weird," Cat's voice giggled.

Dean greeted Maya with a much friendlier tone, which Rohan did not miss.

"Hi, Dean," Maya smiled, and tucked her hair behind her ears the way young girls do when a cute boy smiles at them.

"Hey, Maya. How's it going?"

"Good. Want some pancakes? They're blueberry," she asked as she took some off the stove and plated them.

"Nah, I've eaten already this morning, but thank you."

"Want some coffee?" Rohan asked.

"No, thank you," Dean said politely.

Rohan crossed his arms over, resting his hands in his elbows, and leaned up against the entryway of the kitchen. Dean was definitely being weird.

"What's new?" he asked.

"Not much. You know how it is." Dean kept the conversation to a minimum.

"I hear Connor has his parents' house all torn to shreds."

"Some, not all. Most of the changes were just a few walls coming down on the main floor. Master bathroom got a big remodel. It's mostly done," Dean offered.

"That's cool. I'm sure Olivia will enjoy seeing that house become something. Maybe the house she always kind of wanted it to be."

Dean's jaw clenched and it took everything in him not to turn from where he was standing and push Rohan straight into the hot griddle. It was like getting punched in the gut. Rohan wasn't wrong; Olivia would really love seeing what that house could be in Connor's hands. However, the fact that Rohan got close enough to her for him to know that shot a bolt of heat up his spine. They were obviously still talking. She was contacting him from Thailand. Dean was trying to be a grown-up and remember that Olivia was not actually his. Rohan technically was doing nothing wrong. He was a good guy. Where is Cat?

"Chairs! Yay! Let me see, let me see!" Cat came around the corner, looking pretty casual in shorts and a tank top.

"In my truck. Sign here, and we can go see about setting them up," Dean offered and Cat signed the papers. "Right this way, see ya later Maya."

Rohan watched him offer Maya a genuine smile and then as the two men made eye contact, Dean's smile faded and he just nodded to him. Weird. He could think of no reason why Dean might have been mad about anything, so maybe he was just imagining it. He shook it off and turned his attention back to the pancakes and doing his best air guitar.

Twenty-one

Elle,

I wish you were here. This place is insane. INSANE. I love it. So far, I have seen the Grand Palace, took a Long Boat tour, and explored Chinatown. The palace is fun; everything is super gaudy and way over the top. The boat ride was crazy; he went so fast, I had images of the front of the boat cracking in half as it smacked into the river. There were other boats with trinkets for sale. I bought a small wooden elephant, pretty sure I paid twenty dollars for it. It might be worth three. Chinatown is exactly how it was in my mind. Rows and rows of stalls way too close together, with 200 smells and 5,000 different sounds. It was hot, sweaty, and busy. Next time you go to the store, pick something up and I bet it says, "Made in Thailand." It's all here…in Chinatown. Tomorrow I go to this place called the Jim Thompson house. He was an American who showed them how to export their silk, and now they worship the *ground he walks on. Or walked. Rumor has it he was eaten by a tiger in the jungle in the sixties. So I am going to his house and playing with seven hundred-year-old antiques that he just had laying around.*

More soon! Glad to hear your monster class ended well. Come up to NYC when I get back and we will hit the town to celebrate.

Has Connor died? He hasn't responded to any of my e-mails. I got one that said. "Stove coming today, I might take a nap in it." Check on him, make sure he eats.

—Liv

Elle smiled at her laptop. Olivia was doing it. She actually jumped. Elle could not have been more proud. Olivia wasn't the jumper, Elle was. Olivia was the observer of life. She had always been that way. It was interesting to watch her best friend piece this life together that she had wanted so desperately to live, but then just didn't. A whole life planned and not yet lived. Go live it, baby.

Elle wondered if Olivia knew how essential she was. In a town that she swore she didn't fit in, Olivia's absence was certainly marked. James and Maggie had thrown themselves into their business; it became all real estate all the time. She never saw them in town without it being when they were trying to buy a house, or sell a house, or were talking about buying and selling houses. Even when Connor and Dean opened the business, Maggie still somehow was able to turn the conversation around to what a great find the space was and what a great rate they got. Olivia always had a steadfast rule that there would be no business talk at family events, and with her not around to police it, business talk took over like the climbing ivy plastic plants Maggie loved putting in every empty corner of the house. They were everywhere she turned.

Dean had been hot and cold this last month. Looking back on the last two years, she would have never picked up on the fact that there had been an intimate relationship between him and Olivia. Elle had assumed that Olivia was active and had a couple of boyfriends over time that she spent her evenings with. It floored her when Olivia told her that not only did she sleep with Dean, but that he had been, to date, the only man she had slept with. Now that she knew, she watched him. She watched his reactions. She saw it. She would see him go still for just a beat and take a deep breath whenever anyone mentioned Olivia or how she was doing back in New York or on this trip to Thailand. She watched him do everything humanly possible to have as little contact with Rohan as a person could, which only meant one thing, he was jealous. Now why, if Olivia had thrown herself at Dean and he was as uninterested as Olivia insisted, would he be jealous? Elle would be taking it upon herself to investigate this.

Connor. Perfect, sweet Connor. What was she going to do with him? She had loved the boy with all of her heart since she was in first grade. She fell hard and fast for him, on that evening she had brought a sign to go over the door of the tree house. It was something that hung in her own room, a gift from her grandmother. It was explained to her, and even as little as she was, she understood that it was given to her for protecting her home. Olivia had made her feel like she was home when she was in the tree house. All of them had something there. Olivia had shelves with trinkets that she and Elle played with from time to time. Dean kept some random camping gear there, scissors, rope, and flashlights. And her practical man had kept something completely impractical there. She smiled at the memory of discovering an entire collection of Transformers and Thunder Cats action figures. Somewhere in Connor's eleven-year-old body was actually a child. He'd surprised her. It was time to test the waters. She'd searched her room for something. A crystal? Maybe. A voodoo doll? Perhaps. She looked up at the wood carving and just knew, that was it. That was what was going to make it home for her, too. She'd asked her dad to get it down, and she took it over. She handed it to Connor and he never even hesitated. He asked what it meant, told her that she was weird, and hung it up. No questions asked. He accepted her weirdness, and at seven years old, she knew he was the boy that she was going to marry.

She just had to wait for him to realize that. He had to come to her on his own path, by his own power. He had girlfriends, and though she had thought about putting curses on them, she didn't. She let him love, and she let him lose. She let him break hearts. She wanted him to be fully Connor. While she waited, she experienced love herself. What's a heart that hasn't been scarred a few times? She wanted to be ready for him, having fully experienced everything, so that she could give him anything he needed. Her mind wandered back to the moment they stood in the house that Connor now called home. When she felt the bolt of lightning through her body as his hand closed over hers. She curiously looked deep into his eyes, wondering what switches were being flipped in that mind of his.

"It's time," she said to herself.

She checked her reflection one more time in the mirror. Yes, she thought, this will do nicely. The girl in the mirror was not one she saw every day. Her chestnut hair was swept back sweetly in a loose ponytail. The pink sundress swept her knees and offered a simple neckline with capped sleeves. White strapped sandals gave her tiny five foot frame three more inches of height, and at the center of her collarbone was a simple silver chain with a small white circle. In it, tiny words read Do No Harm, but Take No Shit. Because at the end of the day, she's still Elle.

She pulled her Jetta into the driveway of the next-door neighbor, who had generously offered to let Connor have use of their driveway while the construction was going on and they were away for the last few weeks before school started again. She was sure to tuck the car as far back as she possibly could. She pulled out the three bags of groceries and headed over to his house. She knocked on the door and Caesar, who was overseeing everything, greeted her.

"Oh, hola Miss Elle. How are you today?" He smiled.

"Hi, Caesar! Good, good, everything is good," she offered and shoved a bag into his arms then walked the other two into the house.

"Boss isn't here, he's at his store," Caesar offered as he tried to keep up with her pace into the kitchen.

"I know," she smiled. "The kitchen is all working, right?"

"Yes. It's not done, but it all works," he answered her, with curiosity.

"Good. I'm going to make Connor dinner tonight here. Let's put this kitchen to the test. I'll stay out of your way."

"Oh-kay Miss Elle. We're almost done for the day anyway. We will be gone within the hour. Should I call boss and let him know you are here still?"

"No." She walked over, leaned up against his sweaty shirt, and whispered to him, "It's our little secret, OK?"

"Ahem," he said and took a step back. "Yes, ma'am. I…um…we…um…within the hour."

"Good boy, Caesar. Say hello to Mariela for me." She referred to his daughter, who was a friend of hers.

"Will do," he said as he quickly went anywhere that wasn't the kitchen.

Elle giggled to herself as she unloaded the groceries onto the plywood that would soon be a marble countertop on the island. She pulled out the silver casserole dish and looked at the note in Rohan's handwriting. She had called shortly after she got Olivia's e-mail and her mind had time to think up a good plan. She asked him if he could help plan her a menu. He offered to make chicken in raspberry sauce, which she could just heat up in the oven. He told her what vegetables to get at the store to toss into a salad, and she picked out her own dessert: strawberries, pineapple, marshmallows, and bananas, all to dip into chocolate fondue.

She had the chicken in the oven and used the time to set up a little place for them to eat. There was no furniture on the main floor; it had all been moved to storage. She took her shoes off and sat them out of the way by the front door, and looked all around for the perfect spot. She would love to set up a picnic out back, but the August heat was weighing heavy in the air. It was going to rain soon. So she set a picnic blanket down on the floor exactly in the spot where she would put a table, in the nook by the windows that looked out on the yard. She pulled out real dishes, real silverware, and real glasses from a cloth duffel bag. She lit candles, set them everywhere, and would be turning down the light in the kitchen once she finished chopping the salad and prepping the dessert.

Connor pulled up to the house at exactly six o'clock. The sun was setting, and after a very long day of playing catch up at the store, he was starving. He had stocked the refrigerator with good foods so that he would not have the excuse to hit a drive-thru on the way home. He had done far too much of that after he started the settlement process on the sale of his house and moved into what was no longer his childhood home, but his current home.

He noticed the kitchen light was on. Caesar and crew were done for the day; he would have to remind them to turn the lights off. Things were still sort of in a raw state and he didn't want to accidentally leave anything on if there was nobody there. He let himself in the front door and smelled something amazing. Food. He couldn't see the kitchen from the front door, but he saw a pair of white strappy sandals tucked sweetly in the corner. He followed suit and took his own shoes off and sat them next to the sandals.

"Hello?" he called out to the owner of the sandals. He obviously wasn't being robbed, and he didn't much care what was going on in the kitchen so long as whatever food he was smelling would be shared.

"Hi!" He heard Elle's voice. "I'm in the kitchen."

He rounded the post corner and she came into view. He was about to say something snarky about her being in the kitchen and him not being up to date on his fire insurance, but the second he saw her, he lost the ability to form words. Three vintage pot-lights hung low and illuminated the kitchen island. Elle was standing at the counter, her hair swept back in a ponytail and she was wearing…what was she wearing? A dress? A pink dress? He had never seen her wear anything pink before. All of a sudden, it was his new favorite color. She looked up at him and smiled sweetly.

"How was your day?" she asked.

"Long," he offered. "What in the world are you doing?"

"Making sure that you eat." She smiled at him. "I'm making you dinner."

What words could he say? He found none. It was a sweet gesture; she was a good friend indeed. But his heart could not get past the scene of it all. Coming home, tucking his shoes in next to hers by the front door, finding her in the kitchen happily cooking away with Celtic music quietly sweeping sounds from the radio the crew used for music. Only Elle. She was wearing a pink dress. He died. He must have. He knew he must be laying in the stock room of his store under a heavy box that had crushed him…and this was all some fantasy he was playing out while he waited to go toward the light. He rubbed his chest where the imaginary box was, reminded himself to breathe.

"This is amazing." He smiled and joined her. "You cooked? And my house is still standing."

"Caesar told me where the fire extinguisher is," she quipped as she finished up the salad. "I reheated. Rohan cooked. But I did make the salad all by myself!"

"I'm speechless, Elle."

"Sit." She pointed at the picnic blanket that was set up on the floor with two place settings perfectly arranged. A small vase of flowers was at the center, flowers he recognized from his mother's garden. From his garden.

"Where did you get the dishes? I've been using paper plates, everything is still in storage."

"I borrowed them from my house. We've got salad, made by me. We've got raspberry chicken, made by Rohan, and fresh green beans and carrots that I steamed myself."

"I'm proud of you." He smiled. "You are incredibly sweet, and this is exactly what a day like today needs."

"Good," she smiled.

They sat and ate, talking about his day at work and the work up at the Inn. She rambled on about hearing from Olivia and they compared notes about the e-mails they had each received, wondering what adventures she was off on now. Elle very excitedly set up the fondue pot and put out all the treats to dip. Connor picked up a slice of pineapple and smiled at it.

"Pineapple, huh?"

"I am never going to live that cake down, am I?" Elle asked as she rolled her eyes at the memory of the pineapple upside-down cake she'd excitedly made for everyone the first time she cooked as a young teen…in a broken pot lid that she mistook for a "pineapple upside-down cake pan."

"Not in my lifetime, no." He winked devilishly at her.

They finished dessert, blew out the candles, and started to clean up. They continued to enjoy their easy conversation as he offered to wash the dishes and she dried them as she sat on the kitchen island listening to him chatter on about work plans. As she finished up the last dish, he moved over, lifted her up off the counter, and slowly put her back on her feet.

"I have to say, you were quite the sight when I came home. Coming home from work, the smell of this good dinner with this amazing salad, and you look…you look beautiful in pink."

"Thank you," she smiled.

"You know what I like best, though?" he asked.

"What?" She met his gaze as he slowly laced his fingers under her silver chain. His fingers traced down her collarbone, teasing her skin, and he lifted the small white circle.

"This. You're so weird." He smiled.

She just couldn't stand it anymore. This man could not be more perfect if he tried. She wrapped her arms around his neck and pulled him down to meet his lips with her own. She threw everything into it that she'd been saving up all the years she had waited for him. She wasn't in a hurry, it wasn't furious, but it was deep. It stretched into her soul, and she fed into his. For the first several seconds, Connor was shocked at the turn of events. She was suddenly in his arms, her scent filling the air. Her lips were on his. Elle's lips. Soft, yet fierce…her lips. *What's happening?* He wrapped his arm around her, lifted her off the floor, and sat her back on the kitchen island.

"Um, Elle…you just kissed me. We don't…this is weird." His lips parted from hers and he rested his head on hers to catch his breath.

"No, no, it's not." She smiled. "We've needed to do this for a very long time."

"We have?" he asked, forcing himself to put some space between them. "Elle, this is…"

"What we need Connor. This is what we need," she finished his sentence for him.

In that moment, he looked at her sitting there. She was beautiful. He felt the tug inside, the one that told him he loved everything about this girl. He'd be a fool to stand in the way of whatever path she was currently on. She smiled at him, laid her hand gently on his shirt, and gathered it, pulling him just slightly toward her. Your move. He could see it written all over her face. Could he do this? With her? This was Elle.

This was Elle.

This. Was. Elle.

He shook his head and smiled. He returned to her, his lips tasting her neck and shoulders. She wrapped her legs around him and he picked her up and walked up the unfinished steps to the master bedroom.

"I took your advice," he said.

"Oh?" she asked as he laid her on top of the brand new navy blue duvet on his brand new bed.

"I got a new bed. I hear it's really important that you sleep in the right bed," he said as his hands worked their way up her dress and his mouth worked its way down her neckline.

"Oh, yes. That is true. I did hear that somewhere," she said.

In the quiet of the night, as they lay together completely naked and spent from discovering every inch of each other, Elle trailed her finger over his chest where his heart was beating.

"Can I ask you a question?" he whispered.

"Sure." She smiled as she stretched out her body next to his in a liquid happiness.

"Why me? Why now?" he asked. "I mean, I don't have a fast car. I don't have tattoos or a criminal record. I'm not your usual fare, Elle."

"Because you're perfect. You're the most perfect guy I know, and I love it. I love that you wear a tie to work even when you don't have to. I love that even in the midst of you moving from one construction site to another, your bed was still made when we got up here. I love that you know how to do things, not just with your hands but with your brain. I love your brain, it's so damn sexy."

"You are very weird." He smiled.

"And that. I love that. I'm weird. I don't just march to the beat of my own drum, I dance on my drum. I stomp on it. And you've always been there…to smile and laugh at me, but you've never tried to change me. I wear the pink dress tonight, and you mention you love my necklace."

"It's you," he offered her honestly.

"And it's you. It's always been you who saw that. You like my weird."

"I love your weird." He smiled as he gathered her up and rolled her above him so he could sit up and hold her in his arms. He brushed back her hair that had long since been set loose from her hair tie and nuzzled his mouth into her neck under her chin. "And this part right here, I think it's my favorite."

Twenty-two

Rohan,

Sawadee-kha! Check me out, saying hello in Thai. I can say that and kop-khun-kha, which means thank you. Everyone here is super nice, and most of them speak at least a little English (at least in Bangkok) and are happy to practice their English skills.

Guess what?! I rode on an elephant! Me! They have these benches, kind of like saddles, I guess. It's insane how you have to keep yourself balanced because you go side to side with their walking, it's a little workout. But we walked, or she walked...her name was Daisy. Daisy walked through this ancient city. It was a spectacular experience.

The city is called Ayutthaya, it was the capital until it burned down over the course of several wars. The people leave it standing so that their descendants can see what happened...so they don't ever forget. It's sad and beautiful all at the same time. I could spend a week just here, climbing in and out of burned down wats (temples). There is this sandstone Buddha here, with a tree that has grown around it. I was so excited to see this because it was one of the bigger check boxes on my list of things to see in person. I have taken 987,459,767 pictures...at least. I ate this food called Roti, it was all sorts of bad for me but supper yummy. Look it up the recipe; try it! I'm sure you could do amazing things with it.

I jumped. Thank you for encouraging me to. I still can't believe I'm here.
—Olivia

Rohan sat at his desk and smiled at his laptop. He could feel her happiness through the message. He was glad she was having a good time, and flattered that she felt like he encouraged her. She was a sweet girl; beautiful, too. He had enjoyed getting to know her. He got up, walked through his loft apartment, and picked up the disc off the old steamer trunk that served as a coffee table in front of his leather sofa. He slid it into the laptop and thumbnail shots of Olivia's photos filled his screen.

"Let's see what you see, Olivia."

He saw the pictures he had seen with Cat, of the tree house. He had never seen it in person, but he could just imagine the child versions of these adult he knew spending endless summers in the yard, in that house. He smiled once again at the lovely afternoon she had caught happening with the winemaker, Didier, with his wife and grandchildren.

The next image to fill his screen was breathtaking. The sun was set low, and the space filled with golden light. An older man he recognized from the recent job at the Inn, Henry, was there. Henry was standing next to Dean, and they were smiling. Obviously chatting with each other as their lines were cast, fishing in one of the nearby stocked ponds. It made Rohan miss his dad, and he made note to call him.

Another shot, on an early morning perhaps. A black truck, Dean's black truck, parked under a tree facing a farm's midsummer filed of crops. The next made him laugh; Elle's face caught upside down and between her own legs as she was practicing yoga in the downward dog position. She was sticking her tongue out and crossing her eyes at the camera. Another beautiful shot, one with the camera lady unexpectedly in front of the camera. Her back was to the camera, but he recognized her. She was sitting on a bench swing in a garden, a man at her side. Connor. Her head was on his shoulder and his head was resting on hers. They were watching the sunrise.

There were several from the Inn; she had really covered every square inch of the place for Cat to choose from. He saw each of the eight rooms they offered, including the one that was rumored to be haunted. The Inn rented that room out from time to time to excited tourists or brave locals who were usually in their twenties and had come up specifically for that reason. He knew the history of the house; it had been the home of General George O. Archer before the Civil War. George was married to Sandra, and had several children. George also had an affair with their nursemaid, who found herself pregnant with his child. Sadly, the maid lost the child, but stayed in the home to raise the remainder of the Archer children. This room was the baby suite, and the legend goes that in the quiet of the night you can hear her singing softly, a lullaby for the child lost, as she rocked the children who lived. Rohan himself had never clearly heard singing, but there were far too many nights where, when he passed the room, he felt that odd tingling that starts at the base of your spine and travels up the back of your neck. Cat told him once that Elle had been up there before. Just checking out the vibe. She said it was just sad. The room gave her a sad feeling, and made her want to hug somebody who wasn't exactly there.

He found Dean again in the pictures, sanding what looked like the chairs he had recently delivered to the Inn. The angle was focused more on him, giving the viewer the idea that the picture was more about the power of the man than it was about what he was doing. Another of Dean, looking at the camera with a smirk on his face. Rohan can only imagine what Olivia said to him to cause him to have that "Yes, dear" look on his face.

With Dean's recent chilled demeanor, and the realization that a lot of these photos had Dean in them, little bells started going off in his head. There was unfinished, or at least unspoken, business between Dean Winston and Olivia Reynolds. He wondered if the two of them knew it.

As he flipped through the photos of their Fourth of July event, he found several of himself. Cooking, preparing, and singing to his staff. Happiness, she had captured the happiness of the day. He picked up his phone and punched in the number of a friend he had made through his mother's contacts years ago.

"Santiago. Hey, it's Rohan. Good man, I'm good. Yeah, still in middle of nowhere. How you doing? Good. Listen, we need to have a beer and catch up. I've got something here I want you to look at. Want to see if you see what I do. Great. There's a pub, you know, that Irish one. It's kind of half way between you and me. Can you meet tomorrow for breakfast?"

The ride out of town was quiet; it was early for a Saturday morning. Rohan had packed up his laptop into the sidesaddle of his motorcycle and was enjoying the solitude. Since the construction of new pavilions and gazebos were in full swing and set to be done inside of the month, he was even hearing drills and hammering in his sleep.

He pulled into the parking lot of the little Irish pub. It was an old, large cobblestone building that had hardwood floors and fireplaces so large, you could easily walk into them. Each room was painted a different jewel tone color, and there was a good mix of touristy Irish décor and actual, real Celtic history. He knew the chef as a child, a friend of his father's. Patrick had been the one, in fact, who had put Rohan in contact with Archer's Inn.

He spotted just the guy he was looking for. A man with a golden skin tone and jet-black hair sat with a pint of beer even though it was nine in the morning. His faded brown leather jacket was tossed casually on the chair next to him. His dark hair was spiked up, and his beard suggested he hadn't shaved in about two weeks. He was smiling, turning on that Spanish charm of his with his deep brown eyes for the cute waitress who was talking to him.

"Hi, honey, so sorry I'm late." Rohan smiled and winked at him as he slid into the chair across from Santiago.

"Oh!" The waitress's eyebrows popped up, putting together the lover connection. "Hi. I'm sorry. Can I get you anything to drink?"

"OJ, sweetheart, thank you." He smiled innocently.

"What did I ever do to you?" Santiago shook his head as the waitress scooted off in a hurry.

"I just couldn't help it," Rohan laughed. "You needed to be taken down a notch with your whole Latin lover act you've got going on."

"Natural born talent my friend," he said in his thicker than normal rolling Spanish accent. "I use only what God gave me. It's good to see you."

"You, too. Sorry it's been so long. I guess settling into this little life I've got going in the middle of nowhere has been keeping me busy," Rohan told him.

"You look happy, that's good."

"Yeah, it's good. I've got a loft apartment. It used to be a slaughterhouse for the local meat market."

"Really? Weird. Got any mad cow ghosts?" Santiago asked.

"No." Rohan smiled. "But I do have a really big window that is an old clock on the top of the building."

"Of course you do. I'm not the only one who uses his God-given talents." He smiled as the waitress came back to take their order. "Hi, Grace. I'll take the pancakes. This jackass will take the bacon and eggs."

She looked over to Rohan for approval, unsure if she had interrupted a lover's quarrel or not. He saw the puzzled wonderment all over her face and let out a hearty laugh.

"Sadly, my love is unrequited," he said dramatically and held his hands out to Santiago. "This man's heart belongs to the yet to be determined lovely lady."

"Oh." She could not help but blush. "I'll um…get that order right away for you."

As she walked away, Santiago took a second to appreciate the way her jeans hugged her ass.

"I'm sure those jeans will be on your bedroom floor by tomorrow morning, don't worry," Rohan assured him, as he could not help but appreciate the view himself.

"Maybe." Santiago smiled. "I wouldn't mind that. What did you want to show me?"

"Oh," Rohan said as he pulled the laptop out of the bag he was carrying and turned it on. "I have a…friend. My boss Cat asked her to take some pictures to submit to this travel magazine in hopes we could get a feature article on the Inn. She took a whole bunch of pictures, not just of the Inn, but of the whole town. I think they are good. I want to know what you think, since this is your area."

"A friend?" Santiago smiled and said as he turned the laptop to focus on the pictures.

"A friend. There might be something there, but I don't know. She is the lost kind. Not sure what she's looking for. Not sure where she's going yet," Rohan insisted.

"Sometimes those are the best kind of girl," Santiago said smugly and turned his professional eye onto the pictures. "These are good. She certainly has the eye. These pictures convey a feeling, which is what you want. I think your boss lady is going to have a good chance with these."

"I think so, too. But I think these could be something. Like a book. Small town, USA kind of thing. I think she needs to see it. A book, in her hands. I think she needs to see it to believe she's capable of it."

"Oh. Yeah man, I can do that. I mean, you'd have to get permission from all of these places and of course, the rights to the pictures and…"

"Maybe just something that you can throw together, a rough draft? Something I can just put in her hands?" Rohan asked.

"Oh. I can do that. I can get something together and send it to you. This must be some girl."

"She's special. I want to help her if I can," Rohan said honestly.

"Can I get you boys anything else?" Grace asked as she came by to check on them after she had served them their food.

"Can you tell the cook back there that this bacon is dry?" Rohan smiled and handed her his plate of half-eaten bacon.

"Oh, I'm sorry. I can get you more," she quickly offered.

"It's not your fault, sweetheart. Just a little dry, that's all," he informed her.

"Sure. I'll be right back with another plate," she said as she took the plate and walked quickly back to the kitchen.

"What are you doing? That bacon was good, brother." Santiago said with his dark eyebrow raised.

"It was perfect, which is why I know it's Patrick's. I just want to say hi before I go." Rohan winked at him.

"I'm never going to be able to show my face here again when you're done," Santiago said as he took the last sip of his beer. "I always liked this place."

As if on cue, a tall man with slightly whitening red hair walked out of the kitchen door. In his hand was the same plate of bacon that Grace had walked back with. Grace chose to hang back by the kitchen door as she watched the cook walk toward the two men.

"I'm sorry, sir, but I have to disa…" He stopped mid-word when he saw Rohan smiling ridiculously at him. "Well, son of a bitch! Rohan Kingston, long time no see, boy."

"How you doing Patrick?" he asked as he rose to shake hands and hug Patrick, which instantly put Grace at ease by the kitchen door. When she had gone to get a second plate of bacon, Patrick had slammed his butcher knife into the counter and swiped the plate out of her hand. As he marched into the dining room, she prayed he would keep a rein on his Irish temper.

"There is nothing wrong with this bacon, boy. Did you burn off all your taste buds?" Patrick put the plate down on the table and took a piece of it himself to enjoy.

"Just wanted to say hi, man. Not a soul could make bacon better than this," Rohan agreed as he sat back down and took a piece.

"Are you passing through? How are things up at the Inn?" Patrick asked as he joined them.

"Things are good. Meeting my friend Santiago here. Making use of his photographer's eye for a project," Rohan said as he introduced Santiago.

"Hello. I love the food here, just so you know." Santiago shook Patrick's hand and winked at Grace. "And the service."

"Grace. She's a sweet girl…and staying that way," Patrick gave Santiago a warning grin and returned his attention to Rohan. "Archer treating you good?"

"Yeah, really good. He's still got a strong hand on everything but is looking to retire soon, so he's letting Cat handle things. I think she's doing a good job. She's easy to work with," Rohan said.

"From what I remember, she's easy on the eyes, too. All legs and blonde hair." Patrick smiled.

"And married. She's married. Her husband is equally as tall. They're Ken and Barbie. Or more like, GI Joe and Barbie. He's in the Marines. Good guy."

"Glad it's working out for you, then. I'm sure your pop is happy to hear it."

"That he is. Mom too."

"Give them my best next time you talk to them. It was good to see you. Next time, I'll come to your place and complain about your food."

"Can't. I learned from the best, and had the hardest critic in town on me to make it better." Rohan smiled.

"That is the truth. Oh, your mother. This bacon…she sent it back to me four times before I got it right."

"And now it's perfect," Rohan offered as he ate the last piece.

"It is boy. She's a helluva woman." Patrick agreed.

Twenty-three

Cat—

So glad you liked the pictures. You've done such a good job with the Inn, they would be crazy not to feature it in the magazine. I can't believe that my pictures are sitting somewhere on the desk of some magazine reporter. That's a whole separate kind of excitement. Keep me posted! I've had the best time here. Tonight, I am checking out the nightlife. I can't leave Thailand without my "one night in Bangkok."

God, do not tell Connor I said that if you see him. I hear things are really shaping up there with the new outdoor additions. Awesomeness. If you get word that you got the article, we shall party!

—Olivia

Cat pulled up to the Inn's gate and just sat there. She looked up the line of cherry trees leading to the large red brick house. It wasn't hers, but she was so proud of it. She and the entire staff had worked incredibly hard to make the transition from simple B&B to a place tourists seek out and locals want to escape to.

As she drove up and parked her car, she picked up the singular sheet of paper and looked at it one more time. Mr. Archer had invited her out to dinner the evening before, and she was a ball of nerves as she sat wondering if his news was good or bad. He smiled at her, his handsome face with the perfect outdoorsman's beard, and ordered champagne. It was good news.

> *"Dear Mr. Archer,*
>
> *We are pleased to inform you that your Inn has been selected as our feature Inn for the fall issue of Wanderlust Magazine. As agreed in the terms of your application, one of our staff reporters will visit your Inn at the end of August to chat with you about your fall activities and events. If they are anything like your Fourth of July activities, I am sure our readers will love discovering the magic you seem to capture in your small town.*
>
> *We look forward to working with you. Please contact us at any time if you have any questions."*

"Good morning, Maya," Cat smiled as she came into the Inn through the back door. "I need to call a quick all hands on deck. Are you set for the breakfast run?"

"Yes, ma'am. All is quiet for the next hour, so it's a good time to do it," Maya said as she took off her apron and hung it up.

Cat called out to everyone over the radio system, and within the half hour, every person who worked at the Inn was gathered in one of their conference rooms. Since it was an unscheduled meeting, several of the staffers were whispering about why the meeting was called.

"Thank you, everyone for dropping what you are doing. Especially Dean," she said, looking over to him. "I'm glad you actually happened to be here, since this might affect your schedule, too. Mr. Archer informed me last night that we were picked to be the feature Inn in Wanderlust Magazine."

Her speech was interrupted by whoops, yays, high fives, and congratulations. Hugs were given, and everyone settled back in to listen.

"I'm so excited, and incredibly proud of the work that we did over this Fourth of July. I believe it was the event that pushed us into the win. I knew it was a possibility, and Mr. Archer and I went into it thinking ahead so that if this happened we would not have to scramble. There will be a reporter here on Monday. We have them scheduled to stay with us for at least a few days; we'd blocked out the week in hopes we would need to use it. So that means we have less than a week to get this place in the best shape of its life. I want everyone to work as many hours as they can. Archer has given me free range for hours and pay. We've already put together a list of things that need to be fixed, updated, painted, planted, rotated, and spiffed up. Because we're awesome, it's not a huge list, but it is a formidable one. Carson and I will have the master list, so if you are not doing something, come find one of us and we will give you something to do. Now go, my busy bees! Make your queen proud!" She smiled at everyone.

"What's that leave me as far as time?" Dean asked as everyone filed out, excitingly chatting about the news.

"Can you be done and out by Monday? Is that impossible?" Cat smiled at him, batting her green eyes animatedly.

"Um…" He paused. "I'd have to hire out another crew. If we can do that, I can get it done. But I have to pay them. I mean you have to pay them."

"That's fine. Archer kind of figured that and said if you could get it done, he will pay. Business is good, and we want to keep it that way," Cat agreed.

"Then we can get it done." Dean smiled at her.

"Oh, thank you!" Cat hugged him. Her tall six foot frame always offered him a chance to hug a person without having to dip way down. He loved that about her.

"You're welcome. I'm happy you guys got picked," Dean offered.

"I am sure it was all Livy. That girl is magic with a camera. She took some beautiful pictures. I had a hard time picking the few to represent us."

"Yeah, I guess it sometimes pays off to have always been an observer of life," He said honestly.

"Well, she's living it now. I cannot wait to see what she comes home from Thailand with. I mean, her e-mails are so fun! Everything she describes sounds amazing. Don't you think?" Cat asked.

"I…I'm sure she's having that trip of a lifetime," he said. No e-mails sent. No e-mails received, either. Seems Olivia was keeping up with everyone—except him. "I've got to get to work if we want this thing done."

Dean walked out of the back door of the Inn and over to check on the work on the gazebos. He knew he wouldn't have a problem doubling up on the crew and getting the work complete. They were almost done, and this was good business for their still budding company. Even if he and Connor had to get shovels and work all night themselves, the work would be done.

As he checked though his own personal list of things to do and got into his truck to head back to the shop to check in with Connor and let him know of this latest development, his mind wandered to the night of the Fourth of July party. The silence that came afterward made it seem like a million years ago, yet when he closed his eyes, he could still smell her light floral scent as though she had just left his arms. She was living her life, and he wasn't standing in her way. He knew it was the right thing to do, but he had moments where he thought it just wasn't fair. For as long as he could remember, he was doomed to have this imperfect timing when it came to her. He nearly growled at the radio as Dave Matthews's voice filled the truck signing about wearing nothing so well. It was bad enough that she was haunting his sleep, now it seemed she was starting to haunt his waking hours as well.

He pulled into a spot about a block from his shop on Main Street; he didn't want to take up any spots for local customers. Connor had been oddly quiet the last couple of days, he guessed things were going well. They were passing ships in the night; notes scribbled to each other on a pad of paper by the register had been their only communication for the last several days. They needed to go get a beer. He needed to check in on how much work Connor had done to the house. He knew the main floor was near completion.

As he started to open the door of the store, he caught the shadow of movement in the back room. Connor was very clearly kissing somebody. He stopped, backed up on the sidewalk, and turned around. Who was that? Connor hasn't been seeing anybody. At least, he didn't think Connor had been seeing anyone. Clearly, the notes on the little yellow pad had not been doing this week justice.

The ring of the bell that chimed when their store door opened jingled, and the woman walking out of the door made his jaw just about hit the ground.

"Hey, Dean," Elle gave him a wicked and very sinful smile.

"Elle?" He seemed to be able to only form the one word.

"Yes?" she challenged him, smiling and wondering what he saw. She knew he saw something; the shocked look on his face when she came out of the store was enough of an admission of that.

"Um." Clearly, all his words were gone. "Um…hi."

"Good boy, Dean. It's good to stick to one syllable words when you're in shock. You'll be fine."

She started to walk away, but then turned back to him.

"Have you heard much from Livy?" she asked.

"You haven't heard from her?" Dean asked, surprised.

"Oh, no," she smiled, "I've heard from her. I was just wondering if you had heard from her."

"I…" He wasn't sure where Elle was going with this, or what in the hell was happening. "I haven't really checked my e-mail lately," he lied. He had checked it every day since she had been gone. Sometimes he checked several times in a day.

"Hmm…interesting." She smiled. "See you around."

Dean watched her walk down the street in her white shorts, black sandals, and black top that he was pretty sure said Witches be Trippin'. He slowly opened the door and stared at Connor, who was leaning up against the doorjamb of the back room watching the small exchange between the two on the sidewalk.

"Hey, man," Connor smoothly offered.

"What the fuck ever, Reynolds?! What was that?" Dean asked.

Connor smiled and looked at his feet, thinking of the last few stolen moments with Elle.

"You might have been right, about Elle," he offered.

"When did that happen?" Dean asked.

"Yesterday. A year ago. I don't know." Connor leaned up against the counter. "I found her cooking in my house last night."

"Cooking? As in, she turned on the stove?" Dean asked.

"Yeah, sort of. Rohan supplied us with a meal. A really good one, actually. All she had to do was heat it up. But I get home, walk in the door, and smell dinner. And then I see her there, in a pink dress, chopping up vegetables."

"Are you…did you hit your head? Elle, that Elle, was wearing a pink dress?" Dean asked, incredulous.

"A pink dress. And I just got swept up in it all. She looked so damn…I don't know what. And then I complimented her on her necklace and she jumped me." Connor smiled at the evening playing out again in his mind.

"OK, now that sounds like Elle." Dean smiled. "So, did you…"

"Yeah. A few times. You would think this would weird me out, but it just feels right. As soon as she kissed me, I felt like exactly where she belongs is in my arms. Oh, God. Did I just say that? Out loud?" Connor put his head down on the counter.

"It's OK, brother." Dean gave him a hearty pat on the back. "I'm happy for you. You've been looking at her differently for a while now. I am glad to see that she seems to be on board with that idea. I wouldn't have pegged you for her type."

"Me either. I swear, I'm going to need to get a tattoo or something." He sighed. "I don't even know where to begin with telling Livy."

"You don't think she'll be happy for you?" Dean asked.

"I don't know…I mean, I…crap. She might kill me."

"It will be fine. Why don't you just let Elle handle this one?" Dean suggested.

"Maybe," Connor said. "So, work stuff, let's talk about work stuff."

"Um, Cat told me this morning that they got the magazine spot," Dean offered. "I came in because we need to sit down together and look at the next few weeks."

"They did? Oh, that's great! Livy's going to be so excited," Connor said as he got out the calendar they kept for jobs so they could go over everything together.

"Yup. Somebody's coming out Monday. Which means we need to double up on the crew and pound this thing out."

"Can we do that?" Connor asked, all of a sudden very concerned looking at their already hectic schedule.

"We can if we hire a second crew. That's no problem," Dean answered.

"Ummm…" Connor started to do the calculations.

"Archer's paying. I made that clear. We will be adding to the estimate," Dean said.

"Good. Well, that's awesome. Let's get to it then," Connor said. "Let's go over everything else too while you're here."

"And then we grab a beer. It's been a long week. And I clearly need to see what my best friend has been up to. He's gone off and fallen in love." Dean smiled.

"Yeah. A beer sounds good."

Twenty-four

Connor, Elle–
They picked the Inn! I'm sure you already know, but I got an e-mail from Cat. They also asked if they could use my pictures! Mine! I can't believe it. I have to sign a release form; isn't that amazing?!?! I think I might make a copy of it and frame it.

I am all packed up and headed home. This trip has been amazing. I will call you when I am wheels down and have a shower and some food. The flight is long, I am not looking forward to it.

Love you guys, hope you're staying out of trouble.
–Liv

The entire Inn was on staff Monday morning. Every person was called in, and told to dress to impress. Cat wanted to give this reporter Archer's Inn at its best. Even Mr. Archer showed up, looking very handsome in his brand spanking new jeans, flannel shirt, and trimmed beard. He looked like he could have covered the front page of the most prestigious hunting magazine, which was the exact look he was going for.

Between them, everything had been checked, double checked, and rechecked. Rohan had the kitchen fully stocked with everything they had ever offered on the menu, and he had Maya trying out some new dishes to impress. If anything, this reporter was going to eat like a king. This was also a good opportunity to get his own name out there into the food world. As a young, budding chef, he ran through every door that opened for him.

"She's here!" Cat ran from her office and stopped in the kitchen.

"Who's here?" Rohan asked.

"Wanderlust. The reporter. She's here," Cat said as she smoothed out her slim pencil skirt "How do I look?"

"Like Professional Barbie," Maya smiled.

"Perfect!" Cat winked. "OK…be cool. I'll bring her back. Just be doing your whole 'I'm Rohan and I'm awesome' thing."

"It's a full-time job." He cocked a sexy smile at her.

"That's my boy," she said and scurried out of the kitchen.

The woman standing in the lobby looked like she walked right out of Hollywood. She was tall and trim, wearing a short white dress that framed her slim curves. She was wearing big black sunglasses and carried only one small weekender bag.

"Hello. Welcome to Archer's Inn," Cat came into the lobby and extended her hand. "I'm Cat. You must be…"

"Anna." Anna smiled at her. "Anna Dupond. Thank you for having me."

"We are very excited. I will call up Mr. Archer to come say hello and we can get you settled into a room."

"That would be lovely, it was a bit of a long way round the bend to get here." Anna smiled.

"Where are you coming from?" Cat asked.

"California. I travel all the time of course, and have been slowly making my way east over the last month. This is my last stop, and then back to my own bed in L.A. for a good long time."

"Of course you're from L.A." Cat smiled. "I love that dress."

"Thank you."

Anna settled into her room and looked in the mirror. Of course, you're from L.A. The words resonated in her mind. That was the point, wasn't it? She had worked hard; long hours. She had sorted mail, made coffee, and run errands at four o'clock in the morning. All so she could be an L.A. sort of girl. The writer everyone at the places she evaluated were falling over backward for; her name on the byline in the glossy magazine.

She went into her private adjoining bathroom, a luxury not all the suites had. They had given her their best room, naturally. She spotted the large heart-shaped Jacuzzi bath and sighed. There would be time for this, no matter what. She wiped her face clean of makeup and pinned her hair back in a cute bun. She reapplied makeup, and headed back out to the lobby. The tub would have to wait.

"OK, L.A. girl…it's show time," she said to herself in the mirror.

She found Cat and Mr. Archer waiting for her, and greeted them with her face at least a little fresher.

"Magnus Archer, It's nice to have you here Ms. Dupond." Mr. Archer shook her hand.

"My pleasure. I'm looking forward to this visit, truly. My last stop was on an Amish farm. You have a bathroom, and lights."

"Well, we do try to spoil our guests with such things." He smiled. "Are you up for a tour of the place, or do you have your own plan?"

"A tour would be nice. Based on the pictures you sent and the descriptions, I have a plan of sorts for the next few days, but a tour would certainly help me fine tune my goals."

"Then let's get to it." Mr. Archer offered her his arm and she put her own through it as he led her out the front of the Inn.

"O–M–G," Cat said as she passed by the kitchen back to her office. "She's gorgeous. She must have quite the life. Mr. Archer is giving her a tour; be on the lookout, as they might swing by."

"No problem, boss." Rohan smiled and turned to Maya. "You started the pickling juice right, and the eggs?"

"Rohan Kingston! You are not going to stink up this kitchen…" Cat straightened and stood tall with her hand on her hip.

"Kidding, he's kidding." Maya smiled and shook the bowl of freshly washed strawberries and blueberries. "See?"

Cat rolled her eyes at them and continued on to her office.

"She's going to be fun for the next three days." Maya shook her head and giggled.

"She's terrified. And excited. And terrified," Rohan said as he started to sort through the pots and pans.

"It's a big deal. This could be a big deal for the Inn," Maya reflected.

"It could be. And it could be a big deal for us," Rohan said as he motioned his hand, indicating the two of them. "If we have good food, this girl will write about it. If she writes about it, people will see it. They will come here and stay, and perhaps we can get some foodie magazine's attention or perhaps career opportunities."

"Career? You going somewhere?" Maya asked, surprised.

"It's not my current plan, no. But the doors, we want them to be open. For if and when we want to walk through them. It's a good thing. What about you? You're going to be running this kitchen, or a kitchen, soon enough."

"I'd like that." Maya smiled at the possibility. "But I love it here. This is already the best job in the world…and such a break from culinary school. It's nice to be here, and breathe. And I kind of love that you can't bake like I can. You'd never survive without me."

"This is very true," Rohan agreed.

"Even when we're busy, you guys are so level headed. This is the first time I've seen Cat completely flip her lid," she said as she layered the fresh mixed berries on top of the cooled tart she had baked the night before.

"Yeah, it's kind of awesome." Rohan smiled.

Anna walked with Mr. Archer through the grounds of the Inn, and then down to the old barns and the duck pond. They enjoyed conversation about the history of the house and his family, how they had started taking in boarders to make ends meet during the Depression. Having no children of his own, there wasn't going to be anyone to pass the Inn down to once he retired. It was something that had weighed heavy on his heart until he found Cat. In his words, she had become the daughter he had never had. She had kept him on his toes; challenged him, argued with him, and agreed with him. She had cried with him when his wife passed from cancer, she had been the first person he wanted to call whenever there was bad news or when there was good news.

"She's not my child, but she was born here," he said as he patted his chest. "She will continue all of this."

"That's beautiful, Mister Archer." Anna smiled.

"Magnus."

"I notice that Cat doesn't even call you that," she smiled.

"Nope. I think it's that small town thing. People here, they are raised right. It's a good town. I hope you get to enjoy it. Cat has really worked hard to include a lot of the local businesses within our planned tour days," he offered.

"It's one of the reasons we were interested. A lot of the submissions we got had some really amazing things to offer. Highlighting every inch of their business. But yours, your submission was really focused on the people who come to stay here and what they find. I have to admit, it gave me a bit of my own wanderlust for small town living."

"And that was all Cat. She's my amazing girl. So you're not from a small town?"

"No. San Francisco, actually. But I wanted to write. And I got some opportunities straight out of high school to do so. My parents were supportive, thankfully. I was freelance for a while, traveled all over. I got to spread my wings and fly. Wanderlust found me about three years ago, and I feel like I've been on the road ever since. This vibe that you've got going on here, it's nice."

Magnus Archer very rarely allowed himself to get egotistical, but he was going to take that minute. Here he stood with this beautiful little thing from a big L.A. magazine, and the Inn was more successful than it had ever been. He could have floated away on his pride.

They enjoyed their leisurely walk through the gardens back into the house and he suggested she have some lunch, as he was sure she was starving for a good meal. He opened the back door for her and led her into the kitchen.

Maya was attending to some steaks in pans on the stove and Rohan was walking out of their large pantry with a few serving platters in his arms. He looked up and saw Mr. Archer standing in the doorway, and then his attention was drawn to the woman standing next to him. Her face flooded his entire system and all of the sound went out of the room.

"Anna," he said quietly, to himself. The platters he had been carefully balancing went crashing down on the kitchen island with a loud clatter.

"Rohan," she said as she took a deep breath and stood straight as an arrow.

One…two…three…

"Oh, so you know our Rohan?" Mr. Archer asked.

"I do." She plastered on a fake, friendly smile as she was internally battling a full on meltdown. "We um…"

"Went to high school together." He smiled and wiped his suddenly sweaty palms down the front of his apron, and then took it off as he walked over and offered her a hug. "Hi."

"Hi," she mimicked his slightly unsure greeting and hug.

"Um…yeah. Hi," he said again, then walked back to the safety of the kitchen island.

"What a small world. A piece of Rohan's childhood finds its way here." Maya smiled at them. She wasn't sure who this girl was, but Rohan was instantly off his game. He couldn't stand still, and seemed to forget how his hands worked.

She watched him fumble a bit, stutter a bit. It was like seeing a unicorn. She had known him only a year, but in that time, she knew one thing about him. He was Rohan. He owned it. His motorcycle, the tattoos she had never seen fully but could see peeking out of his sleeve every now and again…teasing the imagination. The most she saw was when he would take off his chef's coat and she could see it went up his arm under his T-shirt. She often wondered where it stopped. He even managed to find a loft apartment that had been converted from an old slaughterhouse for the local meat market. He wasn't just cool, he defined the word cool. And Mr. Cool was acting like a twelve-year-old nervous boy who found himself in the company of his schoolyard crush. Maya smiled as she studied him; she was going to love digging into this one.

"Yeah. Small world," Anna found herself saying.

"Well, maybe you two can catch up. I was just offering Anna some lunch. We have quite a few lovely things on the menu," Mr. Archer offered.

"Chicken salad," Anna interrupted. "Rohan makes the best chicken salad in the world."

Rohan blushed. Maya could not believe her eyes, but the man actually blushed. This girl had superpowers.

"Rohan, I'm going to go run the dining room check and get a few supply things done. Everything for the next run is out," Maya said for the excuse to give them the kitchen. She would have to do her investigating later.

"Yeah, OK," he said as he mentally commanded his feet to move forward to the refrigerator for the supplies.

"I will let you have some peace and quiet. It's been a lovely walk with you, my dear," Mr. Archer said. "I will check in with you tomorrow afternoon, and you feel free to contact me at any time. You have my information, right?"

"I do, thank you." Anna smiled and shook his hand.

Mr. Archer left Anna where she was, in the doorway of the kitchen. She wasn't sure if her feet were going to move or if her knees were going to fail her. She cautiously put one foot in front of the other while Rohan had his back to her gathering supplies.

"Thank you, you don't have to make me chicken salad if you don't want to." She found a stool, slid it up to the island, and sat down. "Am I OK here?"

"You're fine there. We will just have a few wait staff in and out. It's quiet this time of day. I don't mind the chicken salad." He smiled.

"Good. Thanks. I um, I didn't know you worked here." She felt like she needed to tell him that this was a surprise for her, too. "There was no information on the staff in my file."

"I do. I did a few odd jobs since I left…" He paused and thought better of his words. "This was my big break a few years ago. So, you're a reporter?"

"Writer," she corrected. "I was freelance for a while; traveled a bit both in the United States and abroad. I had submitted a handful of things to Wanderlust and they picked me up full time."

Rohan smiled. She looked happy. Sure, her body poured into that dress and her legs were already a million miles without the high heels she was wearing. Beyond her physical appearance, she seemed content. He would bet she had turned out to be the exact person he had known she was going to turn out to be.

"That's great. So, you're doing it," he said quietly.

She sat and watched him prepare the food, something she had seen him do a thousand times. It was the oddest sensation to be watching this man now, the man who looked like a boy she knew once. Standing before her, the boy she knew every inch of. She knew about the scar on his shoulder from a glass bottle that had caught him when he tried to separate two drunk patrons one night at his father's restaurant. She knew about the birthmark he had on his lower back and a small port wine stain the size of a quarter just above his hip. As he chopped up the ingredients and put them into a bowl, she saw the tattoo peeking out of his sleeve. She knew it was tribal art that stretched up his arm, with swirls and jagged edges that covered his shoulder, chest, ribs, and abs on his left side. She knew where the art jetted down, licking the edges of the v-muscle just at his hip that, when trailed with your fingers, led you to the pleasure zone. She knew when he smiled, and when he smiled for real. She knew that if she turned the radio on, the chances of Eddie Vedder's voice serenading her would be very high. Yet, here stood the man, nearly a decade in the making. He was a stranger. She didn't know where he lived, or what kind of car he drove. She didn't know what time he started his day, or what he did to fill it. She didn't even know who he spent his days with, or who he spent his nights with.

"So, what's new?" she asked.

"I guess...everything." His smile was slow and reflective as he continued to mix and create two sandwiches.

"You work here. You live here," she prompted him.

"I work here. I run the kitchen. This is my kitchen." He spread out his arms, "Top to bottom, every piece of food that goes out is up to me."

"That's wonderful." She smiled.

"It is. I'm lucky to have found it. A friend of my father's owns an Irish pub outside of town and put me in contact, as he knew Mr. Archer was looking for somebody."

"Lucky him," Anna said.

"Lucky me," Rohan said honestly. "It's a good job. As for the living part, I've got an apartment closer to the main town. A loft, old building. I've got mad cows haunting me."

"Really?" she said, surprised.

"No. But it used to be a slaughterhouse so there are some very cool bars and pulley systems that look very rustic, and I am sure at some point did something very gross."

"Are you married?" she asked, quickly before she lost her nerve.

There was a large pause, her heart quickened. She reminded herself to knock it off, she wasn't a teenager anymore.

"No. Not married. You?" he asked.

"Um...no." Her eye contact with him broke, and she settled on watching the food that he was preparing.

"Were you married?" he asked at her hesitation.

"No. I was asked once. Good guy, he had a lot to offer me," she said, thinking of Charles.

"What happened?" he asked as he slid the plate under her face.

"He was all the right things, on paper. But the things I found myself needing, they were missing from his family dossier. He's a good man; he's just not my man."

"I'm sorry to hear that," he said, imagining her snuggling up to some GQ guy in a skinny suit as they walked across the lawn of a country club. She certainly would have fit the part looking the way she did. She looked more beautiful than he could have imagined the grown-up version of her to be.

"Don't be. He was a good man, and he knew something was missing too. He wasn't surprised. I think he asked because it was expected of us. I think he was actually relieved when I said no."

Rohan could not imagine anyone being relieved that they would not be marrying Anna Dupond, but he also didn't want to imagine anyone being married to her, so he didn't try too hard.

"So, you're doing the article. We're thrilled that we got picked," he said, trying to keep the chat professional.

"It was the photos. They were beautiful. They really captured the whole feeling of the town and the people in it. The photographer…" she looked back through the notes on she had scribbled as Mr. Archer talked on their walk.

"Olivia. Olivia Reynolds," Rohan offered.

"She was a good hire. She's a really good photographer."

"I think so too, though she's not a photographer," he added. "She grew up here, but kind of did the lost soul thing and wound up in New York two years ago. Her parents died, she happened to be here over the last bit of June and the start of July. Cat knew she took pictures and asked her if she minded taking some for the magazine."

"Oh, my gosh, I am so sorry. I didn't know that. Good for Cat though, good score," Anna said genuinely.

"I think it's been hard on her and Connor, her brother. They are very young to lose parents, especially both of them. Car accident; the other driver fell asleep."

"You know them? You seem to know a lot," Anna remarked.

"I know them. I've known Connor pretty much since I moved here. He's a good, solid guy. Olivia is younger, and I met her when she came from New York. We, um…we spent some time getting to know each other." He suddenly turned his attention to his own sandwich.

"Oh," Anna said. "You're dating her?"

"We've gotten to know a little bit about each other." He smiled softly. "She's in New York and still very young and lost. I think that she's got some things to work out yet."

"You seem happy," Anna said.

"I am. Are you?" he asked.

"Life has been good to me." She smiled and took a bite of her sandwich "This…oh, this, oh my gosh, this is the exact same."

Twenty-five

"I'm alive! And in the United States!"

"Yay!" Elle said into her phone. "How was everything? What'd ya buy? Did you meet any hot tourists while being a tourist? Oh, did you meet somebody at the airport and you had an amazing encounter but sadly he was going to Seattle and you were going to New York?"

"Um…I did not find the love of my life and then leave him at the baggage claim," Olivia confirmed.

"Man, I hate it when that happens. Well, how do you feel? Do you feel like you've conquered the world? Did you find your animal spirit guide?"

"I feel…accomplished. I feel like I've been living that life…for somebody else."

"Good. Did you take a lot of pictures? Oh! Oh! Livy, it's so exciting about the Inn and all those pictures you took. You're famous!" Elle squealed into the phone as her thoughts poured randomly out of her mind.

"I know! I framed my release form. I had no idea they were going to use my pictures," Olivia answered.

"Of course they were going to use your pictures! They're awesomeness wrapped up in amazing."

"Thank you, but you're biased." Olivia smiled into her phone as she laid upside down in her bed with her legs propped against the wall.

"Cat mentioned something about a celebratory bonfire. Will you come down?" Elle asked.

"I would love to, but I've only seen my New York life a handful of days. I need to unpack and sit down and figure out what direction I am going in. I need some time to just be. I'm going to come down for a weekend at least when the article comes out. Plus, Connor wants me to help him go through Mom and Dad's stuff."

"Well, just be. But be here. I have, Livy, I have, um…oh fuck. I need to tell you something."

Olivia's feet stilled. Her heart instantly dropped. Elle was so rarely serious, it made people stop dead in their tracks when she was. On the occasion that she had something to say rather than sing out loud to the world, it usually carried some heavy weight.

"What happened? Is it Dean?" she asked quickly.

"No, but that's an interesting thing you did there by jumping right to Dean. We'll talk about that next. Be ready."

"OK. Are you OK, Elle?" She turned over and sat up, giving her best friend her full attention.

"I'm fine. I'm more than fine, Liv. I'm in love," Elle said. No tone, no singing, no wild sweeping moments.

It wasn't what she said; it was how she said it. It was a matter of fact. She didn't scream it, she didn't growl it, she didn't include the words and I kind of want to lick him. She was being serious.

"With who?" Olivia wondered.

"With…with…oh God, Liv. I'm going to throw up." Elle curled up in a ball on the other end of the line.

"Just tell me!" Olivia insisted.

"Connor!" Elle blurted out before she could suck his name back in.

There was silence. Dead silence. Elle scrunched her body more and covered her head with her hands as she waited for the screaming or the chastising. Olivia Reynold's older brother was wasting his time with the likes of Elle. Is she mad? Is she sad? Did she die of shock? As Elle opened her mouth to ask the silent abyss if Olivia was still there, she heard a giggle. A giggle that opened up into a full gigglefest.

"What's so damn funny?" Elle immediately straightened her body and got defensive.

"Elle. Oh, Elle. Does Connor know?" Olivia asked, smiling and breathing herself back into composure.

"Yes. I mean, no. I mean, I don't know. We, we um…Olivia, I slept with your brother. Totally on purpose. Not even a little bit accidentally," Elle admitted.

The giggles stopped.

"You guys slept together?" she asked seriously.

"Yes. What are you thinking? Walk me through what is happening in your mind," Elle demanded.

"Elle, you've been in love with Connor since we were kids. I thought maybe you were just warming to the idea. I didn't know there was any action on it!"

"Wait, wait, wait…you knew?" Elle whispered loudly into the phone.

"Of course," Olivia said as if it was the most obvious thing in the world.

"How? I never said anything. To anyone." Elle thought of all the years behind her where she had loved Connor from afar.

"Your everything said it when you're around him. Elle, when a boy likes you, you flirt and you tease and you tempt. You are not just Elle, you are Elle loudly. When you like a boy? That's different. You dress in things to catch his attention. You get excited and supportive of his hobbies, no matter how stupid they are. Remember what's his face who had that dumbass car that he drag raced? You sunk every penny you had into funding new tires or speakers."

"Don't remind me," Elle rolled her eyes.

"With Connor, you're just different. When we were kids, it always him you would ask to help you get out of our hot messes. Never Dean, even if Dean was standing right in front of you. I started noticing the little things when we were older. Like one time he told you that you smelled nice, and ever since then, that's the only scent you've worn."

Elle rubbed the pressure points that she did, indeed, still coat with that same scent Connor seemed to like so much.

"When Connor was home from college for the weekend or holiday, all of the sleepovers were suddenly at my house. When he said you looked cute in something, you blushed. Elle Brannigan does not blush. What I did not know was that Connor sees you that way. He's never given me any indication. When did that happen?"

"Is it OK?" Elle asked, sheepishly and quietly.

"What? Of course! If he's happy, then I'm happy. If you're happy, then I'm happy. Tell me, how did this happen?" Olivia asked.

"Well, he's kind of been different around me for the last few months. I kind of got the feeling that maybe he liked me. I decided to do my best friend duty and check on him…make sure he ate. Kill two birds with one stone, see if maybe I could do something to know if he liked me or not. So I went to the house, which looks fan-flipping-tastic by the way. I went to his house and made him some dinner before he got home from work."

"Wait, you cooked? Was somebody supervising?"

"Shut up! Just hush up, now. Rohan. Rohan cooked. I reheated."

"OK, good. Go on." Olivia smiled.

"But I made a salad all by myself, thank you very much," Elle quipped.

"Good, good!" Olivia agreed.

"I put on a dress. A pink one."

Again, there were several seconds of silence.

"Hello?" Elle asked. "No jokes?"

"You wore a pink dress?" Olivia asked, not hiding how touched she was.

"I did. I really like him, Liv." Elle sighed.

"Oh, God. Elle. That's so sweet. But as your best friend, even if he is my brother, I need to remind you not to change yourself," Olivia said seriously.

"That's the thing, Liv." Elle added. "He loved the dress. He loved the dinner. But he traced the chain around my neck with his hand and picked up my little necklace that I got at the Winter Solstice festival last year."

"The do no harm one?" Olivia tried to picture the necklace in her mind.

"Yeah. He picked that up and told me that it was his favorite part of my outfit."

"That's my boy!" Olivia beamed with pride.

"And I lost it. I just couldn't hold it in anymore. I do love him, I love him so much," Elle said.

"I am happy for you. I'm happy for you both."

"So you're OK with me being with your big brother?"

"I will say, I am going to ask you to keep the very descriptive sexiness to a minimum. I don't want to know how big…" Olivia warned.

"Oh, so…" Elle smiled at her memories.

"Stop. Right there, just stop," Olivia interrupted. "Elle, in all seriousness. I don't think I would ever truly think anyone is good enough for him. And I don't think that anyone would ever be truly good enough for you. This, this…is actually pretty damn perfect."

"I love you," Elle said.

"I love you, too, crazy girl." Olivia smiled and then paused. "Have you um…"

"Seen Dean? We're going to talk about Dean now. We need to," Elle finished her sentence for her.

"Yeah."

Olivia had not e-mailed Dean. She had not called him. Her last memory of him was looking at him lying in his bed, naked and sleeping peacefully with his arm around her. It killed her to get up, out of his arms, and get dressed. It killed her to tiptoe down the hall and let herself out in the silence of the middle of the night. It broke her heart as she packed her bags, but she knew she had to. She knew it was the only way. She had always been the one to push the envelope with him, and while she would never regret that he was her first kiss or her first—and only—lover, she knew it would not have happened if she had not thrown herself at him.

She loved him as a teenager, and it wasn't until she found herself in his arms again that she realized how deep that love went. He was it. He was the love of her life, but sadly for her, she was not the love of his. As tears slipped down her face, she looked at him sleeping quietly. She would love him forever. And even a day after that. She had to get away. It wasn't fair, to her, to the abyss she felt in her chest. She just had to get out of town, and she wasn't sure if she'd ever be able to go back.

"Well, I've seen him. I've watched him. I've given some things some thought," Elle said.

"You didn't say anything to him, did you?" Olivia asked.

"Of course not. That's all you. Not mine to tell. I haven't talked to him directly. Just same old seeing somebody around town stuff. He seems edgy and distracted," Elle noted.

"Well, OK." Olivia wasn't upset by the idea of him being edgy about their situation.

"I saw him the other day and asked him if he had heard from you. He seemed to huff at me when I had possibly, maybe insinuated you had been e-mailing everyone accounts of your trip."

"Elle, you did not!" Olivia announced.

"Yes, I sure as hell did," Elle said with determination.

"And?"

"And he played it off like he had been too busy to check his e-mail. Which means I know damn well he was checking. Probably many times a day."

"I didn't e-mail him. I haven't talked to him. I don't know what to say," Olivia said. "He doesn't love me."

"Are you sure about that?" Elle asked.

"Yes. It's always been me. Every part of our relationship has always been me," Olivia said with a sad tone. "I've always been the one who loved him. I've always been the one to seek him out. I've always been the one. It's true that he let me, but I know damn well that this is a one-sided love story."

"Did you know his parents are selling that house?" Elle asked, abruptly changing subjects. On purpose.

"What? How? They can't sell the house. Why would they want to sell that house?"

Olivia realized her voice had bubbled into panic, so she calmed herself down. She didn't mean to yell that into the phone, it wasn't her house. She did have a lot of memories there, though. In the house, running around following behind Connor when she was very young. Helping Sophia in the kitchen when Connor and Dean wouldn't let her keep up with them. The tree house. The tree house where her very best childhood memories were made, and some extremely special not so childhood memories as well, would most likely be taken down. Perhaps it would get a reprieve and another child would make their own memories there. Hers would be erased. The thought of it made her sick.

"Yup. Connor told me. He's actually going to put it on the market next month. They want to downsize. That retirement neighborhood by the library."

"That makes sense. It makes me sad, but that makes sense. How is Dean with it?" she asked.

"Not sure. Connor said he's being very stoic about it. Saying things like 'Whatever Mom and Dad want, I had my childhood there and now another child can get the chance.' Things like that."

Exactly the things that Olivia was thinking. If she was feeling this sick over the idea, she could only imagine how Dean was feeling about it. It made not talking to him all the worse.

He was her friend, she should be there for him. But could she? Could she be his friend and tuck away that little part of her that loved him? She had no idea. She just knew she loved him enough that she needed to try. How was she going to try?

"That sucks," Olivia finally said. "I guess it really isn't up to me though. It was never my house."

Twenty-six

A package sat on the table, with a note from Debi.

Hey love,
This came for you. I signed for it.
–Deb

Olivia opened the package and a black ten by ten book slid out. The cover was a photo she recognized, a small square with a black and white image of the tree house in Dean's backyard. She pulled off the singular sheet of paper that was attached to it.

Olivia,
I took the liberty of having this put together for you. Thought it might be fun for you to have a little book laying around, a coffee table book of your work. The pictures are too beautiful to be unused. I showed these to a professional

photographer friend of mine, who said he knows people
who would be interested in marketing something like this.
I imagine whatever it is that you are looking for in
NYC can be found within these pages. Look at them. Do
you see what I see?
—Rohan
"What lies before us and what lies behind us are small
matters compared to what lies within us. And when you
bring what is within out into the world, miracles happen."
~ Henry David Thoreau

"He quotes Thoreau. He rides a motorcycle and quotes
Thoreau. Oh, Rohan, how I wish my heart was still mine to give
to you," she said to the page and put it down.

She set down the package and looked at the cover of the
book. She took a breath and opened it. Her photos filled the
pages in artistic ways. Simple ways. Beautiful ways. She was
immediately swept up into her own childhood memories when
she saw the snapshot she took at the pool of two girls laying in
their chairs. She could hear the sound of kids playing in the water.
She could imagine the conversation going on between these two
girls. A photo of Connor, leaning in the doorframe of his store.
His tall figure in his button-down shirt and tie. He looked so
grown-up and professional, it made her smile. The yoga photo of
Elle, which made her laugh every time she saw it. As she flipped
through the familiar photos that had been chosen by Rohan, she
noticed that she had taken several images of Dean. It was never
him directly, but he had been in several. Dean working at the Inn
on the construction, Dean building a desk in the workshop area
of their store, Dean's truck...parked in front of a pond. Her
mind swam to him even unconsciously, like he was just sort of
always there. She saw pieces of him, if she looked hard enough, in
many of the photos. Parts of him, shadows of him. She ran her
finger down a page that had an older gentleman riding a tractor

through his summer harvest in the early morning sun. It was the farm across the street from her parents' house. If she closed her eyes, she could feel Dean sitting in the swing next to her, watching the man with her on the day she took that photo.

She had always thought of putting a book together, and had planned on making one with all the pictures that were sitting on her computer from the trip to Thailand. Here it sat though, a book in her hands. It was exactly what she had been looking for.

"Home," she said as she slid her hand over the word on the cover.

She brought the book up to her chest and hugged it, sighing at the storm of emotions running through her. She needed to clear her head. A run would be good. Get lost in Central Park for a while. She grabbed her headphones and turned the music on. She could clear her mind.

As she ran, she thought about the bombshell that Elle had dropped about her and Connor. She wasn't shocked, but she was surprised. Her brother had always been such a solid force in her life, in everyone's life. He was a Boy Scout. Hell, he was an actual, honest to goodness Eagle Scout. Elle was insane. She had been insane for as long as Olivia could remember. But the best kind of insane. The kind that she needed in her life, the kind that Connor needed in his. She shook her head at the idea of them together, but she loved it. They would be good for each other.

As she turned the corner and entered Central Park, she chose a footpath that was more secluded since it was daylight out and there were several people around. She had been trying to tackle the park a little at a time, discovering something new each time she went. Some of the less frequented trails she specifically saved for days like this where there were lots of happenings and she wasn't so alone. She might be getting used to the idea of being a New Yorker, but it was still New York.

Her thoughts turned to Dean and his childhood home. She could only imagine how he felt. The house that she grew up in was a lovely home, and there were lots of memories, but nothing that really attached themselves to the house itself. She could, off the top of her head, name at least half a dozen things about Dean's house that she loved. On the inside of his pantry door were all sorts of colored markings. They had been tracking Dean's height through the years. Marking his height on the New Year, his birthday, the beginning and end of the school year. She smiled at the memory of Connor who had started to mark his own growth inside of his own closet door, and hers too, once she found it and made him add her to it. Lemon sticks. Sophia always had lemon sticks in the summer as they were a very Baltimore-specific treat. Olivia rubbed the tiny scar just under her eye. They had been running around in the house and she caught the edge of a table. She remembered Sophia gathering her up and kissing her all over to make it better. The cut wasn't deep enough for stitches, but when she had any little bit of a tan, she could see a small white line where it once was. The tree house. Where was she even going to begin with that? All her best moments, all her big moments, all the moments that she would carry with her in her heart. When she closed her eyes, every inch of the wooded space was easily recreated. Every aged mark, or mark that came from the hazards of childhood. Her childhood.

The music filled her ears, and she emptied her mind as she picked up her pace and her feet ran along with the beat. These were all the things that she was running away from…and run was exactly what she was going to do.

Twenty-seven

Anna sat in the chair in front of the mirror and brushed her long dark hair. It was her last morning at Archer's Inn, and thus far, the trip had been well more than she had thought it would be. Though she personally had not sorted through the thousands of applications that came into the magazine, she had seen the application on Archer's. She had found herself lost in the idea of this sweet little place' and the pictures they had sent in were amazing.

Over the last few days, she had met every person who worked there, and could clearly see the family that they had made for themselves. She could see the pride in everything, from the large newly built gazebos to the sweet flower in a vase she found on her dresser after the maid had been in to clean up. Her notebook had initially been full of questions that she had put together before she arrived. She interviewed guests, walked the grounds, took a couple of tours. All of her questions had been answered, and then some. It would be a good article.

Her mind wandered to the man she knew was down in the kitchen. Her fingers traced a small imaginary line over her heart. Yup, it was the scar she carried with her. The one that hurt the worst, but she loved the most. Her memories carried her back to the day where he invited her to meet him on the Roman Bridge at Stow Lake. Her hands ached as she closed her eyes and felt him gathering her hands into his and kissing them. His words swirled in her mind, *You are the most amazing girl I have ever met. Good things are happening for you, and you have to be there for them to happen. You have to be. Your dreams are real, and you have this chance. Take it. And I've got this life that calls to me, and I have to live it. I have to let you go. It's not fair to you or to me. I love you, but I have to let you go be the person you are meant to be.* Their fates were taking them in different directions. She knew it, but she didn't want to say the words out loud. Doors were opening for her, and she found herself unsure of if she should go through them or not because of him. If he had not been in her life, she would have leaped through them, but now she remained standing in front of the open doors. Unwilling to go through at the cost. What would happen to them? The East called his name, his desire to make it completely on his own. She understood his need. She understood hearing that call. They had to go, had to experience the lives that awaited them on different sides of the country. It killed her as she stood on the bridge with him. Tears ran down her face, and he kissed them away. They put their heads together, closed their eyes, and just tried to breathe. On her own—she had tried to breathe on her own. She knew it would be good-bye. She knew that she would not be able to stay in touch with him. It already hurt too much. It was good-bye, forever.

"Always," she whispered to herself as she rubbed the little imaginary scar. "I carry you with me, always."

She would have to say good-bye to him again, tomorrow. This would be her last night, and she would enjoy the bonfire with all the people she had met. She would celebrate with them, a job well done. She would return to her apartment and write her article. She was living the life that she once had only dreamed of living. As she looked at her own reflection, the L.A. girl stared back at her. Did she have her dream? Why was she not so sure anymore? She heard a small knock at her door. She opened it, and found Cat happily smiling at her.

"Hi. You ready to party?" Cat smiled.

"I am. Thank you so much for doing this tonight so that I could join you guys," Anna said.

"Oh, sure! I thought it would be fun for you to kind of get to know everyone on a personal level. I mean, you know Rohan, so that's cool. But you can get to know the rest of us a little bit."

"That would be lovely," Anna agreed.

Cat checked in with the front desk once more before she and Anna headed out back. They walked down the main path and past the gardens, to an old barn. Anna could smell the fire that had been lit already, and she could see the chairs waiting for them. The sun would be setting soon, and thankfully, there was enough of a chill in the air that the fire would not be adding to the heat.

"Howdy!" Cat greeted the woman who was helping Rohan set up the food.

"Hey!" Elle smiled. "I'm crashing the party if that's OK. Came with Connor."

"Of course! Elle, have you met Anna?" Cat turned to make introductions.

"No, Hi. I'm Elle." Elle smiled and shook Anna's hand. "You're the reporter from L.A., right?"

"I am."

"Have you had a good time?" Elle asked.

"Yes. This is a lovely place. It's a great little town too," Anna said.

"It is. I like it here." Elle smiled.

"Are you from here?" Anna asked.

"Born and raised. I've had all my best moments here." Elle smiled.

"Sounds like a good life," Anna mused.

At sunset, the group that had gathered found themselves sitting in a circle of chairs by the fire. Rohan had brought all the supplies for S'mores, along with the burger dinners and cold salads. Connor and Dean had filled a couple of coolers with beer and wine, Maya was attending to a cherry cobbler in a Dutch oven nearby. It was shaping up to be a good evening.

"So, Connor, Livy is back. I wish she could have joined us for this," Cat said.

"Me too, but I understand. She's kind of been in nonstop mode since the funeral," Connor said.

"You have been, too. How goes the house?" Cat asked.

"It's good. I didn't do too much to it structurally. I knocked down a few walls, updated the kitchen and the master bath. Then it was just paint and furniture. It's pretty much just aesthetics now. No big deal," he said as he sat in a chair and cracked open what sounded like a well-deserved beer.

"Says the man who went to bed every night at three in the morning with paint in his hair." Elle interrupted, as she sat down on his lap and rubbed his hair. She kissed him softly.

"Wait," Cat said, confused. "What is happening? Are you two…like, a thing?"

"Are we a thing?" Elle asked Connor as she smiled.

"Yeah," Connor smiled back at her, and looked at Cat as he pulled Elle closer to him. "We're a thing."

"Well, well, well…love is in the air." She smiled at Anna. "You can quote me on that."

"I just might," Anna smiled.

"Since when? Since when are you a thing?" Cat asked.

"Since a minute ago. Since a year ago. Since I don't know how long ago…" Connor looked at Elle, rubbing her back.

"Since forever ago," she corrected him.

"Oh you guys…this is just…perfect!" Cat smiled.

Rohan found himself hesitating as he walked over to join the group after setting everything up. Should he sit in the empty chair next to Anna? Should he sit in the empty chair next to Dean? Dean had been a bit off over the last few weeks, and Rohan thought perhaps he had discovered the reason for the undertone within the pictures he had recently flipped through. Anna had been nothing but polite, sweet, and fun since she had arrived. They had interacted several times in the last few days, and she seemed to not mind the dips into nostalgia when they came up. Yet, he wasn't sure if sitting next to her would be safe. He was trying to be a gentleman, or at least a man. She was beautiful, a more defined version of the girl he had once known. The boy who never lost his nerve over anything had not been able to string a coherent sentence together since she arrived. Dean, sit next to Dean.

"Anyone sitting here?" he asked.

"You are," Dean offered as he cracked open his own beer.

"How's it going, man?" Rohan asked, hoping that he could get a friendlier conversation going with Dean.

"It's going. This being done," he waved his hand at the gazebo, "is good. Connor's house being mostly done is good."

"I'm sure, man. It's a beer well deserved. Cheers," he said as they clinked their bottles together.

They sat in silence for a bit and watched the flames take over the woodpile. Everyone seemed to break off into smaller conversations. Anna, Cat, and Elle seemed to be very chatty, and Connor just enjoyed sitting with Elle, being with Elle, in this newly defined role.

"Have you heard from Olivia?" Rohan asked, not sure if Dean would answer him.

Dean didn't answer. He turned and looked at him, clear confusion on his face. Where is it that we're going with this?

"I didn't know about the two of you. I wouldn't have moved in that direction. You know that, right?" Rohan finally said, looking into the fire, and then turning to face Dean.

"There is no two of us. You didn't do anything wrong, man," Dean quipped, sighed, and returned his own attention back to the fire.

"Yes there is. I don't know what it is, but there is a two of you," Rohan said.

Dean sat for a second, watching the flames lick the darkening sky. He wasn't sure of what to say. What would happen if he did? What happens when you call things you know lurk in the shadows out into the light? Was there a two of us? Or were they all just stolen moments?

Rohan turned his attention to the brunette sitting across the big circle of chairs, he smiled as he watched her chat easily with Cat and Elle. The breeze caught her hair and it fluttered gently, sweeping her elbows. The white top that tied around her neck showed off her bronzed shoulders, and if he closed his eyes, he could remember what it was like to touch them. Kiss them. She laughed at something Connor said, and all of a sudden, he felt an ache deep inside his chest.

"You see that woman? Sitting right there?" Rohan asked.

"I do." Dean looked at him and followed his gaze over to Anna.

"When I was eighteen, I woke up one morning thinking that I had some living to do. I needed to just pack my bags and get in my car and see where these two hands were going to get me," he said as he looked at his hands. "And she, she was going places. You just knew it, you could already see it. Scholarships were coming in, people were chattering, she was going to be the one who would do something really big."

"Seems like she has," Dean offered.

"She has. And so have I. But of all the living I have done, and the learning I have done, do you know what I know to be truth?" Rohan asked.

"What's that?" Dean asked as he took a swig of his beer and returned his attention to Rohan.

"Love. Love like that, you only get love like that once. I look at her face, a face I haven't even seen in nearly a decade, and I already know that I would pack my shit and leave with her tonight if I could. If she asked. I know nearly nothing about that woman sitting there in that chair. I have no idea where her day takes her, or what she likes to do in her down time. But I know enough about the girl I see when I look at her that I would go and not even look back. I have lived, I've had those experiences I set out to have…but they are nothing compared to what I could have had. I let her go, and now that I see her sitting there, I realize that I let everything go."

"You don't think you did the right thing by letting her go see the whole big wide world out there that she wanted to see?" Dean asked.

"No, she needed to do that. What I should have done was follow her." He sat back in his chair and took a sip of his beer. "I'm a fool for not following her to the ends of the earth."

The night chill filled the air, and the fire had burned out quietly. Eric and Cat decided to just take a room at the Inn rather than drive home. Maya and Dean had said their good-byes and headed back into town. Connor and Elle slipped away back to his house. Talking to Dean had gotten Rohan really lost in his own feelings. He just wanted a minute with her before she left. Just a minute to be real. She would once again walk out of his life, he knew, but he had to at least tell her that she still meant so much to him. He found her before she slipped back up to her room at the Inn and invited her to take a walk with him.

"I don't even know what it is that I can say about the fate of me walking into your Inn," Anna said.

"Kind of an unexpected turn, but it's good to see you. I can't tell you how thankful I am just to see you. To see that you've done well for yourself," he said.

They had walked down to the pond, and sat on the little dock. Their feet were dangling in the cool water, and Anna was looking up at the night sky.

"I'm leaving tomorrow," she said quietly.

Rohan said nothing. This was a woman he knew nothing about. He felt her arm next to his and found his hand seeking hers. Their fingers linked. She was a woman he might not know, but in this moment, she very much felt like the girl he had never been able to forget. She responded by resting her head on his shoulder as their feet continued to sway slowly in the moonlit water beneath the dock. Time, the last near decade, just slipped away silently. The lifetime between them seemed to be just a minute or two. A silly little nothing.

"Are you happy, Rohan?" she asked.

"Right now, or in general?" He smiled, though both of them continued to keep their focus on the stars above.

"Whichever." She picked her head up and turned to him.

"I've got a good life here," he began. "I came out here wanting to build my career with my own hands. I've done that. And this place is just a bonus. The people here, they're good to me. They've become family."

"That's wonderful," she said as she brushed her hand against his closely shaved head.

"I miss you," he said as his hand reached up and held hers.

"Do you?" she asked.

"Have you had a good life?" he asked.

"I told you that I have," she reminded him.

"Then I don't want to regret it," he offered.

"Regret what?" she asked as she lowered her hand and nervously started to play with the fabric at the bottom of her shirt.

"Leaving. Leaving you. It was the dumbest fucking thing I ever did," he finally said, more to the air around him than to her.

"Rohan," she assured him. "You had a plan. Which worked, apparently."

Hearing him say it, the words that leaving her was a mistake, had her heart fluttering. Just knowing he loved her was enough for her to carry with her.

"Did it? Anna, I swear to God, you've been out of my life a decade and I still smell you in the air around me."

Anna's heart went from the mild flutter to deep thundering beats. *Breathe, just breathe Anna.*

"These last three days…" she began, but then found herself at a loss.

"I almost wish we were butterflies and liv'd but three summer days. Three such days with you I could fill with more delight than fifty common years could ever contain,'" he said.

Her smile was slow and sweet. It was amazing to him, these words were the truth. When she left him tomorrow, the last three days would hold more value to him than any time he had ahead of him.

"Keats," she smiled. "You still read poetry to untangle your mind at night?"

"You've always known all my bad habits," he joked.

"Like pouring a little coffee into your sugar?" she smiled.

Their toes touched under the surface of the water, and rather than jetting out in different directions, they both stayed. Their legs tangled together, and both of them took a deep breath. She looked at him, wishing. Take the moment. And as he had always done, he heard the words that she did not say. He closed the distance between them slowly. His lips touched her, and it was as if the whole world slowed. His kiss was as breathtaking as a first kiss would be, and her stomach fluttered just like the first time he had kissed her so many moons ago. Yet time was erased to her. This was a taste she knew, a smell she knew. A place where she fit, slipped easily into a memory. It was as if the decade that stood between them had been erased the second their lips touched.

"I miss you," she said as his soft touch parted from her.

"Do you? You're living the life, Anna. You did it," he said.

"So did you," she reminded him. "You just said that you miss me. I miss you. I find you in the oddest places. I can't even go into the kitchen section of any store and not feel your arms around me, teaching me how to chop vegetables."

He smiled. It was a silly little thing, but he was glad to be part of those little moments. He had often found her places, in the little things that popped up in his day.

"I didn't even realize how much I've missed you. But I have, so much. And tomorrow I…" she began.

"Go back to missing me," he finished her thought, and stared up at the moon.

"Yeah," she reluctantly agreed.

He grabbed her hand, and she turned into him. He wrapped his arms around her and kissed the top of her head.

"The other side of the country, Anna. Why do you have to be on the other side of the country?" he asked.

"I could ask you the same thing." She looked up at him, and kissed him softly.

"I still wouldn't trade this moment. Right now. Anything that comes after is worth this," he said.

"Do you think…" she began, then pushed him back and straightened herself up. "Do you think that we could keep in touch? For real?" she asked.

"I do," he said, though his face looked like he was asking a question rather than answering one.

"Do you think that maybe we could…I don't know what?" she asked, defeated in her own attempt to make anything for them work.

He smiled. She was an L.A. girl. She had made her living and climbed her mountains. It was incredibly sweet that the girl who sat before him now was the same girl he had left on the bridge so long ago. Looking hopeless and confused. He realized that the fates had given him a chance. Just one chance. He gathered her hands, as he once had. He looked into her eyes as he once did. And he said the words he should have said then, but didn't.

"Anna Dupond, you are the most amazing girl I have ever met. Good things are happening for you, and you have to be there for them to happen. You have to be. Your dreams are real, and you have this chance. Take it. And I've got this life that calls to me, and I have to live it."

Anna recognized the speech immediately, and her hands began to pull back. The man standing in front of her was breaking her heart just like the boy had done so long ago. She could not do this again. When she pulled her hands from him, his hands gripped hers tighter, refusing to let go.

"Look at me, Anna," he said, then added the words that had been on his heart but that he had never said, "I love you. A lifetime can stand between us, and I will still love you. I have no idea how, or where, or when, or why…but if you want me to, I will be right here."

He took her hands, still clasped in his, and pulled her closer.

"Here," he whispered.

"I don't want to let go of you, Rohan. I didn't want to let go of you then," she said honestly.

"I know. But you needed to live your life. You needed to be my L.A. girl." He smiled and kissed her cheek.

"Could we figure it out?" she asked.

"Anna…we will figure it out. I will meet you at the ends of the earth if I have to."

"Tomorrow is going to suck," she offered as she laid her head on his shoulder.

"Yeah, but the day after that might not. Have faith in this." He wrapped his arms around her and pulled her close.

The promise of something. That is all he needed. He had to have faith in that.

Twenty-eight

Dean drove home and slipped into his empty bed. His sleep was dreamless, but when he woke up at four o'clock, he found himself restless.

His mind drifted back to Rohan's words. Love like that only comes once. Was it love? He and Olivia had never actually been together. He had relationships, old girlfriends. He dated a few women for long periods of time, yet when he thinks back on the one who mattered, his mind drifted to the relationship that doesn't even count. He had known her for nearly her whole life. And nearly all of his. She was tangled, by different degrees, in nearly every memory he had.

He closed his eyes and imagined her, living in New York, doing well. And him living the life he had set out to live here. His business was good, as much as he could possibly hope for. He had never lacked for the company of women. Hell, he knew that if he punched in the right combination of numbers, he could have a woman in his bed within the hour. Yet, when he looked at the space next to him, the emptiness would only be truly filled by one.

"Goddamn it all to hell, Livy," he said as he threw the covers off and got out of bed.

This was going to end, now.

The sound of the storm woke her up. Olivia climbed out of bed, and walked to the window to find the city being showered heavily. She had planned to walk to the market to get some fruit and pastries for herself and Debi. That would have to wait. She made herself some tea and did a scavenger hunt for food. Between Debi's long hours with her hospital internship and her recent travels, neither of them had actually been in their apartment for any length of time. She found some stale bread to toast and a few packets of jelly in the fridge.

"Saddest breakfast ever," she said to herself.

Tucked between the couch and the wall, she pulled out a sheet of poster board and laid it down on the floor in front of the sofa. She grabbed her tea and the toast and sat down for her continued heavy thinking.

"OK, Connor," Olivia said to herself as she sat in front of poster board with lines drawn to split it into four categories. "Let's see what we can do with Post-it notes."

She was sitting on the floor with the poster in front of her and her morning tea at her side, leaning on one of Debi's super thick medical books to write on the stack of Post-it notes. She wrote out titles for each category. School full time, Around the world in 80 days, Buy a house, and panic…call Elle and blow it all in Vegas.

Each category had a pro/con list, and because a Connor-style list had to have not only categories, but subcategories, she added those too. She smiled and took a picture of it. She would send it to him later. He would be proud.

"I'd have to pick a major," she said out loud as she wrote. She wavered over whether that would be a pro or con for staying in school full time before she placed it on the board. "Pro."

"See everything," she said as she easily plopped that down in a pro for Around the world.

She continued to list out the pros for all of the categories. "Wise investment" for Buy a house; "What happens in Vegas…" for Panic. Then she also quickly wrote, "Bail money for Elle," and tagged it to the con list. After an hour, she was staring at a board that was equally sprinkled with small Post-it notes. Some of them were very thoughtful, like "Better job with degree," and some were as simple as "Lose it all on one bet at a hot table." She was actually pretty surprised at how many pros the Buy a house category had. She had not really considered buying a house because she was only twenty. But she heard Connor's voice in her head…he was Mr. Sensible.

She looked at the board and was proud. It was pretty, and had lots of little things scrawled out on the notes. Some things were stuck in the middle, neither a pro nor a con. Just information to consider. Her brain kept wandering back to Dean, and her eyes kept wandering over to the book that still lay on her desk. Oh that? Just a little book I did about…home.

"Food. I need real food. Damn the rain," she said as she grabbed her rain boots and jacket out of the closet.

She headed out, opened the door to her building, and immediately stopped in her tracks.

"Dean!" she gasped.

He had no idea how long he had been sitting there letting the rain pour down on him. His shirt was soaked, his jeans were sticking to him. Minutes, hours, who knew? He had thrown the covers off himself nearly eight hours earlier and gotten into his truck. He was mad, he was furious, he was sad, he was lost, he was fearful, and he was every damned emotion he had ever experienced. He drove through the early morning into New York, knowing that he was going to end this game he had been playing with her. He was going to say every single thing they had spent years not saying. He found parking in a nearby hotel garage and stomped on the pavement, rain spouting up around his black work boots. Every damned word they had not said. When they had kissed the first time. When he had spent weeks and months being careful to never be alone with his best friend's little sister afterward. Words never said when they happened to catch each other staring, and the small second of eye contact before a reluctant break and they each returned their attention to the world. Words they never said the night they made love. Words they never said when she showed up madder than hell at him in that little red dress. All the words scattered and screaming inside his mind.

He had taken the steps two at a time and found her name on the resident list. He was going to hit the buzzer so hard he would be sure to break it. Instead, his finger stopped just shy of pressing it. Furious, he shook his hand and went to press it again. Nothing. All of a sudden, he had no idea what he was going to say to her. The noise in his head was so loud, but it was all just scattered nonsense. What happens when you say all the things that have never been said? What happens when you're not sure what they are going to say? What happens if you've made it all up in your mind? What happens? What happens?

He paced a few times up and down the steps. He found it ridiculous that he had never feared anything as much in his life as talking to this five foot three inch woman. He sat on the steps and laid his head in his hands. The rain poured down on him and he closed his eyes…begging for the words that had gotten him to these steps to come back to him now. That was where he had sat for he had no idea how long.

The door swung open. He looked up and saw her standing there with her raincoat and boots. His heart started to pound, his hands began to sweat. This was insane. Just say something.

"What are you doing…" she began.

That's all the words there was going to be. As she stood on the top step, and he stood several down from her, they were nearly eye to eye. He reached his arms out, swooped her up, and crushed her mouth with his. Her hood fell back, and she wrapped her arms around his neck. He pulled her tighter to him, lifting her up off the ground. He turned them both and took a few steps down the steps onto the sidewalk. Her lips were soft, sweet, and wet from the rain. He had never tasted a more glorious combination.

"Hi," he whispered to her. But rather than letting her go on the sidewalk he sat her back down on the steps so they were eye to eye.

"What is happening?" she asked in surprise.

"Us…Olivia, us. We're happening," he said to her.

"We are?" she asked as she studied the odd combination of concentration and anger on his face.

"Yes. I don't care if you don't have room in your grand plans for this," he began.

"I don't have room…" she started to ask.

"No. Be quiet. It's time for the words. All the damn words in the whole damn world. Olivia Grace, I love you. I love you so goddamn much and I have been losing my mind for the last month."

"You love me?" she whispered, more to herself than to him.

"Yes, I love you. I have tried so hard to stay out of your way and let you find whatever the hell it is that you're looking for. I've tried to let you live your life, but I can't breathe. I can't breathe one more minute. So here I am. Deal with it."

A smile crept across her face unconsciously, probably bordering on the ridiculous, since Dean's face looked like he was gearing up for a fight.

"What's so damn funny?" he asked.

"You love me!" she said, wrapping her arms around him, and meeting his lips again. Softly, sweetly.

"I'll move here," he said, his lips still pressed against hers. "I just don't want to be without you for one more damn second of my life."

He slid to the ground on his knees with his arms wrapped around her waist. The rain had finally begun to slow down, and she ran her fingers through his wet dark brown hair.

"You don't have to move here," she said.

"Anywhere. If you need to travel all around the damn globe, then I'll travel all around the damn globe. Marry me. Marry me, and let me follow you."

"Marry you?" she asked surprised. Her heart started to beat wildly and she felt dizzy. "Dean, this is all so…"

"Yes. There's a million words running around inside my head. I have no idea what any of them are saying. Who cares? Just marry me. Those are the only words I can hear. Nothing else matters; just marry me."

"Oh, Dean. I love you so much. I've closed my eyes and wished, wished for you."

"Then why did you leave after the party? Why did I wake up alone? Why did you never say anything, ever? Why do you never say anything?" he asked.

"Because I love you. And there were never any words said. I needed for you to be the one to say them. I needed for you to want me as much as I've wanted you. I've always chased you. I've always thrown myself at you when you weren't ready. I had no idea if the words in my mind were the same as yours, even though I wished them to be. So badly. You were my first love, and no guy since then has held a candle to the way I feel about you. But they were always just my feelings. A little girl's crush, nothing more. But still, I wished. I love you Dean. It's only ever been you I wanted to spend my life with."

"Can we start doing that now?" he asked as he stood for another kiss.

"Yes. Yes. Yes, yes. Yes!" she threw her arms around him.

He picked her up and swung her around.

"Let's get out of this rain." She smiled.

He followed her, holding her hand as she walked up the steps. He pushed her hair to the side and kissed her neck as she slid the key into the door of her apartment. As soon as it shut behind her, he once again picked her up and carried her to the bedroom.

He watched as she removed her clothes and he removed his own. She stood on one side of the bed, he on the other. They both got on the bed on their knees and he wrapped her in his arms. His kiss was slow and soft. Her whole body warmed from the chill that the rain had brought.

"Dean?" she whispered.

"Yes?" he answered, lifting his mouth gently off her neck and then returning to it.

"There's something I want to tell you," she said.

He pulled himself from her warmth, looked at her sweet face, and sat on the bed, pulling her down to sit with him.

"Let's chat. I wasn't doing anything special," he winked as he rubbed his fingers up her bare legs.

"I wanted you to know," she started, then suddenly became conscious of her naked body and pulled her knees up to hold onto her legs.

"Tell me, Olivia. We can't do this if there are any walls," he said seriously.

"You're the only one," she said, and then tucked her head into her arms.

"The only one, what?" he asked as he pulled her face up to look at him.

"The only one I've been with. It's only ever been you. I thought you'd want to know."

The information had him silent. He was the only one?

"What about the last two years? What about Rohan?" he asked.

"There were guys, great guys. Rohan's a wonderful man. He's just not you. It's only ever been you," she said.

He's just not you. Wow. It was all he could do not to scoop her up and never, ever let go.

"OK, I have something to tell you too," he said.

"You do?" She was surprised.

"I watched you get on the bus," he confessed.

"You did? I had hoped you would sleep through the night. How did you even know I was leaving? I didn't know I was leaving."

"Not now. Two years ago. I left because it was going to be so damn hard to watch you go. We made love. It was your first time, and I fell in love with you right then and there," he said quietly. "I knew it was wrong. So wrong."

"You did? Then why did you leave? It wasn't wrong, Dean" she said, her heart starting to pound at the idea of this new information.

"I had to. Have you met you? You were hell bent on getting out of Rising Ridge. Your life was yet to be lived; you made that pretty damn clear. What kind of a man would I be if I stood in your way?"

"Oh, Dean. I would have…"

"No," he said. "You had to go. You had to be this Olivia. You deserved your chance. I just couldn't stand the idea of seeing you off. I had every intention of getting out of town that day, but I just couldn't. I had to. I had to just see you go and tell myself it was the right thing to do."

"I'm so sorry, Dean."

"Did you have a good time in Thailand? Do you feel like it was a needed trip?" he asked.

"Yeah. I mean, I didn't find anything there, like I thought I would. But it was amazing, and I am so happy that I was able to go. I have pictures. So many pictures that I want to show you."

"Then don't be sorry. We found each other again. That's all that matters," he smiled.

"Some strings just refuse to be cut." She smiled at him.

"That they do." He kissed her again. "We found our way back."

He laid her down, pushed back her hair, and traced her face. His kiss was warm, and in no hurry. His lips trailed down her neck, and he found her. He slipped into the warmth that waited for him. Only for him.

In the quiet of the night, she laid in his arms. His fingers were laced in hers, and his breathing was the steady sound that was music to her ears. She had finally made it out to the farmer's market for food, walking through New York with him by her side. They sat at her little desk/table and he asked her about the thought behind each and every Post-it note on her planning board. He added a few, like "Get malaria and die" to the Around the world board, and "Wake up with a tattoo of Elle on my butt" to the Panic side…though he did say that might be a positive depending on how well it was done.

"What's on your mind?" he asked, as he sleepily kissed her shoulder.

"Oh, nothing. Just thinking about how excited Elle is going to be to plan my wedding." She smiled.

"I am not wearing anything weird. Like leather, or a kilt, or a leather kilt," he announced.

She giggled and turned to him.

"You wouldn't wear a leather kilt for me?" she asked sweetly.

"Oh, so not fair…you're so not fair." He smiled and covered her in kisses.

Epilogue

The pop of the champagne cork cued the clatter of cheering voices. Dean slipped out in the middle of the night and returned an engaged man. Better yet, he brought Olivia home with him. The wedding was a mad flutter, with everyone involved. Seemed like the entire town was on board with just a few weeks' notice to put together a wedding. Elle brought in all her light magic to make it happen, and maybe a little bit of dark magic too, but nobody had to know that. Cat had quickly offered up the Inn, and Rohan happily swung Olivia around in a hug and offered to make her whatever food her heart desired. Maya dove in and made a gorgeous cake.

Olivia wore a simple, classic dress. Soft satin with a heart-shaped neckline and a skirt that flowed out into a sweet bell shape. Connor walked her down the aisle to Dean, who was standing under a gazebo that opened into a garden of blooming fall colors. Dean had a classic black suit on, to his great relief.

They partied well into the night, and she and Dean had hopped in his truck with a destination of anywhere for two weeks. They had stopped in nearly every state, and Olivia had a blast taking pictures of wherever the day had taken them. They returned back to his small apartment, and had planned on talking about the reality of how and where they were going to live. Rising Ridge, New York, somewhere in the middle?

"Henry, you have had an amazing career," Connor began. "This town would have possibly figuratively, and most certainly literally, fallen apart without you. Cheers. Cheers to what you have built over the last thirty, and to what Dean and I will continue with you for the next thirty."

"Cheers!" everyone said.

Connor had opened his newly finished home to all their friends to celebrate Henry's official retirement. After the construction, he sat back and let Elle and Olivia have at it with their parents old belongings being mixed in with a lot of new ones. He and Olivia would go through the rest once Olivia and Dean made a decision about where they were going to be living and what she would like to take for herself.

"Thank you, my boys. Both of you. Dean, I am so proud of how hard you have worked and what a fine man you have turned out to be," Henry started and patted Sophia's shoulder as she started to wipe away tears. "Connor, your father was so proud of you. I'm proud of you. Thank you so much for opening up your home so that we can celebrate with my friends…my family."

Olivia chatted with a number of the guests, and happily showed off her wedding ring to those who had not seen it. Dean had given her his grandmother's ring, which Sophia had given him when they returned from New York. A vintage square-cut stone surrounded by smaller diamonds. A simple silver band complemented it on the early September evening that they wed. She smiled when she was taking in everything Connor had done with the house; it was amazing. Her attention was drawn above the front door on the inside. Above the frame, there was a light piece of wood with the words Aon Tintean Mar Do Thintean inside a scrolled border. On each corner of were small Celtic trinity circles. The words, she knew, were Gaelic. The English translation was There's no place like home.

No, there was not. And it looked like soon enough, Elle would be calling this home too. Olivia wandered over to the large set of glass doors in the kitchen that looked out onto the patio. Connor had wound up putting in doors that could be pushed out to the side so the outside could be welcomed in. Her gaze went to the tree house that she could see sitting silently in the setting sun.

"Whatcha thinkin'?" Elle asked as she pushed her hand through Olivia's arm and laid her head on Olivia's shoulder.

Olivia smiled and grabbed Elle's hand. She looked over the silver diamond ring that laid on Elle's left ring finger. The silver twisted and turned to look like tree roots, and the diamond sat at the center of small emeralds surrounding it.

"I'm thinking that I am really going to get along smashingly with my new sister-in-law."

"I hear she's nothing but trouble," Connor said as he joined them, wrapping his arms around both of them.

"You get that from a good source," Elle confirmed as she offered him a sweet kiss.

Dean was mingling with some of the guests. Talking business, talking wedding. He found his mother and wrapped his arm around her.

"You got yourself a good woman there, Dean. I'm so happy you two got your shit together finally," she said as she hugged him.

"Mom!" Dean looked at Sophia in shock. He had never heard her use a curse word in his life. She was always one to say fiddlesticks, and when it was very bad, the reserved oh poop.

She just smiled up at him and winked.

"Did your father tell you?" she asked.

"Tell me what?" he wondered.

"We got an offer on the house this morning." She looked up at him once more.

Dean said nothing. He looked at her, trying to measure the feelings on her face. She looked content. His eyebrows came together in a bit of frustration and he sighed.

"That house has a lot of memories, doesn't it?" she asked as she looked over to Connor, Olivia, and Elle chatting. "We had some crazy kids running around inside those walls."

"You sure did, Mom. It was an amazing home to grow up in." He smiled.

"Thank you for that." She put her hand over her heart.

"I'm sure it will be an amazing home for the next generation, too." She smiled. "Go, go play with your friends."

He left her with his father, and walked over to his wife and, now, his new brother-in-law.

"Mom just told me they got an offer on the house," he informed the group.

"They did. It came in this morning. The buyer said she had to check with her husband, as it was the first house she looked at, but everything seemed to be in order."

"Kind of sucks monkey balls, doesn't it?" Elle asked as she looked up at Dean.

He just smiled and shook his head at her. He was trying to be the better man, but yes. It did very much suck monkey balls. Leave it to Elle to just own the words.

"Yeah. It does. But what can you do?" he asked.

"Well, you can buy it," Olivia offered. "How 'bout it?"

"Huh?" he asked, confused.

"Dean, my love," Olivia said. "I started looking for places for us to live. And it seems the first place I looked at was everything I've been looking for. For a very long time. So I put in an offer. Now, I told the guy I would have to talk with my husband, but…"

"What?" his eyes widened, not trusting the words his new wife was telling him.

He looked at this small group of crazy fools smiling at him like idiots. The world was making no sense.

"Meet my buyer," Connor said, pointing to his sister.

"Us? When? How? Why?" Dean stammered.

"Yes. I called Connor when you were helping me pack up my things in New York and I was looking at my poster of all the possibilities. And it hit me. I'm going to go to school here full time, for photography. My name is already out there, thanks to Anna's article, and Rohan has put me in contact with his photographer friend who has interest in making some of my photos into books."

"But, really? My parent's house. We can live anywhere," he said as he pulled her closer.

"We can, but right there," she pointed across the backyard. "Right there is home. It's home to you, it's home to me, and it will be home to the family we will one day make."

"Are you absolutely sure this is what you want?" he asked.

"It's absolutely what I want. After all, there's no place like home." She wrapped her arms around him and pulled him in for a kiss. "You interested Mr. Winston?"

"Yes, Mrs. Winston." He kissed her. "I can't wait to raise a family there, with you."

Dear Olivia,

Oh, my sweet girl. Today was the hardest day of my life. I had to put you on a bus, and watch you go. My baby, my Olivia. I sit here now, on your bed in your room, and I miss you already. I was mad, so very mad. Why do you want to go to New York? Why do you want to take a year off? Haven't we provided you with the best of the best? A mother has dreams for her child, and it's so hard to remember you might have your own ideas.

I was sitting in the backyard earlier and Sophia came over to give me a pep talk, the way she does. We laughed at the memories of the three of you running around our two yards, not believing that we are now both officially empty nested. It seems like just yesterday we bought this house, and you were the sweetest little baby yet to be. She told me to let you be you, you had to find yourself. She told me that you were always the one who was searching for your spot but never quite seemed to find it.

As I sit here, in this room, I realize that I don't see you here. It's true, you packed up your things to take with you to New York. But even so, I should be able to see you here. I see me. I see the things that I gave you, the things that I wanted for you. I know the size of the bags that you took with you, and there should still be part of you left here. There should be more of you here, and there just isn't.

I wandered out into the yard, and I found you. I found you in the garden, in the strawberries you wanted to plant when you were ten. I found you on the swing, the cushion really only feeling right if I lay like you did all the time, swinging and staring up at the stars. I found you in the tree house. I climbed up those steps, and peeked in. I haven't actually been up there in years, since you and Connor were little. Remember that one time you ran away and we slept in there? I found you there.

Little marks, scratches from the little furniture being moved around. Paint splattered from your artistry, and your little names carved in the wall. Connor, Dean, Olivia, Elle. Little names, little handwriting. I closed my eyes and could hear you, as I often did, chattering away up there.

I'm not sure what it is that you are looking for, but I hope you find it. I don't understand what you think you will find in New York that you can't find here in your own backyard, but I am so proud of you that you are brave

*enough to look. I want you to look. I want you to discover your path, see
yourself in all the little things, the way I have today. If you find Olivia in a
coffee shop off of Fifth Avenue, then so be it. If you find her by the pond in
Central Park, then so be it.*

*Your father and I are going to the lawyer's office tomorrow. Now that
you are eighteen, we need to change a few things. Up until now, Connor
would have been your provider. He was old enough, and lord knows the boy
doesn't have an irresponsible bone in his body, so we knew he would take care
of you. We're leaving him the house. It's his. He's such a part of this town,
and we are so incredibly pleased with the direction that he is taking with his
life. We're leaving him stability so that he can continue to grow the business
he wants to have. We want him to be able to have the tools he needs, this
would be what he would want. If anything happens to us, we want to provide
what you kids want out of life.*

*For you, we are going to leave you what you crave the most. Freedom.
Opportunity. I'm going to continue to sit here and write this check out every
month for your schooling and send you care packages. We will be watching
you, from here, and pray that whatever place you settle in, it will be a happy
one. And as much as it pains me to think about it, should we not be able to
see you finally settle into that happiness, we leave you with your tools. Even
though I don't quite understand what is going on in that head of yours, I still
want you to have the opportunity.*

*Be free. Dream big. Find Olivia. Tell her that I love her, and that I
am proud of her…and even a little bit jealous of her wanderlust. Just don't
forget where home is, my sweet girl.*

I love you always,

Mom

About the Author

Alexa Jacobs was born and raised in Maryland where she has spent the last decade and a half being a wife and mother to her amazing family. As a member of the Romance Writers of America, she enjoys all aspects of the writing process and is an avid reader herself. After spending many years as a freelance writer for various outlets, she introduced her debut novel in 2015.

Find out what Alexa is up to today by visiting her website

www.alexajacobs.com

A Preview
of
The Dreamer

Available in 2016

Claire's eyes opened and immediately she wasn't sure what she was looking at.

Back up, she thought. I need you to back up.

As if the dreamer heard her, she felt herself taking a step back and reaching for the stairs behind her that the dreamer knew were there. Being able to focus more on the image in front of her, she realized it was a door. Her hand touched the door, ran down the antique white wood to the gold brass handle and tried turning it. It did not budge. She turned around on the step she was standing on and looked down the flight leading into an unfinished space that held random things. This was somebody's basement.

Slowly walking down the steps, she noticed that all of the contents of the room were blurry. This happens in dreams when somebody remembers something is there, but not all of the details of the actual item. Or perhaps the details do not matter to the dreamer, Claire wasn't sure yet. There were no windows, just gray cement walls. She noticed a light mint green bike against the back wall. Unlike the other items, this bike was not blurry. Her dreamer knew it very well; it was a very cute beach cruiser bike with a tan seat and wicker basket. Skimming the handlebars, her hands found the silver bike bell. Pushing it, no sound came. Claire didn't expect it to; this was not her dream after all.

As the dreamer wiped her hand lovingly over the bike, Claire caught a break. She was able to see a very obscured reflection in the shiny handlebar surface. Seeing her own reflection, or her dreamer's as it was; a woman with long red hair.

The smell of lilac was in the air, a scent that she had smelled just a few weeks before. The same smell as in weird dream, with the girl in the box. Claire wondered if she was with the same dreamer, and what that lilac smell meant. It was light, and fresh. Lilacs, soft powder, much like a gentle breeze that you would enjoy in a garden.

Claire looked down at her hands and watched her fingers wiggle through the air, and just like before the air had waves silently passing. *This has to be the same dreamer.* She guessed being locked in a basement was an upgrade in accommodations. As her fingers twirled, watching the heat waves dance through the air, she felt the mood settle into her stomach. Fear. This woman was scared, and now Claire was scared.

I need to leave this place, and as quickly as she could. The dreamer took Claire back to the stairs and took them two steps at a time. She grabbed the gold brass handle of the door, turning with all of her effort. Again, it did not move. She took her fist and pounded on the door.

"Hello?" Her voice broke the air, but it sounded strange. The sound had breaks, familiar static feedback. She could barely even hear herself. Her dreamer must have said the word as she thought it, which always caused the sound. Echo, echo, echo. Placing her ear on the door to find out if she could hear anything, she heard same sound as the previous dream, a muffled voice. One word, repeatedly. Just like before, she could not understand it.

Panic bubbled up in her throat and she looked behind her, back down the steps. She could see it now, the fire. Claire wasn't sure when it started, but everything was engulfed. It was an angry fire, with the edges licking at the steps that she was standing on.

"Help!" The dreamer's voice screamed into the air as she continued to pound on the door. "Help me!"

Claire could feel the desperation to get the door open, but she wasn't sure if it was the dreamer's or her own. The fight or flight feeling was deep within them both. She knew the fire was not going to hurt her. It looked hot, it looked hopeless, but for Claire at least, it was harmless. She would wake up, safe in her bed, with no burns to be had…eventually.

Until then, Claire was left with only the feelings. Her heart was pounding, and sweat poured off her neck and back. She knew that this was her own body reacting. In reality, Claire was laying in her bed, her heart pounding and sweating through her nightgown. As she waved her hands through the air, and watched the lines of heat, she thought that this dream might be a recurring dream for this girl. It was different from when she was locked in the box. There, she just felt sadness sticking with her. Here, it was complete fear. The smell of lilac was too coincidental, as were the heat waves in the air. Different place, same problem? Maybe.

She pounded her fists on the door now, and felt the fear driving her. The sound in the air was screaming, she could hear the screaming. Broken sounds, scattered sounds. Somebody was screaming. Was it her? She sat on the step, the air got heavy. It was hard for her to breathe, maybe even hard for the dreamer to breathe if she was imagining the air so thick. Claire focused on the bike that sat on the back wall directly in front of the steps. She could see it so clear among the things that remained blurred, with the fire dancing all around it.

It sat there, silently, and she watched the seat get burned. The wicker basket caught the flames and smoked into nothingness.

I have got to get out of here, she whispered in her thoughts.

"I'm going to die," the dreamer's words came out of her mouth.

Rather than stand up and trying to fight, she remained sitting. She curled up into a ball, and covered her head with her hands. Claire had come close to dying many times in dreams, as one does. Falling from something and waking up at the last minute. *Wake up, wake up.* This was different. Death was looming in the air with the heat that she could not feel. With the fire that she could not stop. This girl was going to die in her own dream. As she closed her eyes, the fear consumed her. The sadness woke her.

The sadness was the same that Claire felt before. This girl was so sad, it felt endless, and Claire ached for her.